Mollywood

L.G. PACE III & MICHELLE PACE

Copyright © 2014 by L.G. Pace III & Michelle Pace
Cover designer: Robin Harper. Wicked By Design.
https://www.facebook.com/WickedByDesignRobinHarper
Cover model: Ruby Franco
https://www.facebook.com/RubyFrancoPage
Formatting by JT Formatting

Printed in the United States of America
First Edition: October 2014
Library of Congress Cataloging-in-Publication Data
  Pace, Michelle & L.G. Pace III
    Mollywood (A Carved Hearts Novel, Book Two) – 1st ed
    ISBN - 13: 978-0-9889418-7-8

1. Mollywood—Fiction 2. Fiction—Romance
3. Fiction—New Adult & College

http://**www.michellepaceauthor.com**
https://**www.facebook.com/LGPaceIII**

For the beta readers...
who simply had to know what was in
the heart-shaped box.
Careful what you wish for.

CHAPTER One

Molly

Something Blue

"MOLLY, YOU ABOUT ready?" Joe's rough voice called to me from the living room.

I paused in my effort to put in my second earring. "Just a second."

"We've gotta hit the road, little girl! This isn't exactly the kind of thing we can be late for." His gravelly baritone sounded commanding, and I'm sure most people would've been quick to respond to his authoritative delivery; however, I'm not most people. I arched an eyebrow and picked up my tube of lipstick.

"Pipe down, Joe." I shot back, and I could hear his exasperated sigh all the way in the back bedroom. Heaving a weighty exhale of my own, I turned away from my vanity and opened my mouth to apologize. But, remembering that he'd been the one to start the argument, I turned back to the mirror. I took my time, applying some coral color to my lips and giving my upswept hair a last onceover. Joe may have won the battle, but dammit...I'd win the war.

Taking a small sip from my sweet tea, I stood and surveyed the damage in my full length mirror. I'm always pretty critical of my appearance, but I felt as ready as I would ever be for the marathon of pictures I was about to be in. My mint green dress was just the sort of flouncy thing that usually picked up my spirits. But now on the day of the big event, the fitted bodice felt snug. Thankfully, it still looked okay despite the extra few pounds I'd gained from all the recent stress.

The last few months had been nothing short of chaotic. We'd just managed to put the legal situation with my ex-husband to rest. Draven had made the prosecuting attorney's job fairly easy by leaving so much physical evidence, including the video of his tirade and the string of text messages to me. Then there was the whole business about him using an app to track my movements. Sadly, none of his shenanigans carried much of a sentence and his plentiful bank accounts had afforded him skilled representation. At least he was behind bars where he belonged, even if it was only for a little while.

Meanwhile, Joe's wood working business, Good Wood, had taken off like a thoroughbred at the sound of a gunshot. When word got out that he was carving again, offers had come in droves. His reputation as a master woodworker had people buzzing. He had to quit his construction gig within weeks of the website going live. Who knew that my sexy carpenter had such a following in the wood working world? People from as far away as Peru had come seeking his special skills.

Between the out of control success of my food trucks and the spike in orders for Joe's shop, we'd had very little time for each other. When we were together, we spent way too much of our time arguing. I guess you could say there was trouble in paradise. I wish I could say we fought about important things, but it seemed like lately it was mostly about trivial bullshit. Neither of us seemed to be able to break this new and disturbing pattern, and it was taking its toll on us both.

Thrusting my worries aside, I turned sideways and sucked in my abdomen. My sleeve of tattoos popped against the green dress giving me at least one thing to smile about. The constricting bodice, however…I needed to get my act together about that. Vowing to immediately cease my morning trips to the bakery down the block, I slung my purse over my shoulder and hurried out to silence my handsome escort.

Joe stood at the window with his back to me. The afternoon sunlight played on the highlights in his honey hair. His broad shoulders filled out his collared shirt perfectly, and the way his ass looked in those slacks was inspirational. He'd draped his gray suit jacket casually over his shoulder, and the pose made him look like he belonged in a Hugo Boss ad. I'd never met a more handsome man, and even though we'd lived together for going on eight months, my breath still caught whenever I saw him.

He must have heard me come into the room, because he turned to look over his shoulder. His eyes widened and swept me from head to toe as he slowly turned.

"Well?" I twirled in a circle so that my skirt flared, revealing my ivory petticoat underneath. Joe blinked twice, and his square jaw dropped. "Worth the wait, Captain Patience?"

"You look…amazing." His smoldering gaze honed in on mine, and he took several steps toward me. Just when I was sure he'd pull a Joe and ravish my lipstick off, he halted and frowned. Raking a hand through his hair, he blew out a frustrated breath. "We *really* do have to go."

"Right." I agreed, trying to keep the disappointment out of my voice. There never seemed to be enough time anymore for the good stuff. I reached for the door handle, and recalling the last time we got carried away my eyes flew wide. "Oh, I almost forgot!"

I crossed the room and scooped up a blue garter belt from the coffee table with my index finger. Holding it up for his inspection, my lips curled in a naughty smile. "Something borrowed *and* blue!"

Joe smirked, probably remembering how he'd taken the garter off with his teeth the night before. The way his brow immediately furrowed again told me we'd be having another one of our "talks" on the way out to Lake Travis. My heart sank in anticipation. Our discussions were beginning to feel a lot like lectures, and it grew harder each time to keep a lid on my temper.

Joe had been after me for several weeks to shut down truck one long enough for him to install an extra air conditioner. He felt that part of the reason I'd been feeling run down was my constant exposure to the 130 degree temperatures in the truck all summer long. I argued back that I couldn't stand to lose the revenue and that if he really wanted to make himself useful, he could install external misters so that customers would linger longer and buy more. It had been over 100 degrees for nearly a month straight and the food truck parks had been like ghost towns. Thankfully, truck one had a permanent home outside of a bar, and that same Texas heat made people thirsty. The truck at Cas's bar more than made up for the slower action at the other location. And more importantly, the heat wave had finally come to an abrupt end. Still, Joe was like a dog with a bone about making the alterations to the older of my two trucks. He just didn't get that I couldn't shut down at the drop of a hat, but he would soon enough now that he had his own employees who depended on him.

It was hard to stay mad at him, though. I'd been lusting after Joe since I was in the ninth grade, but that was "Old happy-go-lucky Joe". That man no longer existed of course, though sometimes my Joe did a fairly convincing impersonation of him. He truly seemed contented most of the time, but "Brooding and

Complicated Joe" returned a bit more with every passing day. I'd wondered more than once if he was skipping his weekly sessions with his psychiatrist.

Joe reached for my hand and laced his fingers in mine, pulling me toward the door. We managed to get all the way to TX-1 Loop N and were on our way out of Austin before he turned the music down and started in.

Again.

"You need to change your phone number." His tone was stone cold. I turned my head in his direction, but he kept his eyes on traffic.

"I've already changed it once." My stomach tied itself in knots. We were revisiting an older fight, and the topic change caught me off guard. Unsnapping my purse, I grabbed the container of mints rather than the bottle of Xanax next to it. If I'd have thought I could have kept it down, I'd have swallowed both. When I spoke again, it sounded like a plea for mercy. "Joe...we've been over this..."

"Baby girl, I *swear* I'm not trying to pick a fight." His voice softened, as he glanced sideways at me. I was a sucker for that sad puppy dog expression and his sexy Texan drawl. I settled into the headrest behind me, swiftly defeated by his time-tested strategy.

"I don't want to fight with you either. Today's supposed to be a happy day." Instead of looking victorious, Joe just seemed even more troubled. I despised seeing him down and knowing I was the cause made it worse Unable to resist, I reached over and stroked the sensitive skin on the back of his neck with my fingertips. He smiled and pulled away.

"Stop that. You're gonna get yourself in trouble." Joe's extreme ticklishness was his Achilles heel, and his neck was my favorite target. Taunting him would usually make him dissolve into fits of laughter or cause him to pull over and have his wicked way with me. As far as I was concerned, either result would be a win. But traffic was thick, so it was in our best interest for him to focus on the road. There'd be plenty of time after the wedding for all manner of kink, so I grudgingly removed my offending digits.

Thankfully my distraction tactics worked and he dropped the subject. We moved on to our other favorite topic, how busy we'd both be in the next few weeks. Joe had recently hired my brother, Mac, initially to keep up with his insane workload. Good Wood was already doing custom furniture and carving but the moment Mac came on board, he opened a whole other product line.

Mac had a special talent for restoration projects and had worked all over the area. He was on the short list of people that did that kind of thing well, which meant when the materials couldn't be used in the restoration, he often had first dibs on salvageable stuff others never got a chance to see. He'd hoarded tons of material that he had salvaged over the years from buildings set for demo. He had a couple of storage units, some things at mom's in her shed, and his garage and shop were overrun with the stuff. His ex-wife, Princess Patron, had once famously threatened to burn their house down just to destroy all his "beloved old shit", as she put it.

Between helping Joe fulfill the already overloaded job requests, Mac had built a birthday present for our mom. An insanely cool coffee table made from the mantle that had once rested over the fireplace at our family's old restaurant, Hildebrandt's. I had my friend and webmaster, Jay, add the pictures of the table to the Good Wood website and people when nuts. Suddenly, everyone wanted repurposed pieces. Francis, Joe's head of sales, had been fielding orders far faster than the guys could build them. Now Joe was looking to add another new employee to keep up with demands. I thought about the long days Joe and Mac were putting in and the hours I'd be covering for Sanchez all next week and groaned.

"*We* need a vacation."

"That we do." Joe agreed, cocking an eyebrow with a sideways glance in my direction. "Where do you wanna go?"

I pursed my lips thoughtfully. "The beach. Somewhere isolated. Just you and me and a hammock under a palm tree. No phones, no computers, completely unplugged. Preferably naked."

Joe snickered, and as if the lightened mood had summoned it, my phone rang. It's funny how your favorite song, when used as your ringtone, can quickly become the most grating sound *ever*. I huffed and yanked the phone out of my purse. I frowned when I saw an unfamiliar number.

"Who is it?" Any sign of amusement had vanished from Joe's chiseled features.

"I don't know." I admitted, aware my answer wouldn't go over well.

His jaw tensed and he inhaled deeply. "Let it go to voicemail."

I clenched my teeth and nodded. He was right, but I've never been a fan of being told what to do. Dropping the phone into my purse, I tossed it back onto the floor.

Joe pulled my car up to our destination, and I fidgeted nervously with my skirt. The Oasis was an imposing four story facility that could seat close to 2500 guests total. It sat overlooking Lake Travis with the most spectacular views imaginable. There were several different spaces they rented for parties, and the one we were destined for was one of the more modest sized rooms. The ceremony was scheduled to be on the terrace at 6:00 p.m. The reception would follow immediately afterward inside The Sunset Villa room. I had to admit, The Oasis was a breathtaking location for a wedding.

Joe opened the door for me, and as we crossed the parking lot to the entrance I felt his hand come to rest on the small of my back. I felt those familiar butterflies in response to his touch. When it came to Joe Jensen, I'd had butterflies for so many years that they felt like old friends.

Even after all these months, it was hard to believe he was really mine. He'd been best pals with my older brothers when they were all in high school, and then they'd all been roommates for a couple years after. Most girls would've been overjoyed to have their brother's leave home, but I was bummed that Joe wouldn't be hanging out in the basement rec room anymore. I found any excuse to go visit them at their shitty rental house. Joe was always sweet to me, though the twins teased me mercilessly for my obvious infatuation. After a couple years of unrequited crushing, I'd finally taken the hint that I was dreaming and moved on to boys my own age.

I sort of lost track of Joe on my march through life. I graduated and ran off to culinary school on the west coast. I'd settled in Seattle, hoping to make a name for myself that had nothing to do with being the daughter of a successful restaurateur. For a while, I was on track to do just that, but got derailed, as so many other young women do, by a smooth talking Prince Charming.

When I got divorced and moved back home to Austin last year, I ran into Joe again while cooking at my brothers' jobsite. I'd been shocked at his dramatic transformation. Though he was still ridiculously good looking, his attitude completely sucked. Sweet Joe had become bitter and brusque. Of course, once I'd learned that he'd lost his wife and unborn baby in a car accident, his war torn demeanor made perfect sense.

Jessica and Jack's untimely deaths always disturbed me, and thinking about it made me feel awfully petulant. Joe had definitely been through hell and come out the other side surprising well adjusted. However, he could be a bit overprotective, but based on his past it was kind of understandable. At least, he was working on his issues rather than ignoring them. Granted, his therapy had been court ordered after he got in one fight too many. Dr. Green was assigned to help him with anger management. It hadn't always been a smooth relationship from what Joe had shared with me, but lately he had made significant progress. So much progress, in fact that Dr. Greene had released him from mandatory therapy months ago. Joe had made the choice to keep going , which I considered a positive sign.

If I was honest with myself, Joe had legitimate reasons to be concerned about me. My ex-husband was a total psycho stalker. But Draven was locked up and serving time and besides...I could take care of myself. I'd been doing so for years before Joe was around.

I found myself looking over at Joe's perfect profile, and felt that familiar ache in my chest. Frustrated at our disjointed state and suddenly overwhelmed with emotion, I stopped in my tracks. Joe turned to face me, a perplexed expression marring his flawlessness. I placed my hands on both of his uncharacteristically smooth cheeks and looked him in the eye.

"I love you, Joe." I felt my throat narrow painfully, and blinked away unexpected tears.

"I love you, too." His frown deepened and he brushed my sweeping bangs away from my eyes. "What's wrong, Molly?"

It was a good question and I wished I had a reasonable explanation. We'd come so far and been through so much, it seemed unfair that we couldn't get it together long enough to enjoy any of it. I'd been wracking my brain for weeks to find the right thing to say, a verbal Band-Aid to slap over a hemorrhaging wound. It made me wish my love life could be as straightforward as my job. A good chef can throw random ingredients into a pot and create something delicious. On rare occasions, fate does the same thing with hearts. With the right combination of elements at just the right time, a couple can fall head over heels in love. That being said, blending two lives can get messier than any kitchen and also a hell of a lot harder to clean up. I wasn't usually such a bawl baby, but when it came to Joe, all bets were off. I was freaked out about "us" just then, and what we were becoming. I pulled his face down to meet mine and kissed his lips delicately, so he wouldn't be covered in my lipstick all night. "Let's try to enjoy ourselves and talk about the ugly stuff afterwards. Okay?"

He nodded, his cheeks flushing. I could tell he needed to vent, too. But this was neither the time nor the place for it.

We entered the grand foyer and I heaved an appreciative sigh. The Oasis truly was breathtaking. Joe whistled. Based on the expression he wore as he looked around, he was also impressed.

"Just how much are you paying these two?" Joe drawled and I elbowed him with a grin. My employees, Stacy and Sanchez, might both be certifiable lunatics, but they had excellent taste.

"They reserved a smaller room upstairs." I pressed the elevator button and the doors immediately popped open. The moment the doors closed, Joe turned and gave me a lecherous smile.

"Mess up my lipstick and I'll kill you." I threatened and he looked away with a wry smirk. A moment later the elevator stopped moving and the door opened.

I spotted Sanchez the moment we stepped off into the sunny room. At 6'5' and 250 pounds of solid muscle, he was kind of hard to miss. Sanch looked surprisingly suave in his black tuxedo and I was relieved to see he'd talked Stacy out of the white tux with tails. There was upscale and then there was plain ridiculous.

"Dirty S!" I squealed, giving my favorite co-worker a huge hug. "You look very sharp, sir!"

"Molly. Thank God you're here. Stacy's starting to freak." His quiet voice quivered a bit and I realized he looked petrified. His dark skin looked rosy around the apples of his cheeks and a crease appeared between his dark brown eyes. Both he and his fiancée worked in my food trucks, Wrapgasmic. Stacy was the cashier and operations manager for truck number one, which was permanently, parked outside of Cas's, a popular bar on East

Sixth. She was also my marketing goddess, and worked social media like she was born to it. Sanchez was my head chef for truck number two, which was usually parked somewhere on South Congress. They were both indispensable to me, having been my first crew when I moved back to Austin and launched the brand. They were each hardworking and gifted in their own way and God knows where I'd be without them. I'd nearly bit my tongue off when they announced their engagement, since Stacy was about as constant as a hummingbird and I was afraid she'd break up our Wrapgasmic family.

Stacy's mom and Dad had been fairly indulgent for their oldest daughter's special day, but they'd wisely drawn the line at an open bar and a sit down meal. Still, the location itself was worth every penny. Stacy had spent all of her savings on her dress and Sanchez had done the same on Stacy's ring. The happy couple originally planned to take a three day honeymoon down to Galveston, but I refused to allow it. I smiled, happy that I could afford to give them a proper getaway as a wedding present. Stacy and Sanch would be flying out to Napa Valley for the next week, and I'd soon be busting my butt covering for Sanchez while they were away.

"I suppose I'd better haul some ass then. Can't keep the bride waiting!" I replied with a grin, and headed off to find Stacy. I wove through the swelling crowd until I reached the room reserved for the guest of honor's preparation. I knocked (shave and a haircut-style), and it was Stacy herself who flung the door open. She looked devastatingly perfect in her plunging sleeveless gown. Her blonde hair was teased to such perfection that Miss Texas herself would've been proud. Her eyes, however, looked wild.

"Did you bring the 'something blue?'" She blurted, and I immediately waved the garter in my hand. I'd expected this greeting. Stacy would happily get married without one of her bridesmaids, but she was far too superstitious to get married without accounting for all her good luck charms.

"Good. Now get the hell in here. We've taken all the pictures we could without you." She demanded, her eyes strategically judging my level of *presentability*. Stacy had graciously allowed each of her attendants to pick her own dress pattern. She made no demands. We were free to be as creative as we liked, as long as our dresses were all the same color and material. It was probably a wise decision, since we were all so different in ages and shapes. Her sixteen year old sister was her maid of honor, and she looked darling in her tea length sleeveless tank-style dress. Sanchez's sister was nearly forty years old, but her buff arms and plentiful cleavage rocked in her strapless floor-length. The last bridesmaid, a high school friend, was a fairly hefty gal. Her choice of sweetheart neckline flattered her well, and her pale skin and red hair looked better in mint green than the rest of us. I couldn't stop admiring her.

After we posed for a series of group photographs and Stacy and I had one of just the two of us, Stacy's mom waltzed into the room. Overly tanned and bleached, I felt like I was getting a sneak peek at Stacy's future self when I saw her. 'Stacy Senior' gestured to her gold watch.

"It's time." She murmured.

"Oh God!" Stacy exclaimed, flushing a deep shade of fuchsia. Her panicked eyes darted to mine. "What if I mess up my vows? What if I cry! Oh God, I'm not wearing waterproof mascara! I can't cry, Molly. *I don't want to cry.*"

I put my hand on her shoulder. "Breathe, Stace. You'll be great. That's Sanchez out there. He looks like a million bucks, by the way. You just think about him waiting under that archway for you. The rest of this fluff isn't important."

My pep talk seemed to do the trick. Stacy plastered on her best customer service smile. Her mother herded us out into the ballroom and lined us up. I found myself paired with Sanchez's younger brother, Pablo. He was an inch shorter than me in my two inch heels, but he was pretty cute and very friendly, so I was content with the situation. We were the first two to head outdoors and down the white-carpeted aisle. As we made our way toward the arch, I gave the crowd my best pageant girl grin. This wasn't my thing, and I inwardly cringed as a flash went off in my face. I inadvertently locked eyes with Joe, who'd been seated on the bride's side. He was two people in from the aisle, but his brilliant green eyes drew my attention as if he were the only thing in focus. His full lips turned upward at the edges when I found him, and I couldn't help but melt. Had I not had scores of people watching my every move, I'd have ditched Pablo on the spot.

Sanchez forced a grin and nervously mopped his brow with a handkerchief as we joined him near the railing. The panoramic view of Lake Travis gave me a tiny touch of vertigo, and I quickly swiveled to look back on the crowd. I could see Joe. Even seated, he towered over Stacy's family members and a crease appeared between his brows. He must have seen something concerning on my face. When I flashed him an easy smile, relief washed over him and I saw him sit back and visibly relax.

After the rest of the couples repeated our ceremonial journey, the string quartet began playing The Wedding March. Everyone stood in a rush, and I noticed the priest shuffle impatiently. Judging by the level of the sun in the sky, it wouldn't set until after this wedding was long over. I saw a few people aggressively fanning themselves with their programs, and was grateful for my sleeveless dress. I'd noticed that Joe had abandoned his suit jacket in the car. The temp was in the eighties, yet by all accounts it was actually quite mild for August in Texas.

Stacy took her trip down the aisle like a boss. There were no sobs or raccoon eyes on her part, though her mother made up for that completely. Stacy was composed and picture perfect and Sanchez lit up like a spotlight the moment she came into view.

Thankfully, the priest kept it short and sweet, and there

were no lengthy poetry readings or warbling soprano soloists. I found myself tearing up as I watched my friends exchange vows, partially because I'm a hopeless romantic, but also because they'd only been a couple for about as long as Joe and I had, and I was certain they'd be divorced within the year. The thought of having to replace either of them made me want to hurl. Far worse was the thought of them breaking each other's hearts.

After the ceremony, we posed for a couple of pictures outside with both the bride and groom and then headed into the arctic blast of air-conditioning. I accepted a glass of punch from Pablo and scanned the crowd for my date. I worried about Joe having someone to talk to while I fulfilled my obligations as a member of the wedding party. My concerns were completely abated when I spotted him at the bar with his former boss, Graham. Joe and Graham were tight. Graham was one of the main reasons Joe had made it through his personal tragedies in one piece.

The two of them laughed uproariously at something Graham's wife was saying. Seeing Joe so happy and carefree coaxed a smile from me, and I wandered off to leave him in more pleasant company. It'd been a while since he'd laughed like that with me, and I didn't want to encroach on his good time. With a bittersweet backward glance in his direction, I took my place beside Sanchez's sister just as the toasts began.

CHAPTER
Two

Joe

Glitterbomb

"IT'S GREAT TO see you, Joe. It's even better to see you looking so *happy*." Graham's wife, Anne, came in for a stealthy hug that took me completely off guard. I smiled, but eyed Graham awkwardly. He shrugged and finished off the last swallow of his beer, his reticent expression implying she did stuff like this all the time. After she patted my back and wandered away, Graham took a seat on the nearest bar stool and I joined him, waving the bartender over.

"Shiner, please. Biggest draft you've got." I glanced at Graham expectantly.

"I'll have the same." He nodded, and turned his probing eyes to assess me. Graham had stepped up to be a surrogate father figure for me, even before my world crumbled. The rift with my own parents had still been the size of The Grand Canyon at the time of Jess's accident, though mom had been trying to weasel her way back in when she'd found out we'd been expecting a child. When both Jess and the baby died, I went a little bit nuts.

Okay...maybe more than a little.

My parents bailed immediately. They had no way to deal with what I was going through or the angry lunatic I had become. They scurried back to Florida and left my older sister, Tamryn, to deal with me and my breakdown. Thankfully, Mason and Mac Hildebrandt, my oldest friends, were around to help her out. They'd had the good sense to bring Graham along, knowing that even in my darkest hour, I'd be willing to listen to him. Who knows where I'd be if Graham hadn't stepped up.

Or if I'd still be around at all...

"So, I hear from Mason that you and Mac are making money hand over fist. I guess I won't be getting any phone calls from the two of you looking for work anytime soon." I glanced over at him and saw the gleam in his eye that belied the surly tone.

"Well, if you ever need any finish work done you know where to find me." I murmured. He clapped his hand on my arm and beamed at me.

"I'm glad to hear you're doing so well. You've been hiding your light under a bushel for far too long, son." Graham had always believed I was too talented to be doing basic carpentry. When I lost my wife and son, I also lost my will to carve. I couldn't tap into my creativity at all, but I still had my carpentry skills and Graham had been willing to hire me on. Even after all the trouble I'd gotten myself into...picking fights on jobsites, showing up still drunk. Graham stuck by me when most of the foremen in Austin had written me off as more trouble than I was worth.

We settled back to our beers and I let me gaze wander over the crowd. Molly looked breathtaking. Her luscious dark hair was piled on top of her head in a way that drew my attention to her exposed neck. I wanted to nibble her, and imagining the sounds she would make caused me serious frustration. She was such a contradiction in her sweet little bridesmaid dress which showed off so many of her tattoos. Like a little lost fairytale princess who Dita Von Teese had taken under her wing. Watching her enjoying herself at the table with the other wedding party members, I felt my heart in my throat. Her beauty was effortless. It didn't matter if she was dressed in my old sweatshirt or was draped in an expensive gown; she always outshone everyone around her.

Graham followed my gaze and chuckled softly. "You've got it bad."

I glanced at him and felt my face flush. "Yeah, I guess I do."

"Molly's a special girl, Joe. I'm happy for you." He replied, sipping his beer.

His words gave me pause. I couldn't talk to Mason and Mac about Molly, so that made Graham my only outlet.

"Between you and me? Even with...Jess...I never felt so...consumed. Sounds crazy...but it's a fact. Does that make any sense at all?"

Nodding he raised his beer and directed my gaze to his own wife, who'd just whispered something in Molly's ear. "It does. The first time I saw the missus, she reached right into my chest and pulled my heart right out. She's had it ever since. Luckily she takes really good care of it." He gave an oversized wink as he said the last bit. I grinned back at him.

"I wake up thinking about Molly. She's on my mind all day. Lately...I wonder if I'm screwing the whole thing up..." I trailed off and stared into the dregs of my mug. I looked up to see Graham watching me over the top of his beer.

"Relationships can be tough. Even the *best* ones. Sometimes it's hard to find the right path and along the way you lose each other. I know you don't believe the same as I do, but if you ever want to try it, I'd be happy to—" I held up a hand and nodded. I knew what he was going to say. Graham and I had been dancing a God vs Heathen waltz for so long that the conversation was almost spoken telepathically. I just couldn't take another heart-felt invitation to visit his church.

"Thanks. I appreciate it. I really do." Graham looked at me contemplatively for a moment, and then shrugged.

"No pressure, Joe. I just put it out there from time to time so that you know the offer still stands." Anne swept up and pulled him out onto the dance floor. She always seemed to know when our conversations were at an awkward stage. I waved as they retreated, and turned to look at the head table again. The sight of Molly tugged at my heart hard enough to hurt. The little man who'd escorted her during the ceremony was working hard to chat her up, and I smirked as I watched her shut him down by abruptly turning away to talk to Stacy.

I hated the awkward place we were right now. Our fighting had become like a reflex and I couldn't see a way out of it. She was so stubborn. To be honest, I was just as bad. I'd begun to worry that we just might be too alike in some ways to be able to make a go of it. Thoughts of that nature tended to lead me to a dark place, and I wanted to try and make it a good day, so I thrust them aside.

Sanchez rose from his place at the table. He waited for the room to quiet and when he spoke it was with a full, loud voice that was startling from the normally soft-spoken man.

"Family and friends, thanks for joining us on our special day. Seeing so many of the people we love here to celebrate with us makes us feel very blessed. I'm lucky to have married the most beautiful and loving woman that a man could ever hope to find. Stacy, every day, for the rest of my life, I'll work hard to be worthy of you." He pulled Stacy's hand up and bent over it, kissing it like a storybook prince. On anyone else it would have looked corny, but somehow Sanchez pulled it off.

Sitting back down, he leaned over and planted one on his

new wife. I felt the ghost of pain flare in my chest. It was hard to be at a wedding without thinking back to the day I'd married Jess. I hadn't been to a wedding since, and that was a decidedly good thing. I sipped my beer and fought a silent battle against the specters from my past.

Mac and Mason had thrown me one hell of a bachelor party. I'd gotten so drunk that I'd nearly missed the wedding. If it hadn't been for their mom sending over one of their cousins to roust us, we might have slept all day. Jessica had seethed at the sight of my bloodshot eyes when I turned up late for the pre wedding pictures, but you'd never know it. Her pictures from that day were radiant. In every shot she looked like an angel, but honestly the ceremony itself was a blur. All I remember is sweating out hard alcohol, which I'm sure made me smell wonderful. All things considered, my wedding was not the special memory that it probably should have been.

I blinked away the reminiscence and motioned to the bartender over, ordering a sweet tea. It would be quite some time before we'd be able to leave, but I wasn't about to chance our safety with even a slightly altered state. I saw Molly watching me from the main table with a wistful look on her face. She looked as ready to go as I was The guy next to her, Pablo I think, put a hand on her bare shoulder and turning, she smiled that faux smile of hers-the one that warned she was about to lose her temper. Part of me roared, wanting nothing more than to walk across the room and snap his arm off at the shoulder. This being socially unacceptable, I instead sat and sipped my tea. A moment later, he bent as if to whisper something in her ear, and Molly handled the issue by smashing a cupcake into his nose frosting side first. Her laughter carried across the room to me.

By the time the speeches were finally done, I was long past ready to go. I impatiently watched as the bride and groom danced their first dance. Then the wedding party all joined them. Her obligations discharged, Molly swept across the floor to me.

"Hey there, Tall, Dark, and Ominous. Come here often?" Without moving from my barstool, I pulled her into my arms and nuzzled her neck.

"Right here? No. But I'm sure there must be a door with a lock somewhere nearby." She allowed me to press against her for a moment before pulling back.

"Behave, caveman. People are watching." She soothed the sting of her rebuke by planting a sweet kiss on my lips. I let her drag me out of my seat and onto the dance floor.

I held her close as we danced to a couple of slow songs. She felt perfect pressed against me, her head resting on my shoulder. I lowered my face to brush against her cheek, breathing in the citrus scent wafting from her hair. Neither of us said a whole lot. Maybe we were afraid we'd kill the moment. Then she promptly ditched me with Sanchez while she helped Stacy gather her things to leave.

"Joe, the trip to Napa... I told Molly it was *way* too much." He blushed and I immediately held up a hand.

"Let me stop you there, dude. I had nothing to do with it. That's one hundred percent her. I got you a gift card to The Home Depot." He smiled and a surprised laugh tumbled from him.

"She's awesome." He admitted, and I nodded in agreement. Molly had a compulsion to nurture that seemed infinite. She was generous to a fault, but I hadn't bothered to argue when she told me her plans to send S&S on a foodie honeymoon. Sanchez truly had Molly's back and had even threatened to kick *my* ass when he thought I might hurt her. That made him good people in my book. Stacy wasn't afraid to stand up for Molly either, as she'd proven when she'd used the stun gun I bought for Molly one night. Some drunk had dared to climb aboard their truck when they were feeding the bar crowd down on Sixth Street. Molly told him to get the hell out, but had barely spoken the words before Stacy lit him up like a Christmas tree. I felt a whole lot better knowing the two of them were on Molly's team.

Sanchez excused himself to change and I found myself left with Pablo for company. He gave me a machismo onceover. I decided it was best not to test my patience and turned back to the bar. I ordered another glass of sweet tea and had almost finished it when Molly reappeared at my side, her face lit with excitement. We joined the gathered crowd in forming a human gauntlet for the newlyweds to run. Someone pressed a bag into my hand and I found myself throwing glitter at the happy couple along with everyone else. *Glitter.* It was like a stag party exploded on them as they left.

With the happy couple's departure complete, our obligation to stay was over. I offered to help carry gifts to Stacy's mother's van, but Molly shook her head and asked if we could go. She wasn't feeling well again, which worried me. Over the last few weeks, she'd complained more frequently of being tired. As usual, she'd resisted all of my suggestions that she take time off and rest. She hadn't even bothered to slow down. That night she looked a bit paler than usual as she leaned into me heavily.

"Come on, big boy." Her playful lilt lacked its usual enthusiasm. "Take me home."

Making our goodbyes, I caught Graham and Anne shooting concerned glances in our direction. I figured we were a few moments away from some sort of an intervention and decided that this day needed to be over. Putting my arm around her, I smiled and waved at them as I led her out to the car. After she'd climbed inside, I leaned across and belted her in. She must have been feeling particularly bad, because what normally would've earned me a snarky comment barely rated an eye roll.

I thought about bringing up the "Elaine issue" again, but one glance at Molly and I chose to save that conversation for later. Her ex-husband's new wife had been calling her phone incessantly, and the tension that bitch had created between us made me want to punch something. Easing through traffic, I concentrated on getting us home smoothly with no quick lane changes. It wasn't an easy feat in Molly's Mini Cooper which handled so well compared to my truck that it begged to be raced. I tried not to let my concern show on my face, but I doubted I was doing a very good job.

We rode for a good distance in a comfortable, peaceful silence. I decided that tonight I would just concentrate on taking care of her. No fights, no arguments. That plan didn't even make it all the way off the drawing board.

We were a few exits away from home when her phone went off. The ring tone, Tainted Love, made me arch an eyebrow. It wasn't a ringtone I'd ever heard from her phone before. The look on Molly's face said everything else. Flipping her finger over the screen, she sent the call to voicemail. Glancing up from her phone, she gave me a guilty look.

"I texted Dan to find out what Elaine's number was. She changed it after I moved. I wanted to know when it was her calling." My chest tightened as rage swelled inside of me. I was still pissed at Dan. He never should have given Molly's new number to Elaine.

I would never have guessed Dan would betray her trust like this.

"So were you planning on telling me about that?" I fumed. She looked away and it was clear she hadn't intended to share this information with me.

"I'm not keeping secrets, Joe. Don't make me wish I was." I didn't like her intimating that I was someone that she couldn't be honest with. Molly kept her eyes locked on mine, not giving an inch. "You may as well just go ahead and say it."

"Say what?"

"The usual. How I lack common sense. How I'm a bad a judge of character. Whatever other little gems you have up your sleeve."

"You said it, not me." I mumbled. I expected an explosion

of anger, but she simply shook her head.

"None of it matters. I made up my mind. I'm going to talk to her."

Frustration consumed me, but I tried to push it away. She was sick and the last thing she needed was me piling an argument on top of that. Then that annoying ring tone started again and I snapped. Reaching out, I plucked the phone from her hand and turned it off. She stared at me in shock and red rose up her skin like the mercury of a thermometer. My heart dropped to my feet.

"Molly, I don't want to start somethin'." She flipped her hand dismissively at me staring straight ahead out of the windshield

"Then quit acting like a controlling jerk!" I could see that I'd really upset her. I fought against the urge to verbally lash out. The whole damn point was that I didn't want Elaine upsetting Molly, and here I was only making it worse.

"I'm sorry." I held her phone out to her. The abruptness of my surrender seemed to take the wind out of her sails, and she gently pulled the phone from my hand. "This whole situation is surreal. She comes to you for help after what she did to you? I know she *was* your friend, but I don't understand why you would put yourself through this."

She blinked at me and I saw tears welling in her eyes. Turning away she wiped her face.

"If it were just her…" Her voice came out soft and guarded. Elaine had been Molly's sous chef before her divorce. She'd even sold that bitch her share of the restaurant in Seattle, before finding out that Elaine had been Draven's mistress. Now that he was in prison for stalking and threatening Molly, Elaine was divorcing him. She was building a case for full custody of their baby, and she'd had the balls to ask for Molly's assistance in doing so.

Molly turned and I could feel the weight of her gaze on me.

"There's a child involved. That bastard has no business anywhere near a little kid. If he gets any sort of visitations or God forbid some sort of custody... Joe, if it will keep Draven away from her son, I'm going to do what I can to help. I'd think you of all people would understand that."

Her delivery was harsh and biting, and I felt my anger flare again. As what she said rolled around in my head, I pictured a brief flash of "the Jack that might have been". It'd been a while since I had dreamed about my dead boy, but the image of him dashed my anger out like a bucket of water on a campfire.

We rode in a much less comfortable silence until we got to our apartment. Putting the car in park, I unclipped my seatbelt and climbed out of the car. I went around to her door and opened it. Offering her my hand, I helped her to her feet and pulled her into my arms.

"I'm sorry, baby." I held her gently against me, stroking her hair. "You should go with your gut. If you think that you need to help then you should. But what if she gives him your new number? It's hard for me to believe you would give her any trust after what she has done. But I'm on your side, never doubt that. I just worry about you. What can I do to make things easier on you?" I stroked her cheek with my thumb, and the sad expression on her face faded into a devilish grin.

"Let's see...you could distract me somehow... take my mind off of all my woes."

I cocked an eyebrow at her and gave her a crooked smile "I think I can help you with that."

Grabbing our things, we headed upstairs to the apartment we shared over my shop. Dropping our stuff just inside the door, I locked the deadbolt and then turned to see a flash of leg disappearing into the bedroom and I set off in pursuit.

By the time I appeared in our bedroom doorway, she'd lit the two candles that sat on top of my dresser. The flickering glow revealed her kicking off her heels one at a time.

"Unzip me?" She asked, presenting her inked shoulders and back to me. I eagerly did as she asked and watched her pastel gown fall to the floor. She pulled the jeweled combs from her hair, and it tumbled down her back in dark, silky waves.

"Baby girl. You are *so* damn beautiful." I whispered, pushing her hair aside and planting several small kisses along the length of her neck.

She peered back at me over her naked shoulder. "You think so?"

"I know so." I tilted my head as I raked my eyes over her porcelain curves. She turned around to face me, her blue eyes sparkling in the candlelight.

"Well? Are you just gonna stand there, or are you going to do something about it?"

CHAPTER Three

Molly

Complications

THANK GOD IT'S Friday.

The lunch rush had just fizzled and I'd managed to only run out back and vomit twice. I used my water bottle to rinse my mouth out and chased that with two pieces of minty gum before I climbed back aboard the truck.

"You need to go home, Molly. I don't have time to be sick." Carly, Sanchez's assistant chef, made a cross with her fingers and held it up at me like I was a vampire coming for her jugular. I didn't hold it against her. Her kids were in high school and if anyone made me look like I wasn't overscheduled, it was Carly.

"I'll live." I replied, washing my hands with extra soap. It felt good to be away from the smoldering grill, but I was still sticky from the humidity outside.

"Molly. There's nobody here. We can handle closing the

day without you." Isaac agreed. He was truck two's version of Stacy: cute, quick with math, and too smooth for his own good.

"You've been working sick all week. Didn't you promise Joe you'd go get a checkup?" Carly placed a fist on her boxy hip and fixed me with a scolding glare.

"She sure did." Joe's voice carried through the food truck's window and caused Isaac to start with surprise. I tilted my head to the side to see Joe's jade eyes peering out from under the black bill of his ball cap.

"Look what the cat dragged in." My eyebrow hitched skyward and I folded my arms.

His full lips twitched with a self-satisfied smile. "You've got an appointment in twenty minutes, so we'd better high tail it."

I shook my head and pursed my lips, but it was impossible to hide how pleased I was to see him. He was concerned enough about me that he'd called the clinic and made an appointment for me. My ex had never done anything like that. But Draven had been a snake. The *poisonous* variety. And Joe...well Joe could be pretty swoony on occasion. "Yes, sir."

Ditching my apron and tossing my purse over my shoulder, I descended the steps of the food truck. Joe snatched me right off the steps and swept me into his arms. I let out a surprised squeal and laughed so hard it hurt my raw throat.

"I've been throwing up all morning and you come along and toss me around like a sack of potatoes? *You* are one brave soul." I wrapped my arms around his neck as he made his way to his truck with me in his arms like some defective Disney princess.

"My truck or the Mini Coop?" He asked, pausing between our two vehicles.

"Truck." I replied, feeling a little lightheaded. When Joe drove my car, he had way too much fun, and the thought of him zipping through traffic like a stunt driver held little appeal. He turned away from the cherry red Mini Cooper and placed me on my feet beside his restored Ford.

"You're too good to me." I murmured. "But you don't need to treat me like a damsel in distress."

"I wouldn't have to if you'd take proper care of yourself." His retort was off the cuff and I was glad I was looking out the window when it came because it made me frown.

Just what the hell did he mean by that, exactly?

I managed to keep my lips clamped shut for the duration of the journey. We got to the clinic about three minutes before I was scheduled to be seen. When they called my name, I climbed to my feet and Joe stood right along with me. I raised my eyebrows and my expression must have been a bit withering, considering his deer in headlights reaction. He slowly sat back down and I trudged away in the direction of the nurse.

I was relieved to see I'd only gained four pounds, not five. Still, it made me cringe. The doctor had warned me it could be a side effect when she started me on the pill. That being said, I was happy that their scale had better numbers than mine. Maybe I'd just lost a pound from all the vomiting. The stomach bug had its advantages.

"So, Molly. Tell me. What brings you in today?" The nurse stuck a thermometer in my ear.

"I'm sleeping too much. I have no appetite. The smell of my own cooking makes me wretch. I think it might be the flu or an ulcer. I've thrown up a few times today. Oh…and my boyfriend thinks I'm depressed."

"Oh yeah?" She smiled at my eye roll.

"Yeah. Or he thinks I have cancer." I sighed. "He's been on Web MD."

She chuckled. "How long have you felt like this?"

"Three weeks, maybe?" I shrugged. "It seems to be getting worse."

She looked at my chart. "That's a bit long for a virus. Are you on any medications?"

"I have a prescription for Xanax, but I haven't used it in over a month. I started taking birth control pills a few weeks ago. I can't remember the name. It should be in my chart."

She took my vitals and said my pulse was a bit fast but that my blood pressure was very good. Then she asked if I felt like I could give her a urine sample.

"I'll try. I haven't been keeping much down..."

"It doesn't have to be much. When you're done just leave it in the window." The nurse instructed. "Then go back and change into the gown, alright?"

"Okay."

After the loveliness of struggling to catch urine midstream was done and I was in my ugly plaid gown, she came back into the room and informed me that the doctor wanted her to draw some blood. It was over before I knew it, but I got a little light-headed afterward and she made me lie down. I started to heave, and as if on instinct, she grabbed a small plastic basin and shoved it in front of me just before I vomited. Somehow I managed not to get any on myself or her, which was something, I guess. When I got myself under control, she asked if I wanted glass of water. I nodded, swiping at my streaming eyes.

"Can you send my boyfriend back here, please?" I asked her on her way out the door. She nodded.

"Which one is he?"

I managed a smirk, but it was a weak one. "He's the super good looking one. You'll find him."

I took several slow deep breaths, but I could feel my heart racing in my chest. Having my blood drawn had never bothered me before and I started to worry that maybe something *really was* wrong with me. There was a rap on the door and the nurse reappeared with Joe, who wore a look that was both surprised and concerned.

He closed the door and looked at me over his shoulder. "I thought you wanted me to stay in the waiting room."

"What if I *do* have cancer?" I blurted. With a heavy sigh, he scooted the chair close to the examine table I was lying on and took a seat.

"Molly, you don't have cancer." He sounded mildly amused and I looked down at my lap. He tipped my chin up to face him, his expression loving and confident. "They'll figure this out."

I nodded. He leaned in, but I turned my face away. I could smell his spicy cologne and thankfully it was the only smell today that didn't make me sick. "Trust me. You don't want to kiss me right now."

Joe gave me a crooked smile and pecked my forehead just as the doctor tapped on the door as she entered.

"Well, hello, Molly. Long time no see." She quipped, giving Joe the same head to toe perusal all straight, red-blooded woman did.

"Yeah." I huffed. "Right."

"I've got good news. I know why you're sick."

"That was fast. I thought you had to send the labs off somewhere." I replied with a frown.

"The urine test was plenty. It's your birth control." She replied, and relief washed over me.

"Okay. So I should stop taking them?" I asked.

"Yep. Pregnant women shouldn't take the pill." She responded dryly, and I recoiled as if she'd struck me.

"What?" Joe's tone was flat and his face expressionless. The doctor cocked an eyebrow at him and took a seat, plugging in her computer.

"There must be some mistake." I stammered, turning from Joe to the doctor.

"HCG in the urine doesn't lie." She tapped at her keys without looking at me. "Remember when I said you needed a backup method for the first month on the pill?"

My stomach dropped like I'd just crested the top of a roller coaster. "Yes."

"That wasn't a suggestion." She scolded. I turned to Joe, whose eyes were wide.

"But...we did." He took the words right out of my mouth. His eyes narrowed and then darted from left to right, as if he were replaying every time we'd ever had sex.

"Every time? For the full four weeks?" The doctor stopped typing and turned to us. She looked doubtful.

"Yes..." I nodded. "Religiously."

"Hmm..." She crossed to me and started pushing on the area below my belly button. "Any condom malfunctions?"

"Not since she's been on the pill." Joe's serious face left no margin for error.

I remembered the broken condom a couple of weeks before I started the pill and when Joe's eyes met mine I could see he did, too.

"Well...we did a urine pregnancy test the day I wrote you the prescription. It's possible that you might have been too early for it to detect the HCG."

"Wait." Joe sat forward, his sharp eyes fixed on her. "Are you saying she's been pregnant since before she started the pill?"

"Based on the size of her uterus, yes." Something on the doctor's face disturbed me. "When was your last period?"

"Umm... June? I've had a little spotting since I started taking the pills, but when I called the office the nurse said it was normal to have some breakthrough bleeding." Thinking about these details stripped the gears of my mind. All I could think was 'baby'.

"I really want you to see an OB/Gyn." She now wore a poker face that made me miss her smart ass comments. "Let me see if they can work you in today."

"Is something wrong?" Joe demanded, and my eyes shot to him. His face looked pale. "Can taking the pill hurt the baby?"

"That's very unlikely. But based on my exam, she really should have seen an OB already. Let me make a call. You can go ahead and get dressed, Molly."

She unplugged her computer and left the room in a flurry. I sat up and stared at the closed door in shock.

"What the hell just happened?" I turned to Joe, whose gaze met mine. He blinked at me blankly.

"I...I guess we're having a baby." He replied. We simply looked at one another for a full minute. Unable to process in my state of shock, I started to dress in a daze. When he spoke again, there was amusement behind his words. "I told you not to open the wrappers with your teeth."

I whipped my head in his direction and the twinkle in his eyes stunned me. "Joe, this isn't funny."

He looked down, appropriately admonished and that made me laugh.

"Okay...it was a little funny. But seriously!" I threw my shirt over my head and felt my cheeks burning. "If it was that night after Mason and Mac's birthday party-"

"It was." Joe raked his hand through his hair and blew out a breath at the ceiling. As I slipped my shoes on, I felt a lump form in my throat. The one time we had a condom tear, it was at the least opportune moment possible. I'd already brought up going on the pill and he'd been understandably in favor of the idea. We just hadn't made time in our schedules to get things done. When the condom broke, Joe freaked out and sprang into action. He'd made an appointment the following morning to get tested for everything since I'd already run that STD marathon after Draven's affair and knew I was clean. Meanwhile, I tried not to panic, but I made an appointment with my doctor for birth control and pregnancy test. I thought we'd covered our bases. I shook my head.

I guess I should have pressed them to draw blood.

As I picked up my purse, I noticed my hands were trembling. I stiffly sat back down on the exam table, afraid to even look in Joe's direction.

"Molly?" There was marked trepidation in his voice.

"Yeah?" I stared at the tile patterns on the floor. I couldn't bring myself to look at him.

He reached out for me and stroked my hair. I nervously shifted my gaze toward him, but I still didn't dare look him in the eye. When he spoke, his voice sounded thick. "It's gonna be okay."

Before I had a chance to respond, the door swung open and the nurse hurried back again. She looked flustered as she handed me a business card.

"Alright. They can work you in as soon as you can get there. But you need to go now."

"Is this really necessary? Can't I just go tomorrow?"

"The doctor said ASAP. The OB/GYN agreed." I may not know anything about medicine, but I know people. She looked nervous. I had a feeling she wasn't telling me everything. She rushed us out the door and once we were outside in the sunshine, the entire event seemed surreal. I forced myself to meet Joe's eyes, and was comforted by the fact that he no longer looked as white as a sheet. He took my hand and started in the direction of the truck.

"Let me see where this place is." Joe held out his hand for the business card. I handed it over to him and when he read the address, he stopped in his tracks. He closed his eyes with a heavy exhale.

"What?" I asked, a feeling of foreboding overtaking me. I was afraid to hear his answer.

"Dr. Myers was Jess's OB." His voice had a rough edge. I cringed a little at the mention of his dead wife and the bite I heard when he said the doctor's name.

"Oh." I whispered. He pinched the bridge of his nose and then looked up at the blue sky as if gathering himself.

"She's a really good doctor." He added, as if he'd sensed my apprehension. I noticed he didn't look in my direction, and I realized just how terrified I was.

"Okay." I responded, climbing into the truck. It was the first time I could remember Joe not opening the door for me. I figured he was distracted and couldn't blame him.

We arrived at the OB/GYN office at 3:30 and scrambled in our bewildered state to fill out the lengthy questionnaires and medical histories. In retrospect, it was probably for the best that we had something to focus on. We were just finishing the last form when they called us back.

The nurse requested more urine from me, weighed me again, and measured my height. Then she hurried us into an exam room.

"New OB visit! How exciting! Congratulations. Can I just say that y'all are a *gorgeous* couple? I'm sure you've made a beautiful baby!" Her toothy grin would have had me laughing along with her any other day. Instead, Joe and I both murmured an awkward 'thanks'. She paused at our lackluster response, and after another quick look at my chart, she shifted gears to an ultra-professional manner.

As she took my vitals, she started in with a barrage of questions. When she asked the first day of my last period, I gave her the information and Joe chimed in that we were pretty sure about the date of conception. She took down both dates and informed us that based on our responses my due date was April 4th. Joe and I simply looked at one another blankly. We responded glumly to all her additional questions until she asked my family history and discovered my brothers were twins.

"Identical or fraternal?"

"Fraternal." I replied and she raised her eyebrows as her fingers flew over her keyboard. I realized I was starving and glanced at my phone to see it was 4:15. I needed to eat something but the thought of throwing up again depressed and exhausted me. She blew through several more questions before we hit another roadblock.

"Are either of you of Jewish decent."

"I am." Joe chimed in. "On my mom's side."

"And you?" She turned to me.

"No." I shook my head, wondering what on earth Joe's being Jewish could have to do with anything relevant. "Not that I know of. Why?"

"There's a genetic disorder called Tay-Sachs associated with Jewish parents. You shouldn't have to worry about it. Both parents have to have the gene. Well, that was the last of the questions. This is for you." She smiled and handed me a bag full of samples and coupons. Then she nodded to the gown on the exam table. "Go ahead and change. The doctor will be in shortly."

I started to undress for the second time in awkward silence. Simply put, I was trying to keep from losing my shit. Joe and I hadn't even talked about kids. We'd been too busy trying to figure how we fit into each other's lives to get into any of the serious conversations. Hell, we'd hardly dated at all before we moved in together, much to the astonishment of most of our friends and family.

Pregnant.

A baby.

This just couldn't be real.

I'd always been careful. I'd been completely anal about taking my birth control when I was married to my ex. Before I realized Draven wasn't parent material, I had most definitely wanted to have kids. Once I saw his temper in action, I was terrified of getting pregnant. I quickly decided I didn't want to bring a defenseless target for his anger into our house. But 'pre-Draven Molly' had wanted to have babies.

Someday.

But that hypothetical 'someday' was usually tied to something stable and permanent, or at least a lot more solid than what I had with Joe. And Joe…well, he was still recovering from losing his son who'd died before he'd even had a chance to hold him. I knew he wasn't ready for this. How could he be? Would he even want me to have it?

I shook my head.

Of course he'll want me to have it. This was Joe.

I felt on the verge of bursting into tears. Joe inhaled like he was about to speak when a loud rap on the door made me jump. A tall, statuesque blonde strode purposefully in and smiled brightly at me.

"Hi, Molly. I'm Kate Myers."

"Hi." My response sounded meek. I was afraid if I said anything else my voice would crack and the floodgates would open. I'd already reached my quota of tears for the decade.

"Sounds like it's been a day full of surprises." Her sapphire eyes were full of empathy and she turned to Joe with an outstretched hand. The smiled on her face immediately vanished. "Joe?"

"What's up, doc?" Joe gave her a soft smile and I felt every hair on my body stand on end. Watching the silent exchange between the two of them was like getting a glimpse into the past. I suddenly felt like an intruder.

"It's great to see you again." She sounded genuine, and Joe managed a nod in return. She turned back to me and she seemed to reassess me, her eyes resting on my forearm tattoos. I assumed I must have been a bit of a shock to her after the fair and lovely Jessica but Dr. Myers smiled at me again, kindness emanating from her.

"Go ahead and lie back for me, Molly. I want to measure your uterus and I need to press on you in order to do that thoroughly. It might be a bit tender, but I promise it won't take long, okay?"

I nodded and did as she asked. She used a cloth tape, measuring and re-measuring. When she pushed on me, it was more pressure than I'd expected and I winced and then bit my lip, afraid I'd look like a wimp.

"Well, I can see why she sent you over. You measure a bit bigger than we'd expect you to for eight weeks."

"How much bigger?" Joe asked, and I shot him a curious look.

"She's measuring like she's about ten or eleven weeks along. We usually like to see our new moms at about ten weeks. I'd like to take you down the hall for an ultrasound so we can make sure we're right about the due date."

"We're pretty sure. It was pretty memorable." I replied with a glance at Joe.

"It might just be a big baby in there, then." She grinned, but she didn't look convinced. "Humor me."

She gave me a robe and I stood on shaky legs to put it on. Joe ran a comforting hand along my back as we followed her down the hall to another room. It was dimly lit, and a butch woman in scrubs was clicking away on the computer. Butch gestured to the table. Joe helped me onto it and the doctor joined the technician on the opposite side. The technician pulled out an apparatus that looked like a large white dildo.

"What the hell is that?" I demanded, turning bulging eyes to Joe. He looked as confused as I did, so I turned back to the doctor expectantly.

"It'll be more accurate if we do the ultrasound transvaginally, Molly." Her kind expression soothed my frayed nerves, but my heart still hammered in my chest. "It'll be a little uncomfortable, but it won't take long."

I nodded, but reached out for Joe. He was right there, immediately leaning onto the table and taking my hand.

"Look at me, Molly." He whispered, and I did. He pulled my hand to his lips as the tech basically violated me with the cold, unyielding wand. I tightened my grip on him, and focused on steadying my breathing.

Joe smiled sympathetically, and I closed my eyes as he softly stroked my cheek. Completely overwhelmed, I swiped at a tear that escaped before I could blink it away. He brushed my bangs off of my forehead and kissed it, his eyes reassuring. Then he glanced over at the two women and I saw his expression sober. I whipped my head in their direction. They exchanged a long, knowing glance.

"What is it?" Joe's gritty voice sounded grim. "What's wrong?"

"Nothing at all. Your due date looks right. About 7 to 8 weeks along." The doctor replied, swiveling the monitor in our direction. Even though I'd never been through an ultrasound before, I'd seen it in the movies. It looked all wrong to me. "See? Two placentas, two heartbeats. Congratulations, you two! You're expecting twins."

Joe unlocked the door and held it open for me. I wandered into the dark apartment, numbly tossing the folders, pamphlets, samples and newly filled prescriptions onto the table. I dropped my purse in the middle of the floor and marched directly to the bathroom. Turning on the bathwater, I poured in too much bubble bath and stripped off all of my clothes. I'd been poked, prodded and completely violated. A warm bath sounded like a cure.

When I'd woken up that morning, I'd been worried I might have an ulcer. Now I was eating for three. All of my mother's war stories about having twins came rushing forward from the dark recesses of my mind. Stretch marks, engorged breasts…sore nipples, weeks without sleep…

I dropped to my knees in front of the toilet and vomited again. This time there wasn't much left in my stomach. We'd driven straight from Dr. Myers's to the pharmacy to get the prenatal vitamins, extra iron supplements and the expensive pills to control my vomiting. We hadn't eaten anything for dinner and I was in no mood to cook.

I forced myself to brush my teeth, though I nearly gagged again and then I slipped into the steaming bath. Exhausted, I rested my head against the cool tile of the wall behind me. Staring down at the pale flesh of my belly, I wondered how my family was going to react to our news. They all loved Joe…probably more than they loved me. Granny was sure to enjoy the opportunity to paint me in a scarlet letter, but it was Mac and Mason I was most concerned about. My brothers had an odd way of reacting to Joe and me, considering they'd all been like The Three Musketeers since forever.

"Molly?" Joe's deep voice resonated through the closed door.

"Come in." I sat up and a small stream of bubbles sloshed over the side of the tub. I tossed my towel onto the spill just as Joe entered the room. He handed me my favorite cup full of ice water and a pill.

"Zofran." He explained, and recognizing the name of the drug, I took it. The doctor had insisted I needed to force fluids and that I had to eat something and keep it down.

"Thanks." His eye held mine and I suddenly felt very shy. Breaking off our stare down, Joe closed the toilet seat and sat down, folding his muscular arms across his chest.

"You know, you have to be careful about how hot that water is…"

"Why?" I knitted my eyebrows, truly confused.

"It's not good for…" He trailed off and I watched his gorgeous eyes migrate to my mid-section. A striking realization hit me. From this moment forward, there would never be another conversation about *us*. From now on, it would always be about *all of us*. "The babies."

I exhaled and settled further under the water. "I'm sorry."

He took a turn looking confused. "For what?"

"That we've just landed in a situation we're not ready for." I felt beads of sweat standing on my upper lip. His warning about the temperature ate at me, and I considered turning on the cold water. The doctor said the babies were about the size of two grains of rice, and here I was already in danger of messing them up.

"Well in that case, I'm sorry too." The matter of fact way he said it made me flinch.

He noticed and unfolded his arms. He sat forward, an apology splashed all over his face.

"Okay, that sounded really bad. Let me start over..."

"You don't need to." I looked away, reaching for the soap.

"Listen to me." He moved to sit on the side of the tub and placed a hand on my knee. "You and me? This... it's what I want. This is not how I imagined us starting a family, but that doesn't mean I don't want it."

"So you're saying you want me to keep them." I looked up at him from under my damp lashes. He blinked in astonishment then a sound escaped him that was like a wounded animal. When he spoke, his voice was thick and husky.

"What the hell kind of a question is that? What kind of monster do you...why wouldn't I..." His voice held enough pain to bring tears streaming out of my eyes. "Don't you?"

"Yes." I said cautiously. His response scared the hell out of me, but from the moment the doctor pointed out the tiny pulsations on the computer screen, I'd had no doubt. "I want them."

Joe's face lit up and he leaned forward, practically falling into the tub with me. He kissed me several times before pulling himself away from me. The outrage and hurt from a moment before had vanished, which I considered more disturbing than their appearance in the first place. "Okay. Let's get married."

I exploded in bewildered laughter, a strange sensation considering the fresh tears hadn't yet dried on my cheeks. I shook my head. "Like hell."

"I'm serious." His smile faltered just a tiny bit.

"So am I." My retort was gentle, but firm. "This is 2014, Joe. I'm not going to roll over and marry you because you've put a couple of buns in my oven."

"You don't want to marry me?" The smile had evaporated and he looked hurt again. That expression on him killed me, but I'd always promised I'd never lie to him.

"Not like this. I don't want some quickie shotgun wedding. It never ends well. It's just a bad idea right now."

"I respectfully disagree." He argued, his soulful eyes imploring me to listen to reason. "Our babies are a perfectly valid reason to take the plunge. And you and I? We love each other. So why the hell not?"

"Wow. What woman could resist such a romantic proposal?" I rolled my eyes and grinned. He flushed beet red, and seeing his reaction made me feel like a total bitch. I reached for his hand, and luckily, he let me take it. "Baby, don't misunderstand me. There's no one else I'd rather have for my 'baby daddy'. It's just…we've already got a major dilemma to contend with. Let's not add another, okay?"

He was quiet for a long moment and I felt breathless, wondering if I'd just pushed him too far. His outburst troubled me, but only a little. Joe was nothing but gentle with me, and it was fair for him to get emotional about this unprecedented debacle. Finally, he looked up from the floor. "So I guess we should call our families."

I groaned at the suggestion and pulled my knees up to my chest. "Can't we just put it on Facebook or something?"

Joe uttered a shocked guffaw. "What? Like a group text?"

"Do you really want to have this conversation more than once?" I leaned my head back and closed my eyes.

"Cowgirl up, darlin'. We've got to tell our parents and siblings before we take out a skywriting ad."

I sighed. He was always the pragmatist. "Can we eat first?"

Joe smiled softly. "You're hungry?"

"Ravenous." I could see why Zofran cost a pretty penny. That shit worked like a charm. As if to punctuate my point, my stomach audibly growled.

Joe glanced at my abdomen with obvious amusement and the smallest hint of pride. When he spoke, there was laughter in his voice. "What sounds good?"

I batted my eyelashes at him innocently and bit my lip. "Loaded nachos and a peanut butter malt."

CHAPTER Four

Joe

Announcements

WE DECIDED TO give ourselves the weekend before we told anyone the news. Two days of peace to just try to absorb our new reality. After failing to teach me how to make blueberry pancakes, Molly dug into all the reading material Dr. Myers had sent home with us. She'd read for a while and then let loose with a string of curse words. Every once in a while she'd blurt something like "You have *got* to be shitting me!" or "I'm only allowed to take *Tylenol?*" Then she'd descend into thoughtful silence.

Thirty minutes after she'd started this effort to educate herself, she jumped up and marched out of the room. I assumed she was headed for the bathroom, since she said she felt like she had to pee every ten minutes. When she didn't come back, I realized she'd gone into the bedroom. I went to check on her, but discovered she'd locked the door. After my attempts at gentle coaxing were ignored, I got frustrated and picked the lock.

I found her face down on the bed sobbing into a pillow. She had her laptop open on the bed and when I looked at the screen I saw a webpage about fetal alcohol syndrome. I intervened, pulling the laptop away from her and sitting it far out of her reach. When she finally calmed down enough to speak, she confessed that she was worried about the few beers she'd had over the last couple of months.

"A couple of beers are no big deal. I'd be more worried about the pills you took." The comment was meant to put her mind at ease, but I could tell by the wide eyed stare she wore that I'd just given her a mountain of new things to worry about. I doubted her occasional Xanax and Ibuprofen would do any significant damage, but I knew my medical opinion wouldn't offer much reassurance. Unsure how else to proceed, I did my best to take her mind off of it with two of her favorite things: slow, sweet sex and a walk down to her favorite Chinese restaurant for orange chicken and some crab rangoon.

I barely slept a wink on Sunday night. Molly and I had agreed to start making the rounds the following day. We'd decided to only tell our family and closest friends what was what. We wouldn't announce anything to the world at large for another month, since twelve weeks was some magic pregnancy safe zone. I texted my sister and asked if they were free the following night. She texted back that they were and I told her to bring the family and meet us at The Salt Lick, our favorite restaurant, at five p.m. The place was close to my sister's ranch, and I figured Molly might be a bit less nervous about telling my sister if she got some pork ribs and potato salad out of the deal.

Knowing our "secret" was about to be revealed brought the entire situation into focus. Anxiety started gnawing at me, and I left a voicemail for Dr. Greene's scheduler asking if I could push up my weekly appointment. I had a feeling he'd be eager to see me once I told him what was up.

After tossing and turning, I finally crawled out of bed at five thirty and started preparing for my day. I figured it couldn't hurt to get a head start on the workday, since the jobs kept rolling in. I was lacing up my steel-toed boots when Molly came out of the bedroom. Her hair was wild from sleep, and she looked adorable. She bent to kiss the top of my head on her way past me into the kitchen, and I caught the scent of her soap and minty mouthwash.

"What are you doing up, little girl? You sick again?

She shook her head with a nonchalant shrug. "No. The munching on crackers before getting out of bed thing really worked."

"I always said I wouldn't kick you out of bed for eating crackers." I joked and her bawdy laughter shifted my mood from anxious to amorous.

"The doctor was so right about taking the vitamins the night before. I feel way better today than yesterday." She turned back to the refrigerator and took out the eggs.

"I didn't wake you, did I?" I asked, troubled that she was up. Stacy and Sanchez had texted her the day before to say they were back from California, so I knew Molly didn't have to be anywhere.

"No. I couldn't sleep for shit. I thought I'd do some baking." She yawned as she preheated the oven and started the coffee pot.

"Careful with that stuff. Only one cup, okay?" I kept my tone light. I was torn between not wanting to sound bossy and worrying about how she'd react when she later learned about the dangers of caffeine.

"Yes, dear." She parroted like a 1950's housewife. Her cheeky smile seemed to imply she was kidding. "Actually, I was planning to bring a couple of thermoses down for you and the boys since you still have that shitty old coffee maker downstairs."

"Huh. Obedient, barefoot *and* in the kitchen! Is it my birthday?" I cracked, crossing the room to kiss her goodbye. She crinkled her nose and reached out for my nipple as if she planned to twist it off. I easily captured her hand and backed her against the refrigerator, pinning it above her. My lips were on hers and her enthusiastic moan against my mouth got my pulse racing.

"Obedient, my ass." She replied between wet kisses and her spirited response was impossible for me to resist. I fisted her hair at the nape of her neck while my other hand slid inside her robe, grabbing a handful of pert breast. Her hands traveled down my back to grab my ass and she pulled me roughly against her. Her eagerness caused the blood to rush from my head to my groin. I picked her up and sat her on the nearby counter, kneeing my way between her legs. The gasping sound that escaped her made me want to take her back to bed, or perhaps just bend her over the counter.

Sadly, I did neither, since the pre heat alarm on the oven dinged and Molly pushed me away. I was tempted to press things, maybe throw her down on the couch and take her. She loved that kind of aggressive shit and she had me pretty worked up. I regretted not doing it an hour later as I replayed the groping session. I tried to shake of the intense memory as I balanced on a ladder while staining a 6 foot tall hutch. Falling because my balance was thrown off by my rock hard erection would have been disastrous.

Even though I had the music turned up fairly loud, I heard Francis and Mac come into the shop through the front door. They were already bickering back and forth.

"Keep on telling yourself that, Mac. Statistics don't lie." Francis scoffed and I instantly knew they were arguing about football. Since I'd told them they could no longer discuss politics in my presence, it was their new go-to.

"Joe! Talk sense into this man, would you? Fran seems to

be under the impression that the Cowboys are going to have a shit team again this year." Mac's eye roll brought an instant smile to my face. Molly's brother looked a lot like her. He had the same dark hair she did, but he had far more of it on his face than on top of his head. That was only because he wore his hair high and tight. It was his twin, Mason, who suffered from male pattern baldness. He'd been thinning in the back since he and Mac's twenty first birthday. Mason had a chip on his shoulder about it, so Mac and I pointed it out whenever we could, of course. Mason wasn't running off to get hair plugs or anything. He just wore a cowboy hat 'round the clock in hopes that no one would notice. Sometimes, I thought Mac and Molly looked more alike than Mason and Mac did. But the twins sure as hell *acted* alike. I'd gotten into more trouble with those two in that first year that we met than I had in previous sixteen years combined.

"That's not what I said." Francis sat down his keys and his leather planner on the front counter and made his way back to join us. He completely outclassed Mac and me in his pressed slacks and his starched collared shirt. "I simply said the Saints were going to totally smoke Dallas."

"Which is basically the same thing." Mac snorted, earning an 'oooo' from me like Mac had landed a scathing burn. Francis laughed good-naturedly.

"You Texans." He chuckled with a pleasant grin. He gestured with his thin arm dramatically, and his gold incisor sparkled in the morning sun. "Mass delusions, I tell ya."

Mac wandered over to inspect my progress on the custom hutch while Francis went back up to the front counter and logged onto his email. He picked up the phone receiver, presumably to check voicemail. Mac and I had moved onto our next project, a bamboo pie safe with tins salvaged from a Victorian saloon, before Francis had completed his daily ritual. He was frowning and shaking his head as he made his way back to the work area once more.

"Well, unless the two of you plan to work sixteen hour days six days a week, I think we need to hire another carpenter." He informed us, and proceeded to give a verbal report of all the requests for custom restorations and builds that had come in over the weekend. We were already estimating that we were booked out a month as it was.

"Or we could just raise our rates." Mac rubbed his hands together with greedy villainous laughter and I grinned. It felt great to be wanted, but we needed to keep up with demand.

We were kicking around a few names of guys we knew who'd be both good enough and ballsy enough to take the job, when I heard the creak of the backstairs. Molly came into view. Her hair was in little pig tails dangling over each shoulder and she wore loose, light clothing. Even without a stitch of makeup on, she was luminous. I noticed she was carrying two thermoses and hurried in her direction.

"Hey, there sweetheart!" Francis called, beating me to her side as I rushed to her assistance. "Stopping in to add a little beauty to our otherwise dreary day?"

Francis had been a Molly fan since the first day she fed him. She was rather partial to him, too. He'd been homeless when we'd met, squatting in the courtyard of a dilapidated hotel that the crew I was working with had been restoring. Molly's food truck showed up one day, and Francis instantly became her number one fan. Being the softie that she is, Molly fed him not only lunch, but bundled up leftovers for him before she closed up shop each night. He'd come a long way in rebuilding a life for himself. I'd given him the apartment across from mine when we had to dismantle his makeshift home near the end of the hotel restoration. My income apartment had been empty since I bought the building and it was too damn cold for him to be outside. Since he'd been a salesman before he started sleeping in abandoned buildings, I offered him a job. The rest, as they say, is history.

Molly graced Francis with a grateful smile as he took both of the thermoses from her.

"Hey, yourself, you dirty flirt. How's Kelly liking the new school?" She asked.

"So far so good." He smiled. Francis's daughter, Kelly had relocated from Detroit just in time for the school year to begin. After months of emails and phone calls, she'd come down to visit with her dad for a couple of weeks over summer break, and had evidently fallen in love with Austin. She taught first grade, and had easily landed a job at a nearby elementary school.

I'd been taken aback when Francis had introduced me to her. Kelly was a petite, doe eyed brunette who came off as painfully shy. I was surprised by her quiet demeanor, since Francis had once told me that Molly reminded him of her. Molly was about as gregarious as they came, and could make friends in a morgue.

"Y'all have coffee cups down here, don't ya?" Molly retreated toward the staircase.

"Yep." I moved to the sink to wash my hands.

"Good, 'cause I need to bring down your breakfast and I can't carry both." She vanished out of sight. She returned a minute later with two plates of mouthwatering muffins and rolls.

"What smells so good?" Mac came out from the other workroom as the scent of Molly's fresh treats wafted throughout the shop.

"Cornbread and bacon muffins and a little something I like to call a 'Sticky Pig'." She replied, handing Mac the plate of muffins.

"The muffins are amazing." I chimed in, remembering them all too well from our first 'morning after'. "I want to try this 'Sticky Pig'."

Molly held out the other plate to me and I took one of the giant rolls, trying to keep all of the gourmet bacon bits from toppling off onto my clothes. The aroma already had me salivating.

"It's a lot like a cinnamon roll, but with real maple syrup folded into the frosting and candied bacon sprinkled on top." She explained as I took a huge bite. As with everything she made, the salty and sweet concoction was inexplicably delicious. Francis took one and turned to Molly.

"What's the occasion? You never bring us breakfast." He tasted the roll as if savoring a fine wine.

"Oh...Joe didn't tell you our news?" Molly's blue eyes flicked to me mischievously and I knew all hell was about to break loose. "We're pregnant. With twins.

Mac spit coffee across the room in a spray fighting not to choke.

"Damn it! Don't say shit like that when I'm drinking." There was a smile on his face and I could tell he thought she was yanking his chain. Francis grinned, but looked thoughtfully between the two of us. His gaze swept over Molly's loose purple blouse, then my face, and he broke into a huge smile.

"Congratulations!" Francis stepped up and Molly grinned as he enfolded her in a friendly hug. Turning to me, Francis shook my hand. Mac looked between Francis and Molly for a moment before the smile fell from his face. He turned to me with a confused expression that was almost comical.

"Wait. She's serious? You knocked her up? What the hell, man! Were you or were you not told to buy rubber bands?" I could tell he was teetering precariously between outrage and amusement and decided to give him a nudge in the right direction.

"We...had a wardrobe malfunction," I trailed off, feeling the blood rush to my face. Mac stared at me for a few seconds and then doubled over with laughter. Tears leaked from his eyes and he held onto the worktable to keep from falling over. I started laughing at the sight of his ridiculous display, and Molly and Francis just exchanged looks of disbelief. Mac struggled to pull in gasps of breath. Molly gave him an annoyed side glance and walked past him to peck me on the cheek.

"Trust me, Mac. Joe has no trouble filling up a condom. In fact, he buys the large ones. And if you ever read the literature you'd know that they're only about 97% effective." Mac's eyes practically bugged out of his head and he looked like he was going to have a fit.

"Ugh! Too much information. I do *not* want to know anything about anything you two do or do not do in the bedroom. Remember I just ate." He gave Molly an incensed look, grabbed a Sticky Pig, and hopped up on top of the workbench. Looking back and forth between the two of us he shook his head.

"So does mom know yet?" An evil grin split his face. "Or granny?"

"No," Molly said, smacking him on the arm. "And don't get any wise ideas. We'll tell people in our own time. Got it?" Mac gave a gaping, and nauseatingly sweet roll filled grin and nodded.

"Your funeral. So does this mean you two are getting hitched?" The look Molly gave him would have killed a lesser man. Turning to me in confusion he glared. "What? My sister's not good enough for you?"

"I've already asked her and she turned me down flat, Mac." I replied, refusing to look in her direction. I watched as Francis's eyes shifted to Molly. I'm pretty sure he saw something on her face that gave him some insight, because he tried to catch Mac's eye. Mac ignored him and wheeled on Molly.

"Are you serious? All of a sudden you don't want to marry him? Shack up with him? Yes. Have babies with him? Sure. But get married? Hell no! That's madness! You practically stalked him your Freshman and Sophomore years. I swear, you need to have your head examined."

"Hey, now." I narrowed my eyes at Mac, my voice sounded cautionary, and dangerous.

Molly's eyes blazed like a blue flame and she stepped toward Mac, but Francis moved between them. The rage on the old man's face snapped Mac's mouth shut like a trap.

"Think before you speak, Mac! Show your sister the respect she deserves. Molly's quite capable of making her own decisions. Family is supposed to support you, not tear you down." Something about the way he said it made me think he wasn't just talking about the current issue with Molly. Mac looked between Francis and Molly and raised his hands in front of him in surrender.

"Okay, okay. I'm sorry. Open mouth and insert foot. You two are grown-ups, I'm sure you will figure it out. Kids have a way of making things more complicated...and somehow a lot simpler all at the same time."

He hopped off of the table, grabbed a cup of coffee and another Sticky Pig and retreated to the far side of the workroom. Francis put a hand on Molly's shoulder and then returned to the front counter. She folded her arms and looked at her feet. I pulled her to me and held her. She was stiff for a moment and then she melted against me. I felt her give a little shudder as if she were fighting against tears.

"Mac is an ass. Don't let him get to you." She shook her head and sniffed.

"He's the shallow end of the pool. I'm in for a world of shit when granny gets ahold of this. She will probably knit me a scarlet letter sweater for my next birthday." I grinned but the miserable way she looked at me took the joke out of her statement.

"I told you already, we could get married." She put her hand up to stop me.

"I really can't have this conversation right now. Okay?" I felt a stab of pain at the way she just dismissed me.

"All right." I forced a light tone, keeping all the hurt out of my voice. She gave me a quick kiss without meeting my eyes and retreated back upstairs. Mac and Francis barely spoke for the rest of the day and I found myself grateful for the quiet. It gave me time to think.

Molly had been sending me mixed signals since we first got together. The self-depreciating remarks, the comments about not being in my league. It was all bullshit and I'd chalked it up to false modestly. Lately, I was starting to see that she actually believed that crap. Somehow this unbelievable woman had gotten the idea in her head that she was anything less than amazing. I felt lucky to have her, but if I couldn't figure out a way to make her believe this, I could lose her.

Pulling out my phone, I saw a missed call from Dr. Greene's office. I called back and his secretary told me he had an afternoon cancellation. I told her I would take it.

I finished what I was working on and pulled Mac into the back office for a quick talk. After I closed the door, I turned to him and saw he looked pale.

He started yammering just like Molly does when she thinks she's in trouble. "I'm sorry if I upset Molly, Joe. She just gets these ideas in her head of perfection and life isn't like that, ya know? Like back when we were kids. Every single year she asked Santa for a white Christmas and a sled. Mom and dad were finally like 'it's figgin' Texas, kid. Deal with it.'"

I shook my head, but I knew exactly what he meant. Molly could get fixated on details, which is why she was such an incredible chef. "Take it up with her, not me. We need to make an action plan for this list of jobs."

I went over what we needed to get done by the end of the week then headed to the makeshift showroom to touch base with Francis. I told him to triple our rates except with repeat customers. Short term it would help control our workload. And if they didn't want to pay our rates they could go to someone else. That got a smile out of him and he set about adjusting the spreadsheet tables on his laptop to the significantly higher rate.

By the time I got back upstairs to the apartment, Molly was sleeping on the couch in front of the television. She looked so damn angelic that I gave her a kiss on the forehead and covered her with a blanket.

My drive across town to Dr. Greene's office was hectic. Every idiot with a car was on the road and by the time I arrived I was in a foul mood. The receptionist waved me through. I glanced at my watch and saw I was ten minutes late. Dr. Greene looked up from behind his desk and something in my face caused him to stand. Crossing to me, he shook my hand and gestured me to a chair.

"Hey, Joe. I was surprised to get your call. What's going on?"

"Molly's pregnant with twins." I hadn't expected to just blurt it out but it was like the words had been under pressure inside of me. The doctor kept his expression neutral but stood back up and grabbed a fresh notebook. Pulling out his pen, he jotted a few things down and then looked up at me.

"I take it from your level of anxiety that this was not a planned pregnancy?" I shook my head. "How far along is she?"

"Eight weeks. It's madness. We were so careful, doc." This statement produced a wry look from the doctor.

"Yes, Joe. The medical books all say the same thing. It only takes one sperm and one egg to make a baby. Or in your case...maybe two." His condescending smile reminded me of Molly's doctor's, and I wondered if they'd attended the same 'bedside manner' class.

My mind slipped back to that crazy night we'd conceived. It was Mac and Mason's thirty second birthday and naturally they wanted to go out drinking. Everyone was talking about Midnight Cowboy, some old speakeasy/brothel that had been recently converted into a swanky cocktail bar. Mason and his wife, Robin, set up the reservation. Robin is a nurse, and let me tell ya, healthcare workers know how to drink. She and her coworkers always know about every new bar in town. Mac, who had been between girlfriends at the time, came stag. The twins had invited

Charlie the Plumber and *his* new girlfriend, and Graham brought Anne along.

Molly chose to wear a very short, strapless dress that night. That little black dress...let's just say it left me conflicted about going out. The way it clung to her curves made me want to wrap her up in my jacket or unwrap her in the bedroom. She'd been in a particularly frisky mood, and made all sorts of lascivious remarks in the cab on the way down to Sixth. She said the idea that our destination used to be a whorehouse *really* turned her on. I thought our cab driver was going to wreck the car the way he kept eyeing her in the rearview mirror. She seemed to pick up on this, and proceeded to taunt me a little more quietly (after I shot her a reproachful look) about what she *wasn't* wearing under her dress and how we should do a little roleplaying when we got home.

Once at Midnight Cowboy, we had a great time. The sexy lighting and taboo ambiance put us all in a thirsty mood. We had a lot of laughs and consumed a considerable amount of alcohol. Molly kept whispering sordid things in my ear...dirty things that made me blush. Throughout the entire evening, her hands wandered recklessly under the table.

By the time we got home, we were ready to rip each other's clothes off and we didn't make it any further than the couch. When the damn condom tore, she'd been straddling me, riding me like a cowgirl. I tried to say something, but I was already on the edge and the feel of her around me had just gone from very good to off the chain.

"Molly." I growled her name and a guttural sound ripped out of my throat. She must have taken this as encouragement (on many levels, if I'm completely honest, *it was*), and she sat all the way upright, driving me further into her. She threw her head back and cried out exuberantly, and I was helpless to stop myself from joining her. Moments later when she caught her breath, she rolled off of me, and her wide eyes told me she'd figured out what happened. There was a lot of mutual panic and deep, semi-drunken discussion on what otherwise could have been a bad-assed Penthouse Forum kind of night.

"Understandably, an unplanned pregnancy can be stressful." Dr. Greene's logical delivery yanked me from the memories into the present. "How are things with Molly?"

"I asked her to marry me." He gave me a blank look. "I brought it up twice. She shot me down."

"And how did that make you feel?" He asked in a cliché tone of voice for his profession.

I flipped him off. It was instinctive and he gave something that sounded like a strangled laugh. He and I had always had a pretty unusual doctor/patient relationship. "How the fuck do you think it made me feel? She thinks the only reason I want to marry her is because I got her pregnant."

"Is it?" His inquisitive expression pissed me off, and I took a moment to get myself in check.

"No. Marrying her is just like asking her to live with me. It makes sense. But she doesn't seem to think it's a good idea. Some bullshit about a shotgun wedding. She still acts like she's not worthy of me. It's like she doesn't understand, no matter how many times I tell her. I love her. I want her with me all the time. I think about her constantly when we're apart and worry about her. Being around her makes me feel lighter. It makes life... just better. You know?"

"How do you mean 'not worthy'?" He kept scribbling furiously in the notebook while I talked. "Explain."

I considered his question. "It started with her comparing herself to Jessica. Then she kept dropping these comments about how I was out of her league. Even after I asked her to come live with me she kept acting like I was going to suddenly change my mind. Like I'd wake up and tell her to hit the road. I don't know. Maybe it has to do with that crush she had on me when she was a kid."

"What have you done to try and put her mind at ease?" He stopped writing and sat back.

"I tell her how I feel all the time. It's exhausting."

"Joe, you and I both know that *telling* isn't always the best way. We also both know Molly has trust issues that have *nothing* to do with you. Look, I can't give you a roadmap here on how to resolve the issue. But I can tell you this. Molly's a bright girl. If she still has doubts maybe she sees something you don't. Something you're holding back?"

Sitting there, I carefully considered what he was saying. There was probably something to it. I wasn't the most introspective person in the world. God knows the doc had hit me over the head with the obvious more than once.

Looking up at him, I shrugged. "I don't know."

"Well think about it and let me know next time if you come up with anything. Now how about you answer the original question?" I looked up at him blankly and he sighed. "I asked you how Molly turning you down made you feel. You said she turned you down twice?"

I grudgingly nodded. "It hurt."

"Why, Joe? Surely even you should be used to the occasional bout of rejection. Did it hurt your pride? To have someone that you love reject you, to tell you they don't want to marry you. That must have caused some reaction other than 'it hurt'." I glowered at him.

"I was crushed, okay? Is that what you want to hear? I tried not to let it spill out, doc. She's overwhelmed by all this. She just found out she is going to give birth to twins and she's totally unprepared. Bogging her down with my bullshit seemed a little childish. How I feel doesn't matter right now." Dr. Greene looked at me and shook his head.

"I sometimes wonder if you are just a giant kid inside a man's body. It doesn't matter? It matters a great deal. You're about to be a father again. You are allowed to be freaked out about this. Based on your past, I am absolutely amazed that you aren't a basket case right now."

"Because of Jack? I am freaking out, doc. But I'm dealing with it. Molly needs me to be strong, she doesn't need me to be falling apart."

"Joe, no good is going to come from you bottling these things up. You're talking about the woman you love. Soon to be mother of your twin babies. Molly needs your support, yes. But you need hers as well. Neither one of you should have to deal with a crisis without the other. The whole idea of having a partner is that there is someone there to help you. Someone to lean on when times get tough. It sounds to me like you're completely focused on being her rock. Who's going to end up being yours?"

I had no response, so I sat mute.

"If you feel comfortable with it, I'd like to visit with Molly sometime. I normally don't do couples counseling, but I think in your case it might make a big difference. That is, if she's willing to come. At the very least, I want you to continue your weekly visits. No more blowing them off, alright?"

"I don't miss that many..." I sounded a bit like a teenager negotiating with his father. The image of Molly in Dr. Greene's office put me on edge. If she knew just how crazy I was, how far down the rabbit hole I'd once been...

"Joe. You've been missing every other week all summer." He came around his desk and perched on the edge. "I know you're busy at work, but this needs to be a priority. Especially now. You follow me?"

I nodded. He'd been right about almost everything he'd ever said to me, and if it meant pulling myself together for Molly, I'd do it. "You got it, doc."

CHAPTER Five

Molly

Carved Hearts and Burnt Ends

"NO FLIPPIN' WAY!" Stacy exclaimed as I took a bite of my wrap. I was starving by the time I woke up from my morning nap and figured I would drive to both food trucks and do a little quality control testing for lunch. Stacy's crew were my newest employees, so I had them fix me the "Cranky Carpenter Wrap", since it was a customer favorite and therefore a staple in our menu. They'd nailed it, and I gave them the thumbs up as I chewed the delicious corned beef.

"It's true." I finally responded taking another bite.

"Omg! When are you due?" She blurted loudly, and the rest of the crew wandered over. Though I'd only planned to tell Stacy, I was faced with no choice but to share our news with them all. They all uttered a collective gasp when I told them about the twins. I was bombarded with a rapid fire series of questions that

I did my best to answer. Most of them were concerned about how this would impact Wrapgasmic. I assured them I had no plans for it to affect the business and that all their jobs were more secure than ever, since I would undoubtedly need more help.

They'd raised a few new concerns I had yet to consider, and flared nerves made my appetite vanish. I tossed the rest of the wrap into the garbage, knowing I had another truck and another session of show and tell to get through. The doctor had advised me to eat small, frequent meals, and warned me if I hadn't gained weight by my next visit, I was in for a lecture.

"Boy, it's a good thing you signed up for that expensive insurance plan." Stacy said as she walked me to my car. "Can you imagine how much you'd be paying out of pocket for pre-natal care?"

"Yeah…" Cost was something else I hadn't considered, and I wondered how much the hospitalization for delivering the babies would be. My mom had advised me to splurge on the best health plan I had access to. She'd said 'you can't afford *not* to, Molly. You're the boss. If you get sick or need surgery, it could bankrupt you. Think of all those employees that depend on you.' Fortunately, for once, I'd taken her advice. I made a mental note to thank her.

"Maybe you should reconsider that deal to make a frozen line." Stacy was a smooth operator, slipping in her agenda like a senator with a new bill. I'd been approached by a local grocery store chain about doing a frozen version of Wrapgasmic's biggest sellers. I hadn't even considered it. I just told the rep I thought it sounded disgusting and hung up on him. Stacy had been very verbal about what a huge mistake she'd thought it had been.

"Smooth, Stace. I'll be just fine without selling my soul." I drolly replied. She lifted her shoulders in a cheeky shrug.

"So Joe's gotta be freaking out, right?" Stacy handed me a

bottle of water as I climbed into my car. I leaned back and cracked the lid, forcing myself to drink a half of it, I'd been warned by Dr. Myers that she might have to hospitalize me if I let myself get dehydrated.

"No. He's not, actually." I admitted.

"That's a little weird." She looked doubtful. "Most guys I know would totally lose their shit, at least at first..." I shrugged and pulled the door shut. Waving to her as she walked back to the food truck I put the car in gear and headed across town.

I considered her comment as I drove through lunch hour traffic to location two. Even in a crisis, Joe was always my rock. I'd breeze around spontaneously doing whatever seemed like a good idea at the moment and he'd quietly ground me. But this? This was game-changing shit here and short of a momentary pause, he'd barely blinked.

Joe hadn't always been this stoic. When we were young, he'd been painfully easy to read. In fact, Mason used to joke that Joe had the worst poker face he'd ever seen. When they were roommates, the twins banished him from their weekly poker games because, as Mason put it, 'it was like kicking a sick puppy behind a dumpster' taking Joe's money.

I smiled when I thought about the kind of a jokester he'd been back in the day. Every time I was at their ramshackle hell-hole they called home, Joe would do all sorts of crazy, goofy shit to make me laugh. The practical joke wars between Mason, Mac, and Joe were still the stuff of legend, and I often found myself tangled up in the fray.

Since I'd come back to town and we'd rediscovered each other, I found Joe to be a much darker version of his former self. One thing hadn't changed, though; he still didn't have much of a filter. He called it like it was. If he said something, there was usually no doubt it was what he meant. So I'd taken his reaction to fatherhood at face value. I chalked it up to him being a few years older than me, and-something I would never admit to him-more mature. Plus there was the fact that he'd been through a pregnancy before...or at least most of one. His wife had been almost full term when she'd had her accident.

I came to a stoplight and glanced around. When I realized I was at the light in front of what used to be my father's restaurant, I nearly choked on the water I was drinking. A large 'for sale' sign was tacked to the building where our Hildebrandt's sign used to stand. Seeing it vacant and neglected, I felt a painful squeeze in my chest. The cement was cracked and weeds sprouted from the small fissures. The turquoise paint was chipping on the outdoor patio my father had once been so proud of. I glanced in the rearview mirror and seeing that no one was behind me, I quickly pulled off and parked on the side of the street.

I wandered over to the front porch of the restaurant and climbing the solid stairs, I peeked into the window. From what I could see, whoever had bought the place from my mom hadn't done much to change the interior. I'd heard that it had been another barbecue joint, but they hadn't even made a go of it for a year. The new owners hadn't been able to get mom to sell them dad's recipes, and I'd always admired her decision to hold onto them. They were dad's legacy and didn't belong in the hands of strangers.

Mom and I were the only ones who knew his entire process and all the ingredients to his sauces and rubs. The twins hadn't learned about the back of the house affairs. They'd never been interested in working in the kitchen, but they'd both taken their turns as servers, mostly in order to meet girls. I, on the other hand, had worked in the kitchen with dad every summer from the time I was old enough until I went off to culinary school. I begged to do it year 'round, but mom had been afraid my grades would suffer and she was probably right about that.

Descending the stairs, I walked around to the outdoor dining patio and gasped in shock at its state of disrepair. I remembered with startling clarity how my brothers and Joe had helped dad's contractor build it the summer after they all graduated from high school. I dutifully brought trays of lemonade and sweet tea out for them. I might have been a bit overenthusiastic, since it was an excuse to drool over Joe, who spent most of the job shirtless. Trust me; even at age eighteen, Joe had been something to see.

Finally, my constant presence had become obnoxious enough that Mason barked at me to get lost and called me 'a pain in the ass'. Mac had laughed about it, which at age fourteen was way more humiliating to me than Mason's rebuke. I remembered rushing back inside the empty restaurant just before I burst into angry and embarrassed tears. My dad found me with my head down in the back booth and pulled me into a hug.

"Shhhh. Don't cry, Mollybelle. Ignore Mason and Mac." He'd whispered pulling out that infectious smile of his. "They're just trying to look cool for the guys. Come on. Help me check the briskets. Mom will be here soon and you can help her slice the pecan pies."

The vivid memory of Daddy choked me up and suddenly many images of him assaulted me. His outrageous laugh that people always compared mine to. His dimpled grin. His wavy hair and silly comb over that I was sure Mason would be imitating soon. The memories sliced me like sharp glass.

A lot of the time, I think my Dad had been at a loss with what to do with a daughter. He only had brothers and most of his cousins were male. Our bonding time was spent in the kitchen, and that was alright with me. My biggest regret besides marrying my ex was moving away and missing Daddy's last few years of life. If I had to do it all over again, I'd have stayed closer to home for culinary school and worked alongside him in the family joint. Hindsight was always 20/20.

I realized my children would never have a chance to know him and it was like I'd lost him all over again. This epiphany really choked me up and I had to sit down on the dilapidated patio and just breathe for a couple of minutes. Daddy's absence for my journey into parenthood hadn't occurred to me until that moment, and I was powerless to stop the tears that followed.

About twenty minutes later I pulled up to truck two. When I climbed aboard the much bigger Wrapgasmic truck, Sanchez greeted me with a giant bear hug.

"Congrats, Little Mama!" He grinned, and Carly and Isaac both smiled from ear to ear. A genuine giggle escaped me, but I wanted to strangle Stacy for not letting me break the news my-self. "So much for sampling that case of wine we shipped you."

"Thanks, Sanch." I replied with a wink. "Wine keeps."

"I knew you were P.G." Carly stated, looking smugly from me to Isaac. "You owe me ten dollars."

I wanted to tell her there was no way she could have known shit, since Joe and I were *there* and didn't suspect it, but I fig-ured it was a pointless conversation and let it drop.

"So how was Napa?" I turned back to Dirty S. in a hurry to change the subject. "Did you have a good time? Get any culinary inspiration?"

"It was his *honeymoon*, Molly! Of course he had fun!" Isaac cracked, and Sanchez turned as red as the food truck's paintjob.

"I tried a new recipe today. Want me to make you one?" He replied, as eager as I was to shift the conversation back to busi-ness.

"Damn straight!" I replied, putting on an apron in order to get a front row view to his demonstration. Sanchez proceeded to paint the inside of a wrap with garlic parmesan butter and as-semble a pasta bolognaise wrap. He'd chopped the pasta into smaller, manageable bites before folding the bolognaise sauce in, and I was proud of my star pupil for intuitively getting the tex-ture issue.

"Voila!" He handed me his invention and I eagerly bit into it.

"Oh, Sanchez!' I cried after several seconds of savoring the superb flavors, "I think I'll retire and put you in charge."

"Hell no. He's way stricter than you are." Isaac chimed in and I snorted.

"Can you email me the recipe so I can teach it to truck one? We'll call it "Bangin' Bolognaise. In honor of your Napa *experience.*" I smirked and Isaac cackled. Sanchez let out an embarrassed groan, but his proud smile told me he was pleased that his creation had made the menu. One of the great things about the business I ran was that my hand picked employees let me get away with what would probably otherwise be considered sexual harassment.

"I have another one to add to the breakfast menu." He offered softly, as I took another mouthful of the delicious wrap. I had to stop after three bites because I knew I'd be hurting if I kept eating.

"Outstanding. Can I try it tomorrow? I really need to fly. Joe and I are breaking the baby news to his sister tonight.

"Sure." He replied. "I'll be here at six a.m. Thought I'd do a test batch and see what the customers thought."

"Do your thing, Dirty S. I trust you. And I'll be here by seven...so save me one."

Checking my phone I saw I had a text from Joe reminding me of when we need to leave. I hurried back to the apartment feeling sticky from the warm weather I wanted a cool shower and to change before we headed out to Driftwood to meet Tamryn's family for dinner.

I stood staring into the closet for a good ten minutes before I decided comfort would win out over vanity. I'd just finished tossing on my lilac maxi dress and flat silver sandals when I heard Joe unlock the front door.

"Hey." I called out, and headed into the living room to greet him.

"Hey." He met me in the hall and gave me a swift peck on the lips. "I'm going to change really fast."

"Sounds good." I replied, trying to muzzle my disappointment at his cool greeting. Since I had a couple extra minutes, I returned to my vanity. I scrunched my damp hair and spritzed on a bit of perfume. I put on a quick coat of mascara and a little lip gloss. My eyes traveled to the heart-shaped wooden box propped on my vanity that Joe had hand carved for me the previous Christmas. It'd taken me a few days to figure out how to open the puzzle box, but once I finally did, I found a gold heart necklace inside. On the inner bottom surface, he'd carved 'Joe loves Molly' as if he was carving it into a tree. I traced my fingers longingly over his words and quickly put the necklace around my neck.

By the time I was done, Joe was already in his dress jeans. I leaned against the doorframe and admired his perfect bare back. Watching him shrug into his black collared shirt was like watching soft-core porn.

"So both my crews know." I announced, mostly to fill the resounding silence in the room.

He caught my eye in the mirror. "Oh yeah?"

"Yeah." I replied. "Stacy has a mighty big mouth."

"How'd they like Napa Valley?" His conversational tone had me on high alert. It was stilted and far too polite.

"Sounds like they had a great time. I'm kinda jealous." I kept my voice playful.

"Good. That's what honeymoons are for." I wondered if this was an intentional dig at me for not agreeing to his not quite marriage proposal.

I sat down on the bed as I watched him slip on his boots. "Where'd you go on your honeymoon?"

He froze, looking up at me for a couple of seconds as if I was a bomb and he was trying to decide which wire to cut. At first, I wasn't sure he'd answer me. He took a deep breath before responding. "Sandals, Nassau."

I nodded, imagining Joe rolling around in the sand with his perfect Barbie Doll wife. "Sounds nice."

He stood upright and crossed to the bed, offering me his hand. I took it and allowed him to help me up. His earthy green eyes dropped to the thin gold chain around my neck. He reached out like he was going to touch my cheek and with a complex frown he pulled away at the last second.

"We'd better get on the road." He turned and walked out of the room, leaving me speechless.

It was a quiet trip out to Driftwood. I'd tried to get into the driver's seat of my car, but Joe shook his head and took the keys from me. Frankly, I hated driving in Austin, so I was relieved. The rolling hills made for lovely scenery on the way out of town, and I allowed my mind to wander back to the business and logistical concerns the crews had voiced earlier.

We turned into the graveled parking lot and pulled up next to the fence facing the vineyard. The familiar smell of our favorite place failed to excite me the way it usually did. Our first date had been here at The Salt Lick. We'd been back once a month since then, but the invisible wall between us killed the mood. I undid my seatbelt and opened the door before he'd even put the car in park,

I felt his hand on my elbow and I froze in my seat, waiting to be scolded for being careless or perhaps immature.

"I love you." He sounded somehow exasperated and sincere simultaneously. I turned to survey his face. He'd apparently developed a poker face after all, because I had no idea what to make of his complicated expression.

"I love you, too." I exhaled, unable to mask my frustration. It had been a long time since I'd felt so alone, and the fact that I felt it with Joe was devastating. I clambered out of the passenger seat and headed in the direction of the tantalizing smoke smell. I choked back the lump forming in my throat. I wouldn't ruin this moment for Joe by collapsing into tears like a blubbering idiot. He caught up to me long before we were at the door and his arm came around me. He tenderly kissed my temple, and I felt a pang of regret for being so reactionary.

We turned the corner and Tamryn and Robbie were milling about by the entrance. Their two daughters were chasing each other around in the grass nearby.

"Hi, y'all!" I called to the girls, as Joe closed the distance and kissed Tamryn on the cheek. He offered his hand to Robbie, who shook it.

"Molly!" Joe's five year old niece, Jamie, ran at me full force. Joe intercepted her, swinging her into the air with one arm.

"I get a hug first." He growled, ruffling her hair. Jamie's older sister, Tressa, approached me for a shy hug.

"You look pretty tonight." I gushed, noticing the way she tugged at her dress self-consciously. She lit in a sunny smile.

"Thanks, Miss Molly. So do you." She sounded like she was thirty years old instead of nine. Joe gave Tressa a loud smacking kiss on the cheek and she wiped at it with an eye roll. He was a completely different person when the girls were around. He lightened up palpably, and I breathed a little easier.

"It's so good to see you. You look great." Tamryn smiled at me and I gave her a halfhearted grin in response. She looked pulled together as always, as if she was ready for a martini night with the girls. Nothing was out of place on the petite brunette, from her beige Jimmy Cho's to her model-tall husband and his perfectly groomed sideburns. Here I was in my floor length knit dress and loose, beachy waves. I hadn't even bothered to cover my tattoos in my spaghetti straps. She was being kind, and I knew it.

"Oh, thanks. It was just too hot for me today..." I laughed, feeling the heat blossom in my cheeks. I should have known better than to underdress. I wanted to go hide in the restroom, but little Jamie grabbed my hand.

"Can I sit by you, Aunt Molly?" She'd never called me that before, and I bit the inside of my lip to contain the hormone rush headed for my tear ducts.

"Of course you can, Sugar." I cooed, flashing her a wide smile.

Since it was a weekday, we didn't have to wait for a table. Our server ushered us past the open pit and into the main dining room. I took my seat and Jamie plopped down beside me.

"Good. I'm on the 'tattoo side'." She said narrowing her eyes to study my full sleeve. I glanced bashfully at Tamryn, who shrugged. Joe scooted in next to me, and he ran his hand delicately down my back.

We ordered and I answered several questions from Jamie regarding my ink, when I heard Tamryn say to Joe, "I love this place. Thanks for inviting us. What's the occasion?"

Joe didn't hesitate. "Molly's pregnant. She's due in April."

Robbie gaped at him and then at me. Tamryn slapped her hands over her mouth and squealed. She jumped to her feet and frolicked around to our side of the table where she threw her arms around me.

"Oh my God! I'm so excited!" She cried, releasing me and wrapping her arms around Joe's neck from behind. Without turning to face her, Joe patted her arm in a patronizing manner that seemed to imply he was expecting this sort of reaction. People at neighboring tables were eyeing us with bemused smiles. "You sneaky little shit! I knew something was up when you texted me!"

"Mom. Language!" Tressa corrected her, and Tamryn shot her a look of reproach.

"You don't look like you're having a baby to me." Jamie sniffed as she stared at my stomach.

"It'll be a little while till you can tell." I replied, though I suspected that was a complete load of bullshit.

Tamryn started back around the table and Joe added. "Tamryn."

"What?" She smiled, and I braced myself when I saw the roguish grin on Joe's face.

"It's twins."

Round two of her wild, squealing jig began just as the servers appeared at our table. She rushed around and plopped down across from me. She reached over and took my hand.

"Two babies!" She released my hand so that the servers could sit down the heaping platters of mouthwatering meat. "I can't wait to tell mom. Oh! Unless you want to, Joe."

Joe shrugged and scooped a forkful of potato salad. "Go for it."

His reaction didn't surprise me. Joe had a rocky past with his parents, and though they were now on speaking terms, it still didn't happen very often.

Tamryn was still beaming as she buttered a roll. "Oh, Molly! I can't wait to throw you a shower! I'll take care of everything. You'll have you hands full with the move."

"Huh?" I asked, reaching greedily for some ribs. Now that I'd laid eyes on the spiced pork and burnt ends, I was ravenous.

"Well, you'll need a bigger place. And obviously one at ground level."

Joe cleared his throat uncomfortably. "Tamryn."

"Joe...you can't seriously think it's gonna be easy for Molly to go up and down those stairs in a few months. And how's she supposed to carry two newborns up and down the stairs all the time." She was using what Joe called her 'arbitrator voice'. Tamryn was no longer practicing trial law, but arguing with her about even the most trivial topic could be brutal. "*One* of those infant carriers was heavy enough to kill my poor back. Is she going to leave one in the car and come back for it later? Seriously..."

I forced myself to swallow the large bite of meat without tasting it at all. I got a mental picture of her hypothetical scenario and felt my pulse accelerate. I looked over at Joe and his uncomfortable glance in my direction made it obvious he'd already considered this.

"So does this mean you'll be making an honest woman of her?" Robbie chimed in. His friendly smile seemed to imply he was trying to shift the conversation back to a happy topic. The look Joe shot him wiped that smile right off the poor man's face.

"We just found out on Friday, y'all. Joe and I have a lot of things to figure out." I put a comforting hand on Joe's shoulder, and he held my eyes. I refused to look away, and his expression softened.

"Well, we're here to help. You just say the word." Robbie offered, and I wanted to hug him for keeping things simple. I mouthed the word 'thanks' and Robbie winked. Tamryn and Joe were in the midst of some private silent exchange, so I turned to the little girl on my left.

"Two babies. One for you and one for me." Jamie said to her older sister. Her serious expression was hysterical. She turned and looked past me at Joe. "Do I get to name one?"

"Nope." He responded without a moment's pause.

"Why not?" She looked genuinely annoyed.

Tamryn burst into a surprised chortle. "They're not kittens, Jamie."

After the fairly painless dinner ended, we said our good-byes, promising to come out to their ranch for brunch soon. Joe fell silent on the way back to the car. I had an ominous feeling of foreboding, but pushed it aside as emotional shrapnel from all we'd been through in the past few days. I decided I'd steel my-self and break the ice. As we pulled out onto the highway, I sucked in a breath.

"I'm sorry if you're still upset with me, but we need to talk about—" My phone rang and it was Elaine's ringtone. Joe huffed. Impulsively, I hit the green button.

"Elaine?" My curt greeting was met with a long pause. I could feel Joe staring but didn't look in his direction.

"Molly. Hi." She sounded breathy and her voice was pitched high which I knew meant she was nervous.

"I got your messages. I've been swamped. What is it you want me to do, exactly?"

"Umm…Molly. I'm really sorry."

"Really?" My sarcasm was blatant, and Joe whipped his head in my direction. "For which part? Fucking my husband behind my back or stealing my restaurant for a song?"

"All of it. I thought we were in love. I believed everything he said about you. I'm such an idiot." She choked on a sob and I rubbed my temple.

I understood all too well how easily Drae could cast a spell on a girl. Even an intelligent girl, and Elaine was a whole lot smarter than me. She was kind of a plain Jane. The unassuming, mousy type who'd be warming the bench at the prom. I imagine she thought she'd won the lottery when Draven turned his attention on her. At least, I always *thought* those things about her and had never considered her any sort of threat. It took balls; I'd never have guessed she'd had for her to start an affair with my husband, and the cutthroat way she'd bought me out of my business was downright Machiavellian.

Elaine let out a deep breath and pressed on. "I hate to bother you with this, but my lawyer has concerns that Draven will get visitation rights. He thinks a statement from you might help my case. I don't think he'd hurt Marco, but…"

Marco.

Drae had told me that they'd had a boy, but hearing that they'd named him after Draven's father somehow jarred me. I was more disturbed a moment later when I heard little Marco jabber in the background. It was the sweetest sound I'd ever heard, and when Elaine murmured softly back to him, any lingering doubts I had about helping her dissipated.

"Look, I'll make a statement if you need me to, but this isn't the best time."

"You will?" She sounded on the verge of tears again.

"Yes. But my schedule is pretty booked. When do you need it?"

"If you could have it for me by the end of next October that would be great. Believe it or not, that asshole is up for early parole." The ice in her voice was unmistakable, and my palm came up to my forehead. I wasn't surprised to hear this news, but I was disappointed.

"I believe it. Consider it done." I cleared my throat anxiously as I heard the familiar beep of another call coming in. "I have another call, but I'll text you when it's done."

"Thanks, Molly. I—" I disconnected the call and answered the other line. Hanging up on her like that was a bit cavalier, but I figured I was entitled to be a little bitchy with her.

"Hello, Ma." Still distracted by the thought of Draven walking around a free man, I closed my eyes and willed myself not to throw up.

"Molly. Where are you?"

"Driving back from Driftwood…why?"

"When are you going to be home?" She sounded giddy.

"Why?" I asked again, turning to Joe. He cocked a curious eyebrow at me and I mouthed the word 'mom'.

"We're sitting outside your apartment…we have something for you."

"Tell Joe to get that fine behind of his home." I heard Granny chime in, and I laid my forearm over my eyes and fell back against the head rest.

"Ma, you know Granny can't climb the stairs." I chided.

"Just hurry up. There's an NCIS Marathon on tonight. You know how I feel about missing Mark Harmon." She hung up and I blinked blankly at the screen of my phone. I turned to Joe an explained the conversation.

"Well, it sounds like your brother let it slip somewhere." He replied.

"Yep. Good news travels fast." My sarcasm was blatant. Joe's eyes slid sideways at me.

"We may as well get this all over with in one night." He picked up his phone and hit one button. "Hey, Mason. Look, I wanted to tell you this in person…"

He trailed off and I could hear my brother murmuring through the phone.

"Yeah. Mac's a shitty little Chatty Cathy, isn't he? Remind me to count his strokes at the golf tournament next weekend." Joe replied, and it confirmed that Mac had already opened his big mouth.

"Thanks, man. Yeah…yeah we're kinda freaking out. But we're excited." Joe sounded sincere as he smoothly lied to my brother. I was impressed, considering he'd made it through so many years of his life without developing the skill. I figured it was his survival instinct kicking in, since Mason had nearly broken Joe's jaw when he found out we were dating.

"Yeah, I know. Yep, I'm working on it." He continued, sounding serious. "I don't have to tell you what a pain in the ass she is."

I glared over at him suspiciously, but he completely ignored me and kept on chatting. I picked up my phone and pulled up Facebook. Ignoring the rest of their conversation, I quickly typed the status "Joe and I are expecting twins in April, y'all!" I figured my friends would be pissed at this type of reveal, but they'd be more pissed if I waited another 4 weeks to tell them. It was better to roll the dice and make it public.

"Yeah. We'll be there. Ok, hold on." He handed me the phone. "Robin."

I took the phone and endured the happy hysteria of my favorite sister-in-law with all the patience I could muster. Once she'd spun down a bit, she shifted in nurse-mode. "I need info.

Identical or fraternal?"

"Fraternal."

"Figures. Fertile Hildebrandts. How far along are you? Mac sucks with details."

"Eight weeks."

"Have you had morning sickness?"

"I've had every time of the *damn* day sickness." I replied, and then decided to make the most of the conversation by asking her a few questions about the drinking and medications I'd taken before I knew about the babies. She told me the same things Joe had, and promised to look up each of the questionable substances and text info on them to me. After agreeing to go to my nephew's soccer game the following weekend, I hung up. I handed Joe his phone.

"Mason asked us to do dinner with them after the soccer game. He thinks we should get married, too." He said levelly, as he slipped his phone in his front shirt pocket.

"It's a good thing I wasn't born in the middle east." I snorted, spotting Mom's car as we passed by the front of our building. "They'd have given you three chickens and a goat to take me off their hands months ago."

Joe braked a bit too enthusiastically as he parked. I shot him a look, but again he wore an unreadable expression. My phone began a steady stream of chiming that I assumed were responses from my Facebook announcement, but I ignored them and hurried toward my mother's van. Both she and Granny were climbing out of it.

"Molly! Get over here!" Granny H. had been on my case since I'd become a teenager and sprouted boobs. She always dropped snide comments about my life choices and on more than one occasion said I reminded her of her when she was my age. Mixed messages were her specialty. I stopped, and then after a brief hesitation, I approached her with apprehension. She reached out for me and yanked me into a sweaty, wrinkly embrace.

"I'm so happy for you, child!" She stunned me with her genuine laugh, which admittedly sounded like mine if my voice had been run through a cheese-grater. "Joe's a hell of a catch!"

"Yes, he is." I mumbled, eyeing Joe from underneath her jiggly arms. His amused eyes shifted from her to me.

"Two babies! Maybe you'll get one of each and knock it out in one shot. Then you'll have a hope of keeping your figure." She added, evidently elated at my prospect of twins. "Mine wasn't wrecked until I had your daddy, bless his heart."

I looked over her shoulder at my mother, who seemed a whole lot less exuberant.

"Oh, honey." She muttered sympathetically, her sheepish expression squelching the sliver of joy I had at Granny's greeting. "I hope you had fun having a social life because that's done for."

Considering she was my subject matter expert on twins, I was immediately conflicted.

"We brought you presents! It's a new mommy goody basket!" Granny overrode my mother, reaching into the back door of her minivan. She pulled out some ridiculously long cylinder that just kept coming and coming like handkerchiefs at a magic show. I blinked at her blankly, as Joe stepped forward and grabbed the end of it from me. "It's a Comfort-U. A special mom-to-be-pillow for when you aren't snuggled up to that sexy man of yours. Trust me, it's hard to get comfortable when your legs start to swell and your belly is the size of a watermelon."

"And here's your gift basket. The salesladies at Motherhood gave us some ideas. They're up on all the newest stuff." Mom chimed in, handing me an oversized basket that Joe ripped out of my grasp. It had books, something called a 'Bellyband', coconut oil lotions, and even Ginger flavored Altoids in it.

"Oh, my goodness. You didn't have to go all out." I replied, unsure of what to make of the incredibly generous nature of their present.

"Don't be ridiculous. You're only a first time mama once." My mother scoffed and came over to hug me. Joe vanished into the building with the basket and three mile long pillow. She whispered in my ear. "How's Joe dealin'?"

"It's hard to say." I whispered in return, hoping Granny couldn't hear me.

"If you ever need me, you know where I am." She kissed my cheek and I felt tears sting my eyes for the seven billionth time.

Joe came out of the building with a couple of bottles of water for them. "Are you sure y'all don't want to come inside?"

"Unless you've put an elevator in that building, darlin', there's no way in hell." Granny laughed.

"I can throw you over my shoulder and carry you." Joe offered dryly, and Granny flushed deep purple. Granny was a bit of a flirt and Joe's appeal transcended generations. I bit the inside of my lip to keep from laughing out loud.

"Mama Hildebrandt, we need to go. Molly's tired." Mom interjected with a conspiratorial wink at me and I wanted to give her another hug.

Minutes later, Joe jumped in the shower and I collapsed into bed. He'd unwrapped the giant body pillow when he brought it inside, and I snuggled into it, instantly seeing the appeal. It coiled around me, supporting my back and cushioning my knees. I'd nearly drifted off when I felt the motion of Joe climbing into bed. There was a shift in the weight of the pillow behind me and I felt his warm, rock solid body spoon against me. His arm came around me, and his fingers splayed over my womb. This simple action slayed my defenses and I relaxed back against him with a huge sense of unexpected relief.

"Baby girl." He murmured into my hair.

"Hmmm?" I shifted slightly, and he rolled me over onto my back so that we could lock eyes.

"I can't wait to see them." His earnestness was undeniable as he took in my face. He ran his thumb across my cheek, and traced his index finger down my nose, "Little pumpkins that are part me and part you...I can't imagine anything more perfect."

His words touched me so deeply that I found I couldn't reply. Instead, I simply tilted my lips up to meet his.

CHAPTER Six

Joe

Patience

"UNFORTUNATELY THAT'S ALL we have time for today." Dr. Greene gestured his head toward the clock and removed his wire-rimmed glasses. His longish greying hair flopped in his eyes and he flipped it away as he looked up from one last scribble in his beloved notebook. "Come back on Monday. That's not a request, Joe. When I asked you to stop skipping appointments, I meant it."

I nodded slowly. I deserved his ass-chewing. It had been a little over a month since I'd told him Molly was pregnant, and it was my first time back. I wasn't ditching on purpose; there was just too damn much to do. Even with two price hikes, we were busier than a one legged man in an ass-kicking contest, and we'd finally been forced to hire another guy.

Graham recommended Nick Marshall, the son of a guy I'd

once worked for back before 'the dark era'. Only twenty years old, Nick was a bit of a punk with his giant ear gauges, Fu Manchu facial hair, and permanent smirk. He'd made quite an impression when he came for his interview. First there was the "Legalize it" t-shirt he opted to show up in. While I was working, I'd observed him take a selfie on his phone with the Good Wood sign out front. Then there was the annoying sound effects of the video game he was playing on his phone while he waited for me. The icing on the cake was the way he reacted when Molly turned up just as we were about to begin the interview.

"Hi, y'all!" She called, sweeping in with a box full of wraps for us. She'd called an hour before and asked what each of us wanted for lunch.

"Hi." Nick blurted, his eyes wide and ecstatic as he took her in.

Molly did a double take at his exuberant response. She walked around to the employee side of the counter and perched the box on its surface. Nick bounded up to the customer side of the counter like an enthusiastic puppy.

"You must be the new guy." Even though I couldn't see her face, Molly's grin came through in her voice.

"I hope to be." His dimples appeared as he went for the modest approach. "I'm Nick."

"Well, hello, Nick." A hint of Texas found its way into her Yankee-fied voice. "I'm Molly."

"Do you work here?" He boldly slogged on, and I had to give the kid an A for effort.

"Nope. Just bringing the boys a lunch delivery. Joe wasn't sure what kind you'd like, so I brought you one of my favorites. It's a California BLT Wrap. I hope you aren't a vegetarian."

He looked taken aback for a moment that she'd brought him lunch, but recovered immediately, giving her a shark-like grin. "Oh no, I'm *definitely* a carnivore."

I hung back for a couple of minutes, cleaning my tools and

watching the show. Nick proceeded to hit on Molly as she passed out the wraps to Francis and Mac. She smiled patiently at him as if he were a toddler climbing a bookshelf and she was going to have to yank him down and scold him.

She handed Nick his wrap and he took a quick bite.

"You made this?" He sounded like the man on the verge of an orgasm.

"Yep." She handed him a wad of napkins. "You like?"

He told her that it was perfection and asked her if she was going to Austin City Limits. He was launching into how he had VIP passes to the main stage when I joined them at the counter.

Molly handed me my wrap. We exchanged a brief glance and my cocked eyebrow elicited a knowing smile from her.

"Well, you'll have a great time, Nick. Eminem puts on a hell of a show. And good luck on your interview. Don't let Joe intimidate you too much. He looks grouchy, but he's a big teddy bear." At that, she slinked into my arms and kissed me goodbye, lingering a little longer than usual for her audience of one. A few feet away, I heard Mac snort. Molly made a show of putting a hand on her already visible baby bump, which she'd finally exposed when she'd discarded the empty cardboard box. "Gotta run, darlin'. The babies are craving Verde Chili Fries from Casino El Camino."

With an innocent little wave to Nick, she breezed out the door. His youthful eyes were the size of saucers as he watched her go and when he turned back to me, he smartly fell all over himself to apologize. I held up a hand and shook my head, wearing a smirk of my own. Between Molly's sassy bounce in her walk and Nick's abject horror at his faux pas, I was genuinely entertained. I'd already decided to let it the entire thing slide.

"Save your breath, kid. You obviously have an eye for perfection. It's a major job requirement for what we do, and if you're going to apprentice with me, you'd damn well better have excellent taste.

Nick and I headed back to my tiny office. We chatted for a while between bites of wraps and it didn't take long for me to get the vibe that he enjoyed building and knew what he was talking about. He'd brought some photos of some carving he'd done, and I was pleasantly surprised at his raw skill. I decided the shop could use an infusion of young blood, and told him I'd give him a shot.

Nick had to give two weeks' notice and was supposed to start late next week. In the meantime, Mac and I had been working a lot of twelve hour days. Mac wasn't complaining; he'd finally broken down and bought the Harley Davidson he'd always wanted. A SuperLow 1200T. It was a pretty sweet ride, I had to admit. As stressed as I was, Mac seemed to thrive in the midst of our slammed workload. He'd always been an adrenaline junkie (both the twins were) and he was getting to spend more time with his son, Malcom Jr. There seemed to be a temporary truce between him and his loony ex-wife. Probably because he was able to pass her a little extra cash beyond the court ordered child support.

Francis got a big bonus from me and was spending his free time shopping for a used car. He'd also begun to pay rent, though I'd told him on numerous occasions that his apartment across the hall from ours was a perk of the job. Things got a little heated when I initially refused to take his money. When I tried to cut the conversation off, he switched tactics and pulled Molly into the argument.

"She's going to have to quit working for a while, Joe. Even if it's just for a few months after the babies are born. You need to start putting something away for that eventuality."

This stopped me in my tracks, and I had no rebuttal. Francis may have lost his way for a while, but he'd always struck me as having uncanny insight. He had a solid foothold on his life again, and who was I to deny him the opportunity to pitch in? The diligent expression he wore as he watched me consider was what actually made me cave. I remembered all too well what it was like to feel like a burden. That dark period of my life was behind me now and I saw just how badly he wanted to put distance between himself and his. So I folded and agreed to let him pay me three hundred dollars a month for rent. Francis cackled at that.

"You can't get a studio in Austin for that, let alone a remodeled two bedroom." He tilted his head and opened his mouth to counter. "Maybe I should ask Molly what she—

I cut him off. "It's my building, not Molly's. Three hundred dollars or nothing. Take it or leave it."

Francis was a smooth talker; it's what I paid him for. But after several years of living on the streets, he had developed excellent survival instincts. He could tell I was a man on the edge and didn't seem like he was anxious to push me off. It didn't take an expert like Dr. Greene to see I was about to go insane.

Molly and I had been franticly house hunting nightly for the past three weeks. To say it wasn't going well was a major understatement. Molly had always been a handful, but trying to agree on a house gave us all new and interesting things to argue about.

At first, Molly approached the subject of moving with extreme caution. I couldn't blame her. I'd been in the apartment above the shop since Jess and Jack died At first it was because I couldn't stand to be in the house I'd remodeled for Jess and being surrounded by her things broke my already mangled heart. Then, I discovered that my late wife had been embezzling from me, and selling the place had become a necessity.

Finding out Jessica had been lying to me the entire time we'd been together destroyed what little faith I had left. Robbed blind by my own wife. It had been humiliating and embarrassing, but it also made me mourn for my memories that I now dissected like some sort of amateur archeologist. It would have been better to have had the illusion that I'd lost my soul mate than the certainty that I'd been living a lie.

Then I found out I wasn't even special in the regard of her

treachery. Jess had been a successful C.P.A and she'd "borrowed" money from several of her clients as well to pay off her various gambling debts. When she was no longer around to keep the plates in the air spinning, her scheme collapsed like a house of cards and all I was left with was my building, my truck, the clothes on my back and two marble tombstones in the local cemetery.

When Molly finally gathered the courage to broach the subject, I had been surprised at how ready I was to make the move. It was pretty straightforward. Before Tamryn opened her big fat mouth, I knew we had to find a new place. Even if we'd been on the ground floor, our place wouldn't have had the space for two children once they were old enough to crawl. Starting my life with Molly invigorated me, and I'd already been thinking hard about our future before we found out about the pregnancy. I knew we had to sort out a few issues, but I'd seen things heading down this path. Now I was beginning to wonder if I'd misread the situation entirely, since she still dismissed the idea of marriage as easily as if I were suggesting we buy leopard print wallpaper.

Finding the right place had proven to be a pain in the ass. I wanted a place that was safe and functional for our new family. Molly wanted a place that felt homey and had mature trees and character. We were butting heads over our wish lists and the joy of the hunt had quickly disappeared.

I could tell that Molly was nearly as nervous about the prospect of homeownership as I was. She mentioned using the money from the sale of her home with her ex to buy a condo or rent a duplex nearby. We were at the doctor's office waiting for our second OB appointment when she brought this up, which probably saved us from having a huge blowout. The way she phrased this idea made it clear that she meant to do this without me.

"There are a few places that aren't far away but would work great for two small kids. I think that the money I have in savings would be enough to cover my move in costs."

"So what? You're ditching me?" I fumed. She whipped her head in my direction, obviously surprised.

"No." The word came out slowly, and she looked at me as if I were a madman. "Where the hell did that come from?"

I tried to keep my voice down as the two other women in the waiting room glanced up from their magazines. "First you don't want to marry me and now you don't want to live with me anymore. How do you expect me to feel?"

She leaned in close to me and locked her pretty eyes on mine, "Of course I want you to come with me. I hope you want to."

She put her arm around the back of my chair and rested her head on my shoulder. Her hair smelled like oranges, and I relaxed as I breathed her in. Even with her calming influence it was an effort to get myself under control. My battered emotions were far too sensitive about rejection when it came to Molly. She spoke softly, as if telling me a secret.

"I didn't want to assume that you'd be ready... you know ...to leave your building after everything. Moving on is a *huge* deal, Joe. That's a lot of change all at once."

"So is having *children* and we're doing that together." My tone softened, but my pulse still raced. Sometimes we were so far apart on our patterns of thinking that she terrified me.

"But it's not like we planned *that*. We still have some *control* over where we live." She'd replied, lifting her head from my shoulder to stare me down. She didn't seem to be challenging me. Her expression reminded me of the one she wore when she was trying to solve the puzzle box I'd made for her for Christmas.

I snapped out of the memory when Dr. Greene slapped his notebook down on the table. He stared at me for a moment and then shook his head.

"I suppose you haven't asked Molly to join us for a session

either." Dr. Greene's body language left little doubt that he al-ready suspected my answer.

"No. But I will." I hadn't mentioned it yet. I felt like a cow-ard, I'd been dragging my feet about asking. Molly's moods were volatile and she flew off the handle about something as basic as a bruised banana. I assumed Molly would jump to the conclusion that I thought she needed therapy, and I didn't want to start yet another fight. Dr. Greene regarded me doubtfully and I put a hand over my heart. "I promise."

"I hope so." He replied suspiciously, as he ushered me to the door. "I think both of you would benefit from a little refereed discussion." Once more I promised to bring Molly to an ap-pointment and slipped out the door.

As I climbed into the truck, I got a text from Molly. Our realtor got us a last minute appointment to see a house that seemed good on paper. She said she'd meet me at the shop and I hurried when I noticed the time.

When I turned onto my block, I spotted Molly's car parked out in front of Good Wood. As I passed the storefront window, I saw her inside leaning on the counter. I swung the door open and there stood my girl, chatting with Francis's daughter, Kelly.

"It was okay... but you're right, it was *no* Salt Lick." Kelly was saying to Molly in her delicate, high pitched voice.

"You should come over some night and taste my brisket. It's my daddy's recipe, but I put my own little spin on it." Molly replied. She was wearing rolled up denim bibs and her hair was in pig tails. She looked like Mary Ann from Gilligan's Island if Mary Ann hung out with Kat Von D. As I snuck up on her, Kelly looked in my direction and her amused eyes gave me away. Mol-ly spun and her lips curled in a smile.

"There's my guy." She drawled, and I pecked her cheek. My hand automatically went to her belly. She was only fourteen weeks along, though because of the twins, the doctor said she measured closer to eighteen. Her faded bib overalls showed off her bump adorably, and had we been alone, I would have kissed her there.

We'd been to her second appointment two weeks before and Dr. Myers said the blood work and ultrasound looked great. Molly's relief was palpable. She'd been reading her new mommy books every night and had freaked herself out about "Vanishing Twin Syndrome. Though she admitted one baby would be a hell of a lot easier on us, she was truly worked up about the idea of something happening to one of them. She'd started to freak me out too, so when the ultrasound tech swiveled the screen in our direction, we were both relieved to see both babies alive and well.

"Hey there, little girl. Hello, Kelly." I put my arm around Molly and nodded to Francis's daughter. I noticed Mac lurking within listening distance of us. He seemed to be taking forever to select a tool, but I pretended not to notice. It was pretty obvious he was checking Kelly out. She was cute: tanned, brown eyed, and her long hair was nearly black. She was the type he always picked out of a crowded bar. But Kelly wasn't the bar crowd type, and I didn't need the workplace drama that would come from razzing him about it.

"Hey, Joe." Kelly's high pitched voice made her seem younger than she was. She turned back to Molly. "I'm doing the Howl-O-Ween 5k. My dad said your food truck is going to be there. Maybe I can try your brisket then."

"Good idea. I'll figure out a way to work it into a wrap." I could see the wheels turning behind Molly's baby blues.

"When's this 5k?" Mac asked. He directed his question at Kelly. He twirled his screwdriver in a nonchalant, yet showy manner as he approached the counter. Kelly turned her doe eyes in his direction.

"October 18th." She replied, with a flirty toss of her waist length hair.

I could no longer resist the urge to flip him shit. "Are you gonna run, Mac?"

Mac's ears turned red, and he folded his tattooed guns across his barreled chest. "Maybe."

Molly snickered and he shot her a look of reproach.

"What?" He looked serious. "I work out."

"Curling a beer bottle in the direction of your mouth isn't going to qualify you for the Boston Marathon." Molly replied with a small laugh.

"Ha ha," He replied. "What about you, prego? Are you going to walk it?"

"I would, but I'll be cooking." Molly responded, her eyes dancing with amusement. "You might want to cut back on that pack a day habit before you take up jogging. You'll have a damn heart attack."

I could tell Mac was biting back some vile comments. "I've been down to a quarter of a pack since January. Show's how much you pay attention."

"My mistake. You're a bad ass, Mac. I can't wait to cheer you on." Molly grinned.

"Ha ha, Short shit. Challenge accepted." He replied. Meanwhile, Kelly glanced back and forth at the squabbling siblings. Mac stole a glance at Kelly and she seemed to be doing the same and caught him looking. She smiled sweetly at him. I felt like an intruder in their moment and looked around for Francis. He was nowhere to be seen.

"Molly. We gotta fly." I murmured, anxious to leave the starry eyed pair alone.

Molly glanced at the time on her phone.

"Oh, shit! See ya later, Kelly! Live strong, Lance!" I huffed in amusement at her as I quickly ushered her out the door. Molly banged on the window and lifted a fist in the spirit of unity to her brother. When Mac flipped her the bird, we both dissolved in laugher.

"He's fixin' to piss Francis off, hitting on his daughter like that." I said as we sped off in the direction of our potential new home.

"She's a grown ass woman. But she's way too nice for Mac." Molly responded, flipping down the visor to check her lipstick in the mirror. "She's *so* friendly, it's kinda creepy. I keep waiting for her to pull out a knife and stab somebody."

Turning down the quiet lane, I gave Molly what I hoped was a comforting smile. The neighborhood was filled with large single family homes interspersed with green lawns and old trees. Tamryn had made a hobby out of finding the best listings and forwarding them to us and our realtor on email. She was pouring stress onto an already difficult situation, but I knew she meant well. Molly would have freaked on me if I told Tamz to stop anyway. It was a delicate situation, balancing Molly's needs versus what I could handle.

"Suburbia… we're really going to do the whole white picket fence thing, huh?" Molly unconsciously pulled her sleeve down a bit to cover her tattoos. Giving an inward sigh, I kept my voice calm and level when I spoke.

"You said the last two places were too urban. This one is in an older neighborhood; it's in a great school district. Let's just take a look okay? There's Thomas." Pulling into an empty spot I waved to our realtor. He'd helped Mac find his house after his split with his ex, and Mac spoke very highly of him. When we called him, Thomas had jumped at the opportunity to help us.

Hopping out of her car, I moved around to get the door and help Molly out. She gave me her patented eye roll, but put a lot of pressure on my arm as she stood up. She shot me an apologetic glance, and taking her hand, I led her down the sidewalk toward Thomas. He shook my hand and gave Molly a chaste hug.

"Hey, you two. Did you have any trouble finding the place?"

"No." Molly's tone was overly chipper which wasn't necessarily a good sign. "But it is kind of out of the way."

Thomas nodded and pulled out a leather bound notebook.

"Side street, good school, old trees, houses with character. Yes, this should have a lot of things that are on your list." He gave her a huge smile and gestured us forward.

I could tell five minutes after we got there that this was not the place. It was all cookie cutter, and the flow was all wrong. With some hard work and sweat equity, we could have made it very livable, but we didn't have that kind of time. I let Molly come to that decision on her own. It took her less than ten minutes.

Thomas took feedback from both of us, mostly from Molly, and made some notes. Promising he would find us something better to look at next time, he left us near our car. I helped Molly back into the passenger seat and slid back behind the wheel. We were half way back to the apartment before Molly spoke.

"We're never going to find a place. Maybe we should just listen to Mac and install an elevator." I'd stopped at a red light and turned to gape at her in shock.

"Wait...did you just agree with Mac? Is that even ... possible?" Her eyes narrowed at my teasing and she turned away to stare out the window.

"I'm just tired of looking at houses. There's always something wrong with them. Either they are too old, or too new. They are on a busy street or way outside of town. The closest we came to agreeing on anything was that funky ranch house but it needed way too much work."

I sighed and placed my hand over hers.

"We could always just build a house. Or I could get some guys together and remodel one." Remodeling was actually the last thing I wanted to do. It reminded me too much of Jessica and Jack. Tempting fate by doing exactly the same thing with my current mate that I had done with my first seemed just...wrong.

"We don't have that kind of time. These babies are going to be here before you know it. What we need is for Thomas to get his head out of his ass and find us what we need!" Her anger was as severe as it was irrational.

"Tell you what. Just in case, I can talk to a few people about putting an elevator into the shop. Just so we have a backup plan." She whirled to look at me with her eyes flashing.

"Like there's room for an elevator. And what happens if there's a power failure? I'm trapped inside with two infants? Oh my God! What if there's a fire. I'd have to try to climb down the fire escape with two babies or just throw them to some random passerby. This is crazy! I can't do this....it's just too damn much." She burst into angry tears.

I immediately veered over to the side of the street and parked. Reaching over, I pulled her into my arms. The console made it awkward but I pressed my side painfully into it so that Molly wouldn't be uncomfortable. She resisted my embrace for a moment and then collapsed into my chest. I knew she sobbed in frustration and fear and I tried my best to soothe her.

"Baby girl, you know you won't be alone. I don't care what it takes I'll make sure that you and the babies have everything you need. Shhh, baby, please don't cry. It's all gonna be okay."

It took almost five minutes but I managed to calm her down. Inside, a part of me was screaming in concert with her concerns. Two babies. Not just one life to try and protect, but two. I'd utterly failed to protect my first, and now I was going to be responsible for the well-being of two more? The tortured animal that lived in the dark corner of my mind howled in protest. But Molly needed me, so I shut it away and ignored the noise.

When we got home, I made her put her feet up and ordered out for some dinner. Thanks to Molly's encyclopedic knowledge of every restaurant in town coupled with Francis' organizational skills I had a mammoth binder that was a veritable compendium of carry out menus. I'd found a service that picks up carry out orders from anywhere and delivers for a fee. I think I was on track to becoming their number one customer.

With the cravings that Molly had been having, it was a Godsend to have a service that would schlep their butts to six different restaurants on their way to my house. The owner and I had been talking about a discount "frequent flyer" rate. Turning from the phone, I discovered that Molly had disappeared into the bathroom. I checked on her and found her lounging in a tub full of bubbles. The water wasn't too hot and she impishly flicked some at me as I ran my hand through it to test the temperature.

"How long 'til the food comes?" Planting a gentle kiss on her forehead I pulled a towel out of the cupboard and put it within reach of her.

"Not long. You should have enough time to soak before it gets here." She smiled and slid down further into the water.

"Joe…." She sighed, her gaze fixed down on her belly. "I'm sorry for being so ridiculous I know it must be getting old. I'm driving myself crazy. But I think the mood swings are starting to get better."

"It's fine, baby. Just try to relax." I kissed her forehead again and went back out into the apartment. Her mood swings weren't getting better. They were less frequent, but the intensity of them was worse. Or maybe my patience was just wearing thin.

Her nausea and vomiting was a lot less frequent, and she seemed to have more energy now that she was in her second trimester. Still, she slept like a rock and when she was doing anything physical, she needed to take a lot of breaks.

Gathering up the scattered dirty clothes I started the washer before heading into the kitchen. I didn't want Molly to have to bother with chores. I was exhausted from working all day, but managed to finish just before the doorbell rang.

Our delivery dude was a heavyset kid with horrible acne. I tossed an extra ten into my planned tip (hoping it might help him afford a dermatologist) and kicked the door shut with my heel. Juggling the carryout containers, I returned to the kitchen and plated up the food. When I came back out into the living room,

Molly was lowering herself onto the couch wearing one of my t-shirts and a white pair of panties.

"Joe, baby, did you clean up?" She glanced around the room with a troubled frown and then back at me.

"Yeah."

"I was going to do that after we ate." She looked a bit defeated, and I doubted it was likely she'd have rallied the energy.

"I wanted to be able to spend time with you tonight, without distractions." I replied, handing her the food. She leaned down and inhaled the aromas rising from her plate.

"Crab Rangoon? Mac and Cheese from Hillside Farmacy? Baby, are you *trying* to turn me into a house?" I smiled and let her sharp tone wash off of my jangled nerves.

"You're tired and I didn't want you to feel like you had to cook. Me cooking isn't exactly the best idea. You don't have to eat it all. I just wanted to give you options." She looked from me to her plate with hesitation, and then picked up her fork and tasted the mac and cheese.

Despite her initial irritation, Molly tore into the meal with gusto. "God, everything's so good. Oh! Tamryn called today. Your parents are coming into town the week before Thanksgiving and they want to meet my family. She'd like to have everyone out to the ranch for dinner and drinks sometime while they're back."

"What did you tell her?" There was a hard edge to my voice and Molly shot me a look of surprise, and then shrugged.

"I told her we'd be there. Why?" It was amazing how much ominous warning she could put in one word. What she said was 'why', but what I heard was 'you got a problem with that bucko?'

Taking a deep mental breath I took a bite of food, buying myself a moment's respite. Tamryn had been trying to get me to call my parents for weeks but I'd managed to dodge her. It pissed me off that she had done an end run around me by going to Molly. *And* that Molly had accepted the invitation without talking to me about it.

For a moment, I was tempted to answer her challenge. Angry Joe, the damaged asshole who squatted in the shadowy recess of my mind, had quite a bit to say on the subject. How she was overstepping her bounds and treating me like crap, for starters. Instead, I pushed it all down and answered in a calm voice.

"Just curious. I've been trying to make some time to call my folks. I've just been so distracted." I could feel her looking at me but kept eating as if I didn't. I struggled with my frustration and where to direct it. I asked myself the most frequent question that crossed my mind in these situations.

What would Dr. Greene tell my stupid ass to do?

I came up with nothing. After a few seconds she sighed, stood up, and took her empty plate into the kitchen.

"That's because you've been picking up *everything,* baby. Don't get me wrong. I appreciate all the help…but I'm not terminally ill. I'm pregnant." Her voice was as delicate as a snowflake and I lifted my eyes in her direction. Her back was to me as she rinsed off her dish and loaded it into the dishwasher.

"I know." My words came out as a tired sigh. "I just need to do *something*, Molly."

She froze, her back still to me, as if pondering this carefully. Then she turned and leaned against the sink. "Baby, I can tell that you're mad at me, but I'm confused about why. After everything you've said to me, I thought you'd want our families to meet."

My family was always a complex topic. My mother had called a couple of times since we'd spoken at Tamryn's Christmas party, but I hadn't talked to my father since that night. I felt like it was his move, and still he refused to play ball. He'd been kind to Molly, which was something. But the thought of him breezing back into my life, trying to play Grandpa of the Year, just pissed me off.

A blended gathering of our families made me uncomfortable. No, that wasn't true. My sister was not part of the problem. Tamryn loved Molly, and Tamz had fit right in with Mac and Mason back when they'd formed a team to save me from myself. But imagining my father having cocktails with Molly's mom and looking down his nose at the entire Hildebrandt clan set my teeth on edge. If he found *me* so unworthy of the family name that he still hadn't reached out to me...

I walked into the kitchen and sat at the island. I held my arms out to Molly. She only hesitated for a fraction of a second before she crossed the kitchen to me. I looked into her reluctant eyes. "Tamryn and Robbie. Yes. The girls? Of course. They'd have a ball with Mac and Mason's kids. But mom and dad..."

She nodded "But they're good to Tressa and Jamie, aren't they?"

"Tamryn seems to think so." I replied, tracing my fingertips up her soft thighs. The familiar citrus smell of her freshly shampooed hair, touching her softness, it all comforted me. She was a marvelous distraction presented at precisely the right time. As usual she made an awful situation easier to bear.

"We'll need all the babysitters we can get." She pulled me closer to her, and my face was practically in her cleavage. I brushed my lips over her nipple which hardened under the thin material of the shirt. She inhaled sharply, but when I glanced up in alarm, she'd thrown her head back and her expression wasn't one of pain. Encouraged by the way she'd arched her back, thrusting herself forward against my lips, I trailed my hand under her t-shirt, and slipped it slowly into her panties.

"Joe." She moaned, and her instant wetness coaxed a rakish smile from me.

"Ready for dessert?" I breathed into the material over her other breast.

"Oh yeah," she gasped as she moved her legs aside to make more room for my hand. I teased her for a while, watching with fascination as the color rose in her cheeks…listening to her tiny gasping breaths. When she moaned loudly in frustration, I pulled my hand away and brought the panties down with me. She blushed and braced herself on my shoulders as she stepped out of them.

"You won't need these anymore tonight." I tossed them over my shoulder and her lips turned upward in a wicked smile. I took her hand, leading her into the bedroom.

CHAPTER

Seven

Molly

Cats and Dogs

"TASTE THIS, DIRTY S." I held out my latest creation for my second in command as he climbed onto the food truck.

"This isn't another one of your 'craving' wraps, is it?" He gave me a skeptical glance, but he inhaled the smell and his expression shifted to curiosity. The crews of both trucks had been teasing me about some of my special lunch requests lately. I still failed to see what was funny about sizzling rice soup with toasted pimento cheese sandwiches.

We'd had a rough couple of weeks. Some asshole tried to demand six months of free food after claiming he'd found a bug in his wrap. Stacy handled it, which was good, because if *I* had been there I would have called him a fucking liar to his face.

Then there was the abysmal replacement chef we'd tried to train in preparation of my maternity leave. Sanchez and I had interviewed six people and chose to hire two part timers instead of one full timer. Ian turned out to be a great choice. He was fun and a very fast learner. Darla, on the other hand, had *supposedly* trained at Le Cordon Bleu. It was painfully clear after two days that she'd either faked her resume or taken a head injury since leaving the culinary institute. She kept saying "I know" every time Sanchez instructed her on anything and finally I snapped.

"No...you don't know or he wouldn't have to keep telling you all the damn time." I shouted. She clammed up for the rest of the day and never came back. Due to this incident and a few more of my hormonal tantrums, the staff was now referring to me as 'Gordon Ramsey' behind my back. They didn't think I knew, but what fun is coming to work if you can't rag on the boss? Especially when she deserves it.

"Really, Sanch. Try it." I insisted. Taking the wrap from me, he sampled a decent sized bite and chewed slowly.

"I call it the Gangsta Wrap. It's my spin on dad's brisket with some of his cole slaw. What do you think?" I'd spent all day brining, smoking, and slow cooking the meat at the commercial kitchen I rented for occasions when we needed advanced prep that the food trucks couldn't facilitate. It was kind of fun getting back to my barbecue roots, though sitting around waiting for them to cook gave me way too much to think, which wasn't ideal these days.

Sanchez paused, took another enormous bite, and chewed with a blissful expression on his face. When he finally swallowed he held the wrap away from my outstretched hands refusing to relinquish it.

"I think this just might be the best thing you've ever made." He went in for a third bite and nodded. "Really, little mama. This is a winner."

"Fabulous. We'll make it tonight's special. We have an hour before the runners line up at the starting line. That should be plenty of time to go over the slaw with you". I frowned as I looked past him and saw no one around. "Where's Stacy?"

Sanchez's dark eyes wandered. "Isaac is working the window tonight. Stacy had a conflict."

"Oh." I could tell there was a story behind this change of plans. Stacy had been the one who'd gotten us involved with the race organizers in the first place. She'd been pimping Wrapgasmic's appearance at the Howl-O-Ween 5K on Twitter and Facebook nonstop since October first. The way Sanch hurried away to the sink to wash his hands clued me in that he was dubious about discussing Stacy.

"Should I be concerned?" I asked, trying and failing to make eye contact with him.

"No. it's all good." He replied, tossing on his apron. Oh, how I hated that phrase. People usually said it was 'all good' when things in their life were decidedly a clusterfuck.

"Okay. If you want to talk about it, you know where to find me." I offered, wondering if the honeymoon was already over. He nodded and then changed the subject back to food. He told me he had an idea for a deep fried wrap with egg roll filling. It sounded insanely good, and we kicked the filling ideas back and forth, agreeing to try a pork and a chicken version later in the week for a test market on South Congress. That demographic was a more reliable crowd to get feedback from than the drunks on Sixth.

As we went through the Gangsta Wrap recipe, I marveled at Sanchez's talent. His knife skills were impressive when you considered he'd never taken a culinary class in his life. He was like a savant, the Mozart of the mobile restaurant world.

It helped that he'd been born with an amazing palate, and could taste even the most subtle change. His consistency was far better than my own, but I tended to get bored easily and then, in turn, get creative. I'd been surprised when he started proposing new recipes. I was thrilled, but I wondered how long it would be before he realized just how talented he really was and I lost him to some high roller with bottomless pockets.

I didn't think I needed to worry too much. Sanchez was fiercely loyal to me and he had staunch principals. Everything he'd learned about cooking he'd learned either in prison or from me. His parole had ended in the spring, and that very day he'd proposed to Stacy. Never one to think before she acted, Stacy immediately said yes and shouted their news to the world. But that was Stacy's approach to life; when I put the status about my pregnancy on Facebook, she took a screenshot of it and put it on the Wrapgasmic page and tweeted about it. The following week I was inundated with gifts from vendors and some of my more loyal customers. I had to call Joe twice to come help me load up the flowers, edible arrangements, gift cards and presents from Motherhood and BabiesRUs.

Sanchez and I threw ourselves into our prep, making two large batches of slaw and the fixin's for three other standard menu options. I'd was about to review the recipe for my brisket with him, when Mac turned up at the window. The sight of him without his beard, made me do a double take. He'd had one since he was twenty years old, but he actually looked better without it. However, his neon green running clothes and a sweat band around his head nearly made me pee my pants. He'd even borrowed Mason's hound dog for the race. Bones wagged his tail at me, obviously enthused to be out in public. He was at least ten years old and was as unlikely to finish the race as Mac was. I struggled to keep a straight face.

"Have you seen Kelly?" He asked eagerly, and I bit my lip to stifle a guffaw.

"This is the finish line, dumbass!" I replied and when I saw the panicked look in his eyes, I felt a little pang of guilt. It'd been years since I'd seen him look so vulnerable, and I quickly explained where he needed to go to register and get his number.

As Mac drove off, I texted Joe, who was working late. Before he left for work that morning, he'd mentioned coming down for dinner.

I waited for five minutes before his response came through.

Joe: *Maybe. I'm still working on something.*

I felt my lips purse in a pout. He'd been living in the shop for the last couple of weeks. I really wanted to see him, so I decided to tempt him and texted back

I made a new wrap tonight. It's barbecue. A lot like daddy used to make.

His response was immediate.

Joe: *I'll be down in an hour, or so, baby girl. Luv you.*

Smiling, I stuffed my phone into my pocket as Isaac pulled up in his ancient economy car and trudged in our direction.

"Hey, y'all." He fussed with his hair in the mirror above the sink and set about washing his hands. He seemed out of his element, working the night shift. "What's the delectable smell?"

We prepped as much as we could and served the few early birds who'd come to cheer their loved ones on at the finish line. The majority of customers were ordering the special and one older gentleman even came up to the window to tell me my daddy would be proud of the brisket. I was thanking him for the lovely compliment when my cell phone rang. I looked down to see it was my friend, Dan calling.

"I'll be back in a second." I said to Sanchez and Isaac, and stepped off the truck.

"Hi. How's life in Margaritaville" I answered, sounding cheery. Dan had a condo with a view of The Gulf that I'd been dying to visit. I'd taken to referring to him as 'the beach bum'.

"Hey, sweetie. You doin' alright?" He had a hang dog tone to his speech, and I knew he was regretting the entire Elaine business before he even had a chance to bring it up.

"I'm doing very well. Thanks for askin'." And I was. The nausea and vomiting were almost entirely gone. My energy was back, as was my sex drive. I chose to focus on the positive.

"Has Elaine stopped bugging you yet?" He sounded like he was walking on eggshells, and I immediately wanted to put him at ease. Dan was one of my dearest friends, and I couldn't handle any rift with him. I felt the intense need to circle the wagons, and presumed that this compulsion might be my version of nesting. Besides, talking to him always improved my mood.

"We talked. She said Draven has a parole hearing coming up."

"I'm so sorry she ambushed you. I know I should have talked to you first, but she just sounded so desperate."

"She's just looking out for her son." While I was cooking the briskets low and slow, I'd put the finishing touches on my letter about Draven. As I read it over, I'd realized how angry I was. Not at Draven, though thanks to him I still jumped out of my skin at loud noises and had bouts of paranoia when I drove home. My anger wasn't even directed at Elaine, who I really *had* considered a friend. I was furious with *me*. I knew something wasn't right about Draven when he first started to pursue me. I knew something was off when he proposed just weeks after we met. When things seem too good to be true, you really *should* check the back seat.

"Honestly, I think she's mad because Draven's little tirade proves he's still in love with you." Dan drawled. "I think this is more about revenge for that than protecting their spawn."

"Draven doesn't know the definition of the word love." Dan had been my shoulder to cry on during my entire marriage to Draven Cirone. Even so, I'd kept a majority of the truth from even him. I'd confided a little to Dan and a little to Mason's wife Robin, but I'd kept most of Draven's crazy to myself. Joe and I had had a wicked fight about me helping Elaine, since Draven had his lawyer contact me and assure me that he'd leave town and serve his probation with an ankle bracelet in Seattle if I stayed silent. He wanted to focus on his new wife and kid. Joe was all for it; he wanted Draven as far away from us as possible. I told Joe I couldn't in good conscious because of Elaine's baby, but that was a lie.

What I hadn't told Joe...what I hadn't told anyone...was just how much Draven terrified me. It would have been impossible to explain to anyone just how twisted the man was. The thought of him being anywhere near a defenseless child. Or God help me, being able to mold the child into a new version of himself. I had spent the afternoon revisiting the years of methodical brainwashing that he had inflicted on me.

He'd get pissed at me for not hopping out of bed when he did, even though I'd hardly slept since I worked nights and weekends. He'd snap me with his towel on his way out of the shower at six a.m. Some of the welts left by the towel would hurt for days. It got to the point where the sound of him in the shower would yank me from sleep like a conditioned response. I'd drag myself from the bed and prepare a gourmet breakfast for him. But I wouldn't dare to try to go back to sleep until he had left the house.

The most disturbing thing he'd ever done, the thing that haunted me and made me fear for Elaine, had to do with my love for hot baths. I used to love to soak in the tub after long nights in the restaurant. We had one of those bowl type tubs in our ultra-modern 'Draven Cirone' style house, and it seemed like a damn shame not to take advantage of it. Drae said only 'lazy sloths' soaked in the tub, and that it was a waste of water and our time together. Mostly, I think he wanted me in bed servicing him.

One night, I was particularly exhausted after a seven day stretch, and I actually fell asleep in the tub. I remember him bursting into the bathroom (I am certain I locked the door) and grabbing me by the ankles. He yanked me under the water in one fell swoop.

The surprise and the momentum were my undoing, and I involuntarily sucked water into my lungs. I don't remember much after that. When I came to, he was hovering over me, looking relieved and afraid. He kept telling me I fell asleep in the tub and had almost drown. Had I not confirmed the splintered door jam the following morning, I would have doubted my memory of him bursting in. I would have believed his bullshit and not really understood how much danger I was really in being in that house. Again, Draven the hero saved me from a situation he created.

"Molly? Are you still there?" Dan asked, sounding irritated. It pulled me from the traumatic recollections.

I blew out a frustrated breath. "I'm sure it wasn't easy for her to come to me for help. She's got be really worried."

"Well, I'm sorry that she used me to get to you. And I'm sorry they didn't lock him up and throw away the key."

"I get it, Dan. I'm helping her out...or at least I'm doing what I can. Joe's still got his panties in a twist about it, but he'll get over it." I considered how Joe would react if he knew about Draven nearly drowning me. He already hovered and worried. I couldn't stand to see him fretting about me, and was glad I never told anyone about just how disturbing my ex-husband really was.

"How are those babies doing?" I was thrilled that he'd moved on to another topic.

"They're good. Growing like wildflowers,"

"Do we get pictures soon? Are you doing one of those 4-D Ultrasounds? You'd better send me a dvd!"

"We have another ultrasound in about three weeks. It's *the big one*...where we get to find out the sex." When the subject came up, I told Joe I couldn't wait to know if they were boys or girls. I was itching to see my babies and how they'd grown, and every time I thought about it, I had a hard time containing my enthusiasm.

Dan chuckled happily. "Good. I'm *so* ready to shop for tiny little booties and I want to know whether to buy bonnets or baseball caps."

"You and me both." I took a long drink of my sweet tea. I knew Joe would be on me about it, but I was in desperate need of the sugar and caffeine. It was the first I'd had all day and I needed the boost since I wasn't used to working in the evenings.

"You wanna come down for a visit?" Dan's thick Louisiana accent was like cool water on a sultry day.

"I could use some sun. Why?"

"David bought a bar." Dan's brother, David owned a posh French restaurant on Galveston Island. Dan had left Seattle to come down and be his sommelier.

"What? That man's crazy as hell. Doesn't he have his hands full with Madeline's?"

Dan sighed "He gets bored easily, just like you. I'm gonna level with you. He'll make it worth your while. He wants to talk to you about franchising Wrapgasmic."

"As in a Galveston Wrapgasmic?"

"Yes. But without wheels *and* with a liquor license." Dan replied.

I leaned back against the warm steel of the food truck and tried to imagine a brick and mortar place that sold margaritas and my wraps. I could see the concept working well in the land of wide brimmed hats and sandy flip flops.

"Sounds interesting. I should be able to head that way after my next appointment."

"I'll get the guest room ready. And I'll buy all of your favorite treats. Should I stock up on pickles and ice-cream?" He'd no more said the words when I felt as if a gold fish was swimming in my abdomen. I gasped and put my hand on my lower left side.

"Molly?" Dan sounded alarmed, and the sensation happened again, this time more centralized and stronger than the time before. I let out a tickled squeal. "What in gay hell?"

"I think I just felt the babies move for the first time!" I

blurted into the phone.

"Seriously?" I could imagine his jovial expression.

"Seriously!"

"Oh my God!" He exclaimed. "See? It's a sign that you need to get down here and hang out. Knowing you, you haven't been putting your feet up like you should."

"Oh, trust me. I've been very lazy."

He laughed melodiously. "What did your doctor say about drinking wine?"

I felt the fluttering feeling travel all the way across my lower abdomen and I chewed my lip to keep from giggling. "Dan, let me call you back. I really want to call Joe and tell him about the babies."

"Of course. I'll tell David to start getting his proposal together."

"Sounds good. We'll talk soon." I hung up and immediately dialed Joe, pacing with excitement.

"Hello?" His gruff greeting barely registered.

"Hey, guess what?" I was bubbling over with glee.

"Molly...I really don't have time for guessing games." He sighed so heavily it seemed to come from the depths of his soul. I felt my smile evaporate. It was clear that I was pestering him. His rebuke stung, and I'd never been so caught off guard by a reaction of Joe's.

"Oh...okay." My voice sounded too high, and hollow. I felt a little lightheaded and realized I'd been holding my breath.

"I'm sorry, babe. I'm in the middle of something kind of complicated. What'd you need?" He pressed on, still all business.

"It c...can wait. I'll see you soon." I hung up. His reaction to me had stolen all the joy from the moment.

Hurrying back into the truck, I jumped in to help Sanchez. I hadn't wanted to think about the changes I was seeing in Joe. I'd been trying to tell myself it was all in my head. A product of my insecurities and remnants of my time with Draven. But something was undeniably shifting. For the past couple of weeks he seemed to be avoiding me. Some days everything felt normal...happy even. Then on a dime, he'd pull away. I felt my grip on him slipping and it seemed like the more I tried to talk about it the more he'd retreat. The more he acted like nothing was wrong the louder his silence seemed.

Sanchez and I worked through another mini rush, and all the while I found myself feeling numb. Shifting from shock to anger, I was about to call Joe back right before my brother Mason turned up at the window with his wife, Robin and their three kids.

"Hey! I smell Hildebrandts Barbecue" He called in his booming voice, His referral to my father's old restaurant made me grin. He tipped his cowboy hat out of his eyes and smiled.

"Hey. I didn't know you were coming!" I called over the sounds of the grill.

"You think I'd miss Mac victory lap? Hell no!" He pulled out his wallet and asked the kids what they wanted.

"Put your money away, Mason." I stared at him emphatically, and then turned my attention to the kids. "Y'all just tell me what you want."

We'd finally sorted out their orders as the first wave of finishers and their dogs began to appear.

"Molly...you have to make this more often." Mason proclaimed, then his eyes widened. "Better yet! Ribs!"

"It is so good! I wanna take a bath in this sauce." Robin said around a mouthful of wrap, She nodded in the direction of the athletes sprinting toward the finish line. "Oh, we'd better head over!"

Mason snorted. "I think we've got a little time. Somehow I think Mac'll be bringing up the rear."

"Yeah...carting Bones across his shoulders like a casualty of war." I agreed and Mason fist bumped me. Robin made a scolding sound with her tongue and tossed her highlighted mane out of her face.

"Oh, ye of little faith." She drawled. Considering she was Mason's wife, it was comical how Robin always defended Mac. "Miss Betty says he's been training every day."

"That's our mom...the next sports commentator for CNN." Imaging my mother in a blazer with a microphone and camera crew made me giggle.

"Two weeks on a treadmill won't make up for the fact that he hasn't done cardio since high school." Mason laughed.

"You two are downright awful." Robin replied to her husband, giving him a sly smile and a paradoxical kiss on the lips. Mason Eskimo kissed her in return, and I found myself jealous of this airy and uncomplicated interaction. Mason squinted off in the direction of the parking lot and grinned. "Here comes Joe."

A westerly wind barreled into us and I pulled my open hoodie tight around me. I turned and didn't see him at first. Then I noticed heads turning, and knew to follow the female adoration. Joe sauntered in our direction, completely oblivious to the female population of Austin drooling in his wake. Soccer moms and teenage girls stopped to stare at him as he passed, and I didn't need to see him from that vantage point to know the view was equally good behind him. His casual bow legged gait served to showcase his perfect ass.

Joe held up a hand in greeting when he spotted us, and I realized Francis was with him. Francis gave me a friendly wave. Mason took a few steps in their direction so he and Joe could do their usually hand shake/clap-on-the-back greeting.

"What's up, Broseph." Mason called enthusiastically, and Joe gave him his signature lopsided grin. "Little sis hasn't talked you into running off to Vegas, yet? You'd better get a ring on that finger of his, Molly. The cougars are starting to circle!"

Joe eyes pinned mine and when I pried mine angrily away, I shot Mason a dismal glare. My oldest brother's smile faltered as he realized he'd just stepped in some shit. I could almost see him backpedaling. Mason turned to Francis. "Francis, how ya been? Are we going golfing before the weather turns?"

I shook my head and looked at Robin with a huff. She was staring at my belly with eager eyes. "Molly. Girl, you're already so damn *big*!"

"Robin, I love you. You're my favorite sister-in-law…" I cautioned.

"I'm your only sister in law." She interjected, and her tone was punchy.

"But I'm about to grab a fist full of your hair and yank it clean out." I smiled like I was joking, but her comment hit home. The way Joe was acting, I already felt like some inconvenient burden. With Robin's jab, I felt like an undesirable one at that. It was the last thing I'd needed to hear, and the look on my face must've been wretched, because she frowned.

Seeming in a hurry to redirect me, Robin launched into nurse-mode with twenty questions about the progression of my pregnancy. My rapid-fire responses seemed to satisfy all of her second trimester requirement. Her last question gave me pause.

"How's Joe?" Her seasoned eyes penetrated me when I hesitated. In my defense, what reply could I give?

Detached…silent…smokin' hot?

It was a sobering revelation that I would have responded to her the same way almost a year before. Yes, we lived together now. Yes, we were about to bring new lives into the world. No…I had no idea how Joe was or what was happening behind those mossy green eyes of his. I found this deeply disturbing and I recalled something he'd said during the first real conversation as adults.

"You never really know anyone."

Luckily, my nephew intercepted the conversation and ran with it.

"Look! There's Uncle Mac!"

I turned and shielded my eyes against the last rays of the setting sun. Sure enough, my brother's neon green Under Armor stood out like a festering eyesore. Bones trotted along ahead of him and Mac was booking along at a surprising clip. Robin and I exchanged a baffled glance.

"Hurry, y'all!" My bombshell sister-in-law called over her shoulder, grabbing her son by the hand. We rushed in the direction of the finish line. We were about 20 yards away, when I felt a familiar large and calloused hand grasp mine. I slowed, and tried to turn toward him. This was a simple maneuver that I would normally have executed flawlessly. Instead, I nearly tripped, since my center of gravity had been hijacked by two avocado sized babies.

"Whoa, there, Crash." Joe chuckled, and displaying all of the grace that I lacked, he rescued me easily with one arm. When he didn't release me, I tried to wriggle away. He held me firm, and I was left with no alternative but to look up at him. He wore the puppy dog eyes that could usually disarm me, and the two sides of my personality held a brief tug of war. Joe's avoidance wounded me, and I was tired of acting like there was nothing the matter with us. Part of me wanted to stand and fight and part of me wanted to brush it all under the rug with a cliché girl response like 'I'm fine'. For the first time in a long time, I struggled with which course of action was best for us. I wanted my choices to be best for us, especially since fate continued to throw Molotov cocktails in our direction. Lost in my own indecision, I stared absently at his chest, trying figure out my next move.

"Molly." His soft chide had a condescending edge that I'm sure he thought was playful. It instantly pissed me off, which I later assumed had a lot more to do with remnants of Draven than Joe... My face felt like it was on fire. I tried to pull away, but he didn't loosen his grip.

"I felt the babies move today. That's why I called you." Joe stiffened and then heaved a heavy sigh. He reached his hand up toward my face and I twisted out of his grasp. "Mac's about to finish the race." I rushed after Robin and the kids. I despised hurting Joe. My personal battle since we'd moved in together had been balancing my compulsion to take care of him with the need to retain my own identity. Though Joe was nothing like my ex, I vowed not to make the same mistakes with him, namely molding my life entirely to suit his. Destiny, it seemed, took this mission of mine as some sort of a challenge.

I narrowed my eyes and threw my hood over my head. Joe needed a taste of his own medicine. Admittedly, I was feeling particularly vulnerable. Rehashing Draven's betrayal and the evisceration of my self-worth all day long had exposed a lot of raw nerves. Joe had been so hot and cold I didn't know what to expect from one interaction to the next. Worst was his repeated refusal to interact with me at all.

My chest ached, but I didn't look over my shoulder at him. I felt like a petty child for how I had told him about feeling the babies move. What should have been a joyous, important milestone, with him was yet another example of our dysfunction. Instead of feeling close to him I felt further apart.

As I neared the finish line, I saw Mac was running in stride with Kelly. I tried to contain my wonderment, but I couldn't help but be impressed. I can't say that seeing him compete was a foreign experience. Mac had always been a natural athlete, a great football player in school and still pretty sought after when it came time to pick players in his softball league. Granted, he'd also partied hard for a lot of years, which explained a great deal about his catastrophic marriage. His ex-liked to party even more than he did, and situations like theirs never end well.

Mac murmured something to Kelly and her dark eyes narrowed in a fierce and competitive manner.

Hmmm...maybe I underestimated this girl.

Her plump lips curled in a wry grin and they both broke into a final sprint. The two of them made a striking looking pair, and

I wondered if I'd missed the mark when I assumed they were incompatible.

We all whooped and hollered as they crossed the finish line. Mason and Joe crept up behind Mac as he walked off the pain, and I couldn't help but laugh when they teamed up and dumped a half full water cooler over his head. Kelly laughed too, and Mac pulled her into an exaggerated bear hug, squishing his sopping clothes against hers. This made her squeal in mock outrage. Mason's children fell into giggle fits and Mac proceeded to chase after them, as if to do the same to each one of them.

"Don't even think about it, Malcolm!" Robin shouted after him. "Those hellions have to ride home with me and I just had the minivan detailed."

I noticed Francis's pensive expression as he watched Kelly interact with Mac. It was obvious that he was picking up on their chemistry, but how he felt about it was uncertain. Unlike Joe, Francis could have made a killing at Caesar's Palace.

My phone rang, and I saw it was Isaac calling.

"SOS." He blurted into the phone when I answered, and I knew they needed me back at the truck.

"I gotta go y'all. If you want some brisket, sounds like you'd better head this way, too." I announced, my traitorous eyes slipping toward Joe. He looked up from brushing off his jeans, which had caught some splatter from his prank on Mac. I started up the hill, and the wriggling below my belly button kicked in again. My hand went to my bump and for a fraction of a second, I slowed my step.

"Is something wrong?" It was Francis, not Joe, who appeared beside me. I searched the crowd and saw Joe had hung back, still chatting with the twins. He caught me watching him, and when our eyes met, he quickly looked away.

"Nope. Not at all." I forced a smile, and the aftertaste of that lie stayed with me the rest of the night.

Joe

Boiling Point

"WHERE'S NICK?" MAC'S question interrupted my carving for the third time in an hour, and I rolled my head back with a heavy sigh.

"I thought he was helping you." I tossed down my straight chisel and cracked my knuckles.

"That kid has ADD." Mac grumbled. "I swear he takes more breaks than the rest of us combined."

Mac had been in a fairly chipper mood of late between all the money rolling into the shop and the increasingly common visits he received from Kelly. That was until I put him in charge of training Nick, and he did a complete 180. Mac had tried to shoot me down, but I wouldn't take no for an answer.

"I hate to play the boss card, dude." I'd said to him last

week. "But consider it played. I'll be out for at least 6 weeks when Molly has the twins and you'll be stuck with him."

The kid was good for his age, but he had a lot to learn. I'd told Mac I'd take him one day a week and Mac would have him the rest of the time for now. Since Nick and Mac were both a couple of smart ass rebels, I figured they'd eventually hit it off and gang up on me, but now I wasn't so sure.

"He was just in the entryway talking to Molly a minute ago." Francis called from the showroom. Popping up out of my seat, I stretched my aching back muscles. The long hours had begun taking their toll. If Nick didn't end up working out and we had to retrain someone, we were going to be too far behind for me to have the time off I wanted. I checked the parking lot and the back alley to see if he had ducked out for a cigarette and came up empty.

Mac was grumbling under his breath as I came back inside, saying something about dropping the kid in the nearest manhole cover. Not that I blamed him, but the last thing I needed was more fucking stress at that point. Instead, I needed Mac to step up and handle things, not come crying to me when his underling pulled a quick fade.

Twenty minutes later Nick reappeared and Mac pulled him aside for a talk. I was in the middle of a complex carving, so I let him handle it.

When this particular job had come in, we were already swamped. But the money was too good to pass up, and besides it was restoring a piece of history. The Baker Hotel in Mineral Wells had been *the* destination spa back in the twenties and thirties. They'd even boasted the first Olympic sized swimming pool in the state. The town had decided to restore it before it fell down, but the building had been open to the elements for a long time. Most of the woodwork needed heavy restoration or replacement.

My project was a large carving from the ballroom. After

studying some original plans, old photographs and some recent ones they'd sent, I had almost finished it. Now I was fitting it all together and each part had to fit perfectly. I'd already had to re-make one piece when Molly called me unexpectedly on the day of Mac's big race.

She'd broken my train of thought when she called and I'd lost my temper. The way I'd spoken to her was unacceptable, and when I went to apologize she dropped the bomb that she'd been calling about the babies. She'd felt them move for the first time, and her first thought was to call me. My response was to snap at her, and the shame wasn't something I could just shrug off. Imagining how much my shitty reaction must have stung her and made her doubt me really got under my skin.

Since that night, I'd put my phone on vibrate, or turned it off entirely if she was upstairs. The amount of money the hotel job paid was impressive and would help us with a down payment if we could ever find a house worth bidding on. I had to finish the project, but once it was done I could turn my focus to Molly. It was the hardest piece I'd worked on in years, and I was going to be glad to set it aside.

By the time I had everything clamped together for the glue to dry, Mac was back at his workstation. I walked over and raised an eyebrow to him.

"So?"

Mac looked uncomfortable for a minute and then shrugged.

"Short Shit asked him to run an errand. I told him to let me know next time or I'll dock his pay." He looked at me as if waiting for me to correct him but I just nodded.

"That sounds fair." He blinked in surprise. "Mac, I told you. I'm gonna be out for a while. So I need you to step up take on the management of our woodworking staff."

"Our woodworking staff of one?" He cracked, and I nodded. He grinned. "Well at least they don't outnumber me."

I gave him some final instructions on some of the current

projects and headed upstairs.

I took a large breath as I stood outside the apartment door, in limbo between work and home, thinking.

What the hell was she talking to Nick about? And where the hell did she send him? If she wants something she should ask me, not some young buck who drools all over her, pregnant or not.

I felt irrational anger at the thought of Nick sharing secrets with Molly and almost walked back down to the shop. Then I pushed the bad shit down into the imaginary tank where I was keeping all my other bullshit and slammed the lid.

Coming into the apartment, I saw Molly hurriedly sweep something off the kitchen counter and toss it into the garbage. Acting like I didn't notice, I crossed the room and took her into my arms. She looked startled but pleased when I pulled her close and planted a kiss on the base of her neck. Glancing over her shoulder, I caught a glimpse of what she'd thrown in the trash and I felt my stomach tighten painfully.

An empty container from Amy's Ice Cream.

She'd sent my assistant out to get her a treat from Amy's ...probably because she'd been afraid to ask me. Scared that I would freak out or maybe just flat out refuse. Amy's had been Jessica's and my place. We'd met there, and we'd gone there all the time. I hadn't set foot inside the joint since the night of the accident, and couldn't even look at the place no matter which location it was. I just couldn't bring myself to face it. It served as another example of how I was failing Molly without even being asked to try. Anger blossomed in my chest, but the anger was directed inward, and I held onto her tightly while I got the emotions squashed down and tucked away where they belonged.

"Amy's? Where did you get that?" I asked, as if I'd just noticed the bag. She yanked back, looking a little freaked and a slight bit guilty. Then she exhaled as if defeated and squared her shoulders.

"I had a really strong craving for Mexican Vanilla." She refused to meet my eyes so I dipped down to meet hers and smiled at her reassuringly.

"Is that's where Nick went?" The humiliated look on her face told me all I needed to know. "Babe...I appreciate why you asked someone else, but if you want something you should send me."

Molly's face fell into a troubled frown and reached up to put her hands on either side of my face. She looked into my eyes for an inordinately long time.

"Joe...where are you?" Her question confused me and it must have shown. "The last time I even mentioned the place, you almost had a panic attack. Now you can...what? Just flip a switch and run down there?"

"Babe, I'll do whatever you need me to do." I heaved a reluctant sigh, knowing in my heart that going into Amy's wouldn't be as simple as that.

Her eyes flashed and she stalked past me. Halfway across the room, she whirled and her arms came across her chest. "Jesus, Joe! I'm sick of this shit. I feel like I'm talking to a brick wall. I don't know what you think you're doing...but I want the man I love back, not some God damn Stepford Joe."

Her sudden hostility was startling, but it was something I was getting used to. Her attempt to goad me into opening up by attacking me held a certain irony, but the doc and I had worked hard at managing my anger and I refused to lose my temper on Molly of all people. I leaned back against the counter and crossed my arms before forcing out a chuckle.

"I'm just trying to keep things on an even keel. Your hormones have been all over the place and it's made you really unpredictable." It was the truth, but not all of the truth.

Her eyes grew wide and she looked a little unbalanced. When she fired back, it was with both barrels. *"I'm* unpredictable? Me? Really?"

I covered my eyes with both hands, too fatigued to put up a

good defense. "I want you to ask me for stuff, not one of my employees who can't keep his eyes from wandering all over you. Yes, it would be difficult to go to Amy's...but I'd do it for you in a second."

Unshed tears stood in her eyes as she crossed the room to me. Pulling me into a fierce embrace, she held me with surprising force.

"Dammit, Joe," Her whisper matched the intensity of her grip. "I'd never ask you to put yourself through that just because I can't control my sweet tooth."

I pulled back so I could see her eyes and felt my chilly heart melt at the love I saw reflected there. "Listen up, little girl. I love you. More than I've ever loved *anyone*."

I held her gaze, making sure my statement carried the weight it was intended to. Her doubtful eyes made me totally berserk, but I pressed on. "I would walk through fire for you, or hell, sit through a marathon of Gossip Girl."

The tears that had begun to spill were interrupted by a snorting laugh escaping her. A second later, her expression grew somber once more. "I love you, too, Joe. I can tell you're bottling a lot of things up and I'm worried. It's not good for you and it's not good for us. I *need* you. All of you. I need you to level with me. I promise I can take whatever it is that you need to dish out."

I blinked at her uncanny assessment of what I'd been going through...what I thought I'd been hiding so well. I stammered in response. "I...I'm just trying to keep from stressing you out."

"Your attempt to 'not stressing me out'? *It's stressing* me out." Staring pointedly into my eyes, she seemed to be searching for some answer to an undefined question. I was uncomfortable with the way she seemed to see through me. My need to break the tension overwhelmed me, and I pulled her into an explorative kiss. I wanted to take her mind off of this pointless argument...and off of me. She sighed deeply, breathing into me through our kiss. Her body seemed to resonate with relief against mine. She returned the kiss tenfold, and the taste of vanilla and spice on her tongue caught me off guard. The flavor had been Jess's favorite as well, but it tasted so different on Molly. Her tongue softly grazed mine, and minutes later we were escalating in a deliciously familiar direction. Unable and unwilling to tap the breaks, I swept her off her feet and carried her down the hall.

"Joe, you're gonna hurt yourself." Her cheeks reddened, and I realized she seriously thought lifting her was pressing my limits.

"Baby, I have boots that weigh more than you." My dismissive response didn't seem to convince her.

Once in our bedroom, I placed her on her feet and grabbed handfuls of the pale orange material of her dress. It was soft to the touch, like a well broken in t-shirt, and the color reminded me of the icy treats my mother used to buy from the ice cream man.

"You're wearing way too many clothes." My voice sounded husky, and the flirtatious curl of her lips awoke the beast within me. "Arms up."

She blinked up at me from under her dark lashes, and her eyes glittered with heated promise. Her face, neck, and chest rapidly flushed a pretty shade of pink. However, she immediately did as she was told. Molly Hildebrandt *hated* to be told what to do. The only exception seemed to be in the bedroom. This had been one hell of a discovery, and a hell of a lot of fun to explore. Sex with Molly was an athletic experience from the get-go. She had more of a libido than most guys in their heyday, and I considered myself a very lucky man.

My girl also had a kinky side. She liked things a bit rough a lot of the time, and after a great deal of coaxing, I'd proceeded cautiously down that road with her. I had concerns due to her violent experiences with her ex and trepidation not knowing where her boundaries were. Now there was the pregnancy to consider as well, and I was even more leery about playing rough. The last thing I wanted to do was hurt her.

When it came to sex, Molly wasn't afraid to ask for what she wanted. She was a far cry from submissive. She gave as well as she got, and had no problem taking control of me whenever the mood took her.

I slowly stripped off her dress and made short work of removing her bra. Her incredible breasts were even larger now, and her erect nipples a darker shade of red. She looked a bit uncomfortable as my eyes wandered over her changing figure, and she actually moved her hands up as if to cover herself. Before I knew what I was doing, my hands were entangled in her hair and I backed her slowly against the bed.

"Don't even think about it." I growled, between greedy kisses. I lowered her carefully onto the bed. "I *want* to look at you, do you understand me?"

She nodded mutely, and I sat up, letting my eyes wander over her flawless pale flesh. It had pinked with her arousal and her porcelain curves made my mouth water. She was perfection and I trailed kisses from her thick dark hair framing her expressive pale eyes to the tips of her pink polished toes.

"Joe…" She giggled and squirmed. A bashful look transformed her face, making her look surprisingly young. "You're giving me a complex. Get up here and kiss me "

"You're perfect." I traced my finger from the hollow of her neck to her naval, which sparkled with a tiny diamond.

She rolled her eyes and cocked a dark brow. "You're out of your damn mind. My belly looks like a volleyball."

"If you think you're any *less* beautiful to me carrying my children, *you're* out of *your* damn mind." I replied, dropping onto one elbow. She tried to look away, but I tilted her chin so that she could see my sincerity. "Kiss me, baby girl."

She pulled my mouth to hers, and her lips captured mine. The heat between us flared white hot as always, and I felt my tension simply roll away with each kiss and caress. We made love, naturally adapting to her transforming body. I was slow and careful with her, forcing her to ask me for faster, harder, more. Soon she cried out louder and shuddered harder than I'd ever seen. Watching her face as she came was the biggest fucking turn-on, and knowing she was satisfied, I relaxed and succumbed to her.

We lay in comfortable silence, and I felt more connected to her than I had in weeks, maybe months. I must have drifted off because I woke to find myself spooning her. Smiling, I reached across her and placed my hand on the spot where our babies nestled within her. Rolling over to face me, Molly's expression was complex and pensive as she regarded me in silence. Reaching down, she took my hand off of her womb and pulled it to her lips, kissing my knuckles.

"I want you to make an appointment for us to go see Dr. Greene together." She said. I felt my brow wrinkle, but she pushed on before I could respond. "I know he's your doctor, but I think it is important for me to at least talk to him. For *us* to talk to him. We can't keep going on like this."

"Like what? I thought things were better." The look she gave me made me realize that I hadn't been fooling her at all. It just proved that she knew me better than anyone else did.

"Don't. Just don't. Pretending like everything is okay isn't working. Fake it until you make it doesn't work with kids, and it won't work with me. I need us to be able to deal with things openly. Isn't that what you want?"

My throat had been tightening the more she talked. It felt like an elephant was sitting on my chest, it was so hard to breathe. I flipped up to sit on the side of the bed and leaned forward, hoping not to hyperventilate. Molly moved up behind me and her hand caressed my back. Her gentle touch calmed the demon that was shaking the bars of his cage inside my head. She was right, I couldn't keep doing this. And I needed honesty. After all the lies and the secrets Jessica kept from me, the last thing I wanted was to go down that path with Molly. It was long past time we went to see the doc.

"He asked me to bring you a while back." I admitted, looking over my shoulder at her. "But we've both been so busy…"

I stopped. That was a lie. I wouldn't lie like that. Not to her. I took a shuddering breath. "I thought you'd be pissed."

"Why would I be pissed?" She was up on her knees behind me, which put us eye to eye. A crease appeared between her eyebrows. Unwilling to look into her eyes when I confessed my real motivation, I turned away.

"I didn't want you to think I thought you needed therapy." I spoke the words quietly, and waited for an explosion. Instead, she wrapped her arms around my neck and resting her chin on my shoulder. She pressed her velvety cheek against mine. When she spoke, I could feel her jaw move against my bare flesh.

"Of course I need therapy." Her voice was like silk, but her words sounded firm, reticent. "*We all* need therapy. Baby, *promise* me you'll call him. I don't care about the schedule. It doesn't matter when he's avalable, set up and appointment and I'll clear my schedule."

We spent the rest of the afternoon together curled up on the bed. I talked into her bellybutton for a while to see if I could make the babies kick and it seemed to have the opposite effect. Then Molly crafted us some chili and cornbread and we ate it on the couch, spending the remainder of the evening searching Realtor.com for new listings. I never made it back down to the shop, but I figured now was as good a time as any for the boys to get used to me being gone more.

The next morning I called Dr. Greene's office, figuring I would get an appointment in a day or so. The receptionist put me on hold and then came back on the line to inform me that we were set for a one o'clock appointment that same day.

"Ahhh…" I stammered.

"Is that too soon?"

"No. No…it's fine."

"The doctor asked if you'll be bringing a guest."

I covered my face with my hand, wondering what the fall-out of this meeting of the minds might be. "Tell him that she'll be with me."

All day long I worried about what might come out during the session and why Dr. Greene wanted me to bring Molly. By the time Molly and I were getting ready to leave the apartment, I was really keyed up. I think she might have been, too. She grew quieter as the minutes passed, and though I was waiting for her with keys in hand she was dawdling and moody. We nearly got into it when she refused to put on her winter jacket, even though it was drizzling rain and windy as hell outside.

"Molly. Your coat."

"I'm good."

"*Now* you are. In ten minutes you'll be freezing and I'll have to give you *my* coat." I put my hands on my hips and tilted my head.

"Oh, alright." She mumbled and disappeared into the bedroom. She returned, shrugging into a heavy sweater. "Satisfied?"

"Baby girl, you can't wear flip-flops. It's November." I folded my arms and glanced at my watch.

"But they're cozy." She complained, with a sigh, kicking them off.

Thirty minutes later, we walked into Dr. Greene's reception area hand in hand. Molly looked as nervous as I felt, her cheeks all flush with her dewy pregnancy glow. She was wearing one of my flannel shirts and it hung low over her maternity jeans which she'd stuffed into some crazy looking, furry boots just to spite me. They looked like they were made of a skinned raccoon and came all the way up to her knees.

I couldn't decide if having her with me was making me anxious or if I was just anxious. Her long hair fell loose over her shoulders like chocolate waves, and I stroked it nervously as we sat waiting our turn. I did this a lot. It was a nervous habit, my treating her like a security blanket, or a prized stuffed animal. My eyes scanned the empty waiting room, and I noticed the receptionist, typically a very icy individual, eyeing Molly's protruding belly, and smiling.

"So, are you excited for Friday?" Molly asked. I looked at her blankly and after about three seconds of confusion, I realized she was referring to the upcoming ultrasound.

"Oh. Yeah." I murmured, and she slowly blinked at me.

"Yeah. I can tell." She scoffed, and turned away to pick up a magazine from the table next to her.

"Molly." I admonished, and she huffed and dropped the magazine onto her lap. She looked sideways at me, her annoyance as obvious as the stud in her nose. "I am. It's just all a bit weird with you here. My worlds are colliding, that's all. I'm distracted, not disinterested."

She nodded thoughtfully, and the receptionist's phone beeped. She carried on a quiet conversation, then hung up and turned to us.

"Dr. Greene will see you now." She said, and I led Molly into his office. The doc stood up the minute we entered the room, and I felt a tug as Molly, who was still holding my hand, slowed her step

'Hello, Molly." Dr. Greene wore a sheepish grin. Molly narrowed her eyes at him, obviously surprised that she'd met him many times before. She put a hand on her hip and then shook her head with a bemused smile.

"Will." She replied and then followed up in a mocking tone. "Or should I call you Dr. Greene?"

"Why start now?" His retort was swift and their familiar timing reminded me of vaudevillian actors. When Molly and I first started seeing each other, I'd recommended that Dr. Greene try her food. Since then, he'd informed me that he'd been back many times. He'd never revealed his identity to her, doctor/patient confidentiality I assumed, and I figured where he chose to eat was his business, so I never mentioned it to Molly.

"Well...now that we have *that* out of the way..." I muttered, and instead of taking my usual seat next to his desk, I sat down on the couch with her.

"I'm glad Joe finally asked you to come." Dr. Greene came around the desk, leaving his trusty notebook closed and untouched. I could feel the tension in my jaw as I felt Molly's eyes on me.

"He didn't invite me." Molly replied, her disappointment blatant. "I *asked* to come."

"Very well." The doc's telling sigh almost made me wince. Molly's eyes flicked from him to me and then away again. "What's brings you in, Molly."

She fidgeted a bit and looked from me to him. "I want to start off by saying things were good. They weren't perfect, but neither of us would've trusted perfect anyway."

"*Were*? Past tense?" Dr. Greene asked, focusing on Molly. I saw her nod in my peripheral vision.

"Before this." She indicated to her baby bump as if she were discussing an unfortunate grape juice spill on a snow white carpet. "Joe and I were figuring our shit out. We'd moved from the 'everything's perfect' phase to the 'how the hell do we fit this puzzle together' phase. But that's real life. We were working out how to be Molly and Joe. We had fights, pretty regularly...but that's normal, right?"

Dr. Greene shrugged in a non-committal manner as if he considered the question rhetorical.

"Then it all stopped. When we found out about the babies."

"What stopped?" He asked, and I turned to look at her in surprise. I couldn't believe how easily she spoke to the doctor. Much more easily than she spoke to me, that was for damn sure. She furrowed her brow apologetically, and looked away.

Apprehension was plastered on her face, but she pressed on. "The progress."

"We shifted gears." I offered, as if this explained all of our issues in one phrase. Deep inside the back of my brain something nervously stirred. "It's understandable. We found out about the babies and our focus changed."

"You've completely checked out on me, Joe." Molly turned, adjusting herself on the couch so she was able to face me head on.

I inhaled through my nose and exhaled through my mouth. The urge to lose my temper and tell her exactly what I was think-ing was almost overwhelming. She was glossing over everything like the babies were our downfall and it was far from the truth. We'd been busy and I'd been busy getting things ready for the babies. She blew this all off as if it didn't matter. Somehow I suppressed the urge to explode, when I really wanted to shake some sense into her. With serious effort I kept my voice level. "I'm right here, Molly."

"Sure, now you are…but you've been avoiding me for a while. I'm not sure what I did that made you climb back inside your shell. You told me you *wanted* me to have the twins."

"I do." I snapped, unable to keep the exasperation out of my reply. I glared at her in silence, and she flushed bright red and turned back to face Dr. Greene.

She looked down at her hands and her voice quivered just a little when she spoke "I feel really alone. Even when he's with me. He knows things are off, but he acts like I'm imagining things. I just can't understand why he won't talk to me and I was hoping you could help."

Dr. Greene looked at me and raised that damndable eye-brow of his. This was my cue to have some grand revelation, some epiphany that would show my inner growth. But that was Dr. Phil bullshit and it wasn't fair to have them both back me into a corner.

I knew I needed to dig deep and be frank. 'For my own good' they said. 'Let it all out' they said. That was a bunch of bullshit. People didn't really want you to do that. What they wanted was for you to be all right so that they didn't have to feel bad about your pain. It was a shitty way to be treated and honestly all this pressure was the last thing I expected from Molly. Dr. Greene? Yeah, he was an asshole at times, but never Molly.

"Joe," Dr. Greene leaned back in his chair and looked at me. "Molly has told me how she feels, can you do the same?"

"Well, my girlfriend just said that I make her feel abandoned and alone. How do you think that makes me feel?" The venom I spewed didn't ease the sting I felt,

I had very little reserve left and this meeting was going in a very bad direction. Dr. Myers had lectured us both that Molly needed to avoid stress. Having twins automatically classified her as high risk, so the last thing she needed was an angry outburst or any of my grief bullshit. Dr. Greene pursed his lips and I recognized the look. He wasn't going to be put off by my dodge. Heaving a deep sigh I threw my hands up.

"What the hell do you guys want from me?" It came out softly, as I tried to keep from raising my voice in anger. "You both know about my past... the things I carry with me. So I'm trying to take care of Molly and make sure she isn't stressed and yet, I fail...again."

Molly leaned over and put her hand on the side of my face, turning it toward her. Leaning forward she pinned my gaze.

"Joe, I'm not trying to pick on you. Please don't feel that way. I wasted a lot of time making myself into something I'm not just to try and please someone else. I don't want to do the same thing again...but I don't want *you* to do that either."

"I'm not doing that. All I'm trying to do is take care of you. And you fight me every step of the way." Molly reacted in angry surprise, but I hurried on before she could interrupt. "You work too hard, on your feet all day and in the heat. It worries me.

When I try to help, you yell at me. I set up multiple house show-ings after searching for places we both might like and you talk about getting a place by yourself. You push me away constantly and then get angry at me for not losing my temper with you. Ex-actly what is it that you want me to do?"

I slammed my lips together, stopping the verbal barrage be-fore it got any worse. My stomach had become a painful, twist-ing weight of nausea. I waited for Dr. Greene to berate me or for Molly to burst out crying. Instead, both of them looked at me in shock with a touch of approval.

"It's a valid question, Molly," Dr. Greene interjected. "What is it that you want Joe to do?"

Molly paused, and actually seemed to ponder his question. Perhaps she was just selecting her words.

"For one," She replied red face and haughty, "I want him to realize I'm not a damn China doll. I'm not going to break just because I'm pregnant."

"That's a very common complaint, Molly." Dr. Greene's at-tempt to unruffle her feathers caused her to sit back and fold her arms. "Most pregnant women I've known struggle with when to accept help and how to gracefully reject unwanted coddling. Joe's not dysfunctional in this regard."

Molly pinked noticeably, and nodded reluctantly. Turning in my direction, she gently touched my thigh. "Joe, I *want* to be with you. These babies need both their parents. But in order to work things out we need to be a team. Not Mighty Joe and his swooning damsel in distress. Do I need help sometimes? Abso-lutely. But guess what? So do you."

There was an air of desperation to her voice that helped to keep my anger in check. I saw the fear she normally kept hidden threatening to overfill and spill from her like a forgotten faucet. Tears welled in the corner of her eyes and I pulled her into my arms, forgetting Dr. Greene was even in the room

"I love you, Molly. I want to protect you, and I want to protect the twins. Even if it's impossible, I need to try. I won't apologize for that. And I don't plan to stop trying, *ever*, so you'd better get used to it."

She graced me with a tremulous smile, and I felt the need to add another caveat. "I know I'm not doing any of this right, but how I'm behaving isn't meant to make you unhappy. I'll try to meet you somewhere in the middle. That's all I can promise."

We talked for a few more minutes, the doc asking a few more detailed questions even picking up his notebook to jot down his notes as always. The questions seemed mostly about my behavior and my reactions. Finally, Dr. Greene tossed down his pen and pulled off his glasses.

"The most important thing is that you both came here to build a healthy relationship. The fact that you're both committed to that goal is a very big deal. We're just about out of time, but if you don't mind, Joe, I'd like a few minutes alone with Molly. She's at a severe disadvantage considering all the hours we've logged together. Do you mind?"

I minded.

I minded a lot.

There was a definitive roar of anger that issued forth from the dark cave in the back of my head at the thought.

"Sure." I shrugged, barely suppressing the violent urge to throw the nearest chair through his window. The thought of Molly confiding in anyone but me was abhorrent, but I'd learned the hard way that change was both painful and necessary. Additionally, Molly sat relaxed, as if she had no intention of leaving until she had talked to Dr. Greene alone no matter what my response was. I climbed out of my seat and stalked in the direction of the door. I didn't stop, nor did I look back as I spoke. "I'll be in the truck."

"There's mama! Are you ready to see those babies?" The tech asked, as Molly came out of the restroom where she'd just changed into a gown. She looked the fit little redhead up and down and I swore I saw her shoulders slumped.

"All I can think about is how much I need to pee. I'm seriously about to piss myself." The tech blatted a surprised laugh and slapped a hand over her mouth.

"You can go on in and relieve your bladder a little. Just don't empty it completely. With two babies, you don't need to retain nearly as much urine for us to get good images."

Molly didn't have to be told twice. She instantly vanished back into the restroom. I slumped back in my chair and glanced around the dimly lit room. There was nothing at all to look at, and when I glanced in her direction, the ultrasound tech smiled at me in a flirty manner. I nodded at her, a completely neutral expression locked on my face. Had Molly been there, I was sure she would've gone ballistic. Luckily, she was tucked away in the restroom rather than psychoanalyzing my every move.

All week long, Molly had been watching me, studying every expression that crossed my face. Then she'd press me on what I was thinking and how I was feeling. I found her arm chair psychoanalysis unnerving, and it was actually a relief not to be in the same room with her. The minute I acknowledged this murky thought, I was consumed with guilt. The scrub clad girl leaned provocatively across from me, deliberately displaying the waistband of her thong. She glanced over her shoulder seductively and cocked an auburn eyebrow. I flushed and looked away, immediately ashamed. I wondered if I was giving off some vibe that made her think it was acceptable to hit on me and felt like a tool.

The bathroom door swung open and Molly appeared again with a near-orgasmic sigh.

"So much better!" She beamed, her bright smile searing into me like a brand. When her eyes met mine, the smile evaporated.

"What's wrong, baby?"

"Nothing." In a hurry to have her as a human shield, I stood and helped her onto the table with a sly grin. "I'm just anxious to see Thing 1 and Thing 2."

She snorted. "I didn't peg *you* for a Dr. Seuss fan."

"Isn't everyone? You better get on board, little girl, because kids love 'The Seuss'." I leaned in and kissed her nose. Trying to lighten the mood, I decided to revisit the conversation we had about baby names on the way over. "So...if they're boys, what about Han Solo and Obi-wan Kenobi Jensen?"

"Keep dreaming, fanboy." Molly chuckled until the overly-friendly tech, who was scowling at Molly, squirted way too much gel onto her belly. "Ahhh! That's freezing!"

"Sorry." The girl muttered unconvincingly, and scurried to the keyboard. Molly frowned after her and turned to me, shaking her head as if she thought the girl were an idiot. After a minute of typing in information, the tech began to move the Doppler over Molly's belly.

I rolled my stool as close to the exam table as I could get and reached for Molly's hand. She smiled as I took it and pulled it to my lips. I leaned in close and together we settled in and watched the screen intently.

As the monitor lit up with the familiar black and white image, I felt a memory stir. The first time I had seen this...with Jack...I'd been surprised that it looked like a live X-ray. The vivid recollection about Jack was like a lightning bolt burning through my heart. My hand clenched Molly's as the room flickered back and forth in my vision. Molly wavered out of focus for a moment and Jessica suddenly lay on the bed before me. The false image lasted for just an instant, but it left me breathless.

The flash of the past wasn't about Jess, well, at least not most of it. I had spent a lot of hours staring at the last few swallows in whiskey bottles thinking about her. Her beauty, the way she whispered to me in the dark. Her betrayal was something I figured I would learn to live with eventually. But Jack was an entirely different story. I ached for Jack, and I long ago realized his loss was permanent damage that would never heal. The intense memory of Jack's ultrasound...the vision of Jessica on the table...it felt like an omen. A warning of danger to come. Molly flinched on the table and when she winced, it felt like my heart stopped beating.

"What is it?" The words came out a little sharper than I intended and both Molly and the tech looked up at me in alarm.

"Nothing Joe, it just feels a little...uncomfortable doesn't begin to cover it. Awkward is a better word." Molly sounded calm and she ran her thumb over my knuckles as she silently scrutinized me. The tech tried to give me a reassuring smile and nodded to the screen.

"You wanted to know the sex of the babies, right?"

"Yes!" Molly blurted whipping her head in the direction of the monitor and the tech raised her eyebrows, turning to me as if for confirmation.

"You heard the lady." I bit my lip nervously, and she nodded. She pressed the device further into Molly belly. Molly gripped me a little harder, but her eyes remained glued to the screen. I turned my attention reluctantly away from her to the monitor, and saw the profile of one of our babies. I broke into gooseflesh and my jaw dropped as I stared in awe. I could see every bone in its spine and I broke into a sweat as I watched the tiny person squirm fitfully. The tech seemed bothered by the hyperactive little squirt and actually wiggled the wand in her hand.

"Come on, little baby. Turn around just a little bit further." The girl mumbled to herself, squinting at the screen and typing several keystrokes. Occasionally, she'd click the mouse and she seemed to be taking measurements of various bones.

"Okay," She said a couple of minutes later. Her voice oozed confidence, "Do you see this?"

She indicated to the screen and Molly and I both leaned in. I squinted to make sense of the picture.

"Yeah?" I replied completely clueless, my anxious tone urging her to go on.

"Baby A is most definitely a boy." She announced proudly, as if she were about to whip out bubble gum cigars.

My heart rate, which had just returned to normal, after my acid free flashback, shot up and leapt into my throat. I turned to Molly, whose eyes were wide with wonder. She wrapped her arm around my neck and squeezed, but I barely felt it.

"Are you sure?" I turned back to the tech in what seemed like slow motion. It felt like I was outside of myself, and was vaguely aware of Molly sniffling beside me.

"Yeah...he's not being shy about it." The tech replied with a rueful grin.

"Ahhh. He already takes after his daddy." Molly giggled, but her voice trembled with emotion. I just blinked at her, completely dumbstruck. My mind raced at the thought of wagon rides and tossing the football in the back yard. It seemed unbelievable, even with the evidence right there in front of my eyes. I wasn't sure whether to laugh or cry at the thought of having another son.

"Well, alright then..." the tech mused, unable to repress an appreciative smile at Molly's dig. "Let's move on to Baby B."

The image on the screen continued to be the first baby as my boy seemed to be showing off for the camera. It took a bit of finagling on the techs part but she finally revealed the second baby, a tiny thing sucking its thumb. She repeated her thorough measurements and finally exhaled loudly.

"This little one's a bit shyer, but I finally have a clear picture. Congratulations. She's a girl," the tech looked back at us with a wide smile.

My heart thundered in my ears. I felt lightheaded and knew a stupid grin was plastered across my face. I turned to look at Molly, and saw tears standing in her sky blue eyes. She looked at me and smiled. When she blinked her dark lashes, matching tears streamed down both of her rosy cheeks. In that moment, all I could think about was how beautiful she was. Even her glistening tears were as perfectly symmetrical as a Monarch butterfly's wings.

"So I guess we'll call them Luke and Leia instead." I quipped, and Molly giggled, in spite of her tears.

Later in the apartment, Molly slept with her head nestled on my lap, and my hand resting gently on the curve of her stomach. A boy and a girl. The news had sent a shockwave through my system. The love for them consumed me and I wasn't prepared at all for its intensity. Each milestone in the pregnancy just made things that much more real and I seemed incapable of coping. The nagging voice of doom in the back of my head had begun taunting me with self-doubt before we even left the parking lot.

The babies shifted under my hand and my heart leapt in wonder. Beneath my palm the wiggling stilled and Molly stirred in her sleep. Reaching down I pulled the blanket up to her shoulder and she settled back. Gently, I slid out from beneath her head, gliding a pillow into my place. I thought she might wake at my movement, but she must have been more exhausted than I had realized. She turned over and stilled under the blanket.

I went to the kitchen and grabbed a beer out of the fridge. Slipping out of the apartment I ended up on the roof. The patio I had built up there was one of Molly's favorite places. She hadn't been up there in a while, and I guessed the stairs were probably getting to be too much for her. Sitting down, I kicked my feet up and watched cars driving in the distance. The ice cold beer calmed the burning in my throat, too bad I couldn't have poured it into my chest.

My heart ached with so many conflicting emotions; I felt like it would tear itself to pieces. Joy rolled to a rapid boil at the thought of the two little ones growing inside Molly. It was swiftly followed by a swirling tangle of pain because of the memories that this journey stirred up. It was hard to think about a future with my son and daughter without thinking about the infant boy that I had lost.

Jack was alive for twenty seven minutes outside of Jessica's body. Twenty seven minutes of desperate struggle for life. I remember one of the doctors telling another that he was shocked the baby had been able to survive as long as he had. They tried to keep me from hearing the truth, but Tamryn fought for me to get a copy of the autopsy. I got to see it in the end and it seemed to confirm my worst suspicions. Hypoxia. Lack of oxygen. I did that to him. I fucked up and because of it my boy died. I picked his lying mother when forced to choose between them. I made the worst mistake of my life that day and because of that the son that might have been right here sitting beside me died in an anti-septic smelling hospital room.

The day replayed itself as it always did when I allowed myself think about it. Jessica had severe brain bleeding. The doctors had needed to act. The choice was made pretty clear. They operate and save one at risk to the other. I thought if Jess was okay the baby would be too. Part of me knew what I was doing. The chicken shit coward that was afraid of being left alone with a baby, that pathetic coward, made the call; and because I let him I was left without either of them.

Sitting on the roof looking out at the city, I let tears flow down my face while I drank the beer. I could see Jack in my mind just as clearly as if he'd lived. Dressed in a little league uniform, a Halloween costume, Boy Scout camping gear.

For years, I'd be minding my business, at the park or in the mall and I'd encounter other children and imagine my son's face. I had told the doc about it and he'd pressed me to talk about it at length. He never really said anything more about it, just asked questions. Most of the work we did at his office seemed directed toward getting me to deal with my shit with varying results.

The private visit between him and Molly set my god damn teeth on edge. Part of me wanted to know what they talked about. Another part dreaded knowing, and I was glad I'd left the room. Was she finally getting a pictured of what damaged goods she was stuck with? If so, that might explain why she seemed to have no interest in getting married. I can understand not wanting to get married right away. But to just flat out refuse and act like it was a stupid idea…how the fuck was I supposed to take that?

My beer was empty, but I didn't feel like going back downstairs. Being in the apartment with Molly felt too intimate just then…too claustrophobic. I needed to decompress a little. Up here, at least for a bit longer, I could pretend that my life was less complicated. That the woman I loved *wanted* to marry me and was happy to be having my babies.

The way I felt about Molly was beyond what I had ever imagined love to be. The fact that she made comparisons, and somehow felt she was inferior to my dead wife, was crazy to me. My relationship with Jess had been childishly uncomplicated and I realized that part of me mourned the simplicity of what we had. Thinking about Jess like that irritated me. It was like part of her was stuck in me like a jagged shard of glass. A sliver of pain that twisted from time to time just to remind me it was there. Pain laced with shame and self-recrimination.

The guilt that haunted me was shoved rudely aside by something far worse, truth. The painful realization that I had never really known Jess, at least not like I knew Molly. The difference was that I wanted to know Molly better every day. We had learned more about each other in the time we had been reacquainted than I had ever known about Jess.

I could lie to myself and say that my marriage to Jess, all of our happiness, had just been a delusion. But it wasn't true. The truth, as hard as it was to swallow, was that I hadn't been in love with Jess. At the time I had thought I was in love, that *we* were in love. We had fun together, were compatible, and had a good relationship. But when I compared it to what I had with Molly it was a feeble candle next to a roaring bonfire.

Molly and I were equals. She didn't bullshit me or try to handle me like Jess had. She was honest and let the chips fall where they may. Life was more tumultuous with her, but better than it ever had been.

The view from the roof suddenly was a lot less appealing. I had the overwhelming desire to hold Molly in my arms. Things might not be perfect between us. Hell, they probably never would be. But I would take the most fucked up day with her versus the best day without her. Tossing my beer in the trash near the stairs and headed back inside to take Molly to bed.

A few days later, I had been work in the shop trying to perfect a hand carved buffet table when Francis called back to tell me that I had a visitor. I thought this was weird, because most people I know would have just come on back to where I was working. The pointed way that Francis announced this, coupled with the fact that Mac had suddenly disappeared put me on high alert. When I rounded the buffet and got in view of the counter, I could see what had everyone on edge. The man standing at the counter looked as out of place in my shop as a banker in a stockyard.

My father was dressed in what he considered 'business casual'. Tan slacks with a crease you could slice bread with, paired with a button down starched cotton shirt. He had a red handkerchief stuck in his breast pocket and was holding a tan hat in his hand. Though I'd rarely seen him costumed in this manner, I understood that for my father this was authentic, traditional apology gear. He was literally showing up with a hat in his hand. I was instantly annoyed at his theatrics, and I suppressed the urge to turn on my heel and walk back to my workstation. Regardless of what he wanted to talk about, it was better to get it all out of the way. I had enough rubble to sift through without adding parental bullshit to the mix.

"Hello, dad. What can I do for you? Looking for a custom desk perhaps?" He smiled ruefully and though I was totally validated for calling him out, I felt like a dumbass. He shook his head.

"Hello, Joe. No, I don't need any wood work done, thought from what I keep hearing, it sounds like you would be the best one to do it." The compliment was unexpected and his humble demeanor was off putting. He defied every notion I'd formed of him, and it actually pissed me off. I'd grown comfortable with my father being a dark and distant figure in my life. Any alternative meant retraining my overburdened brain, and I was pretty sure I didn't have the reserves for that.

He seemed nervous. My father had *never* been anything other than confident. Seeing him off balance had me concerned.

"Is something wrong?"

He looked up at my alarmed tone of voice and waved his hand with a small shake of his head.

"What? Oh, no...no there isn't anything wrong." He paused, and took a deep breath. "I know you're busy, son, but I wondered if you might have time to grab a little lunch with me?" His fingers tightly gripped the hat in his hands, seeming to unconsciously clench and unclench. It was obvious that being here took real effort.

I glanced over at Francis who gave me a meaningful look. It was no surprise that a guy working so diligently to patch up things with his daughter would encourage me to do the same with my estranged dad. Rolling my eyes and shooting Francis a knowing glance, I dropped the tool I was holding on the table.

"Francis? You mind putting that back for me? Just put it on my workbench. I'll be back in a little bit." He dutifully scooped up the chisel.

"Sure thing, Joe. Take your time. We'll hold down the fort." Francis responded. Turning back to my father, I motioned toward the door and followed him out onto the sidewalk.

I led him down the block to the bakery. They did a decent lunch, so we placed our order and took a number and our drinks outside. Without discussing it, we chose the covered patio for a modicum of privacy. My father was famous for his showboating, but when it came to family, he was private like me.

We banded around some small talk until the food arrived.

"So this dinner with Molly's family." He suddenly shifted gears, "I hope you're okay with it. Tamryn is a bit zealous about the entire thing, which naturally comes as no surprise."

Tamryn never shied away from what she wanted. Hell, it was her need to explore our Jewish heritage that spurred us to enter public school her senior year, I was in eighth grade, and all I cared about was that my Lacrosse buddies said the girls in public school were all easy.

"It's time y'all met." I agreed, trying to hide my distaste at the thought that Molly and I might not end up having a wedding for them to toast at. "Better now than at the babies' graduation."

"I must confess, I've been dying to meet the Hildebrandt's since you started getting into trouble with the twins in high school." He continued, seemingly oblivious to my stilted response.

"They're good people." I replied, sipping my sweet tea. We ate in silence. I started to wonder why exactly he'd bothered to ask me to lunch. I waited and waited for the dreaded 'serious talk" and it never came. My mind wandered to Molly, and I wondered if my constant silence left her with the same exasperated feeling I was presently consumed by. It was a disturbing thought. Finally, I decided I'd had enough and it was time to head back.

"Well dad, thanks for lunch. I probably should get back to the shop…"

"Joe, wait. Please." His sudden, pleading tone took me by surprise and I collapsed back in to the chair. Taking in my father's appearance, I was struck for the first time at how he was beginning to look old. There were soft edges to the hard man that I had always faced off against.

"What is it, dad?" My tone was sharper than I'd intended it to be. He flinched a bit and I saw the flare of anger in his eyes. I'd seen that look many times in the mirror, and the realization sickened me. Then he sighed heavily and the tension went out of his frame.

"Joseph, I know I'm not the easiest man to love." His woeful eyes cut me to the quick and my jaw hit the floor. This was not the way my father talked. My father talked about fiscal responsibility and the importance of serving the public. Love wasn't a word I'd ever heard him say. "I had a hard life growing up. We were poor. So incredibly poor. I determined that I would make something of myself and that my children would never go to bed hungry…or want for anything. However, in my pursuit of success, I failed to give you and Tamryn the one thing that I now realize you two most likely wanted from me. My unconditional love."

I sat there, immoveable and as used up as a crash test dummy at the end of a long shift. I had been prepared for an argument. Our usual squabbling. Some sort of backhanded compliment about my "little" shop or a lecture in regards to my pregnant girlfriend and the lack of a ring on her finger. The last thing I'd expected was my father going sentimental on my ass.

"Your sister has grown into a remarkable woman. But she's god damn relentless. She called me last week at the behest of your mother. The two of them have been conspiring against me and they both are lobbying for us to sell the house in Naples and move back to Austin. She said it was time for me to 'be the bigger man' and cross the line that you and I had both drawn in the sand."

I gaped at him, utterly astonished. I couldn't imagine my parents in Austin again after all this time. The prospect of this was stressful in its own right, but from my vantage point on the hill I was already dying on, it had me teetering on the edge.

"I know it must sound absurd, but I never wanted anything but the very best for you. Just for you to be happy. When you told me that you were not going to follow me into the practice of law, I was blinded by my anger. I felt slighted, somehow, and I now realize that my wounded pride has cost me you. I was never there for you in the ways that I should have been. I thank God every day that you found such wonderful people to support you where I failed."

"Good lord, dad. Are you dyin'?" There was an edge of sarcastic vitriol that I was unable to keep out of my voice. It would be just like my dad to decide to settle his debts if he found out he was terminal. That at least would make sense. He laughed, but it trumpeted out of him a sharp, humorless sound.

"No, Joe. I'm not dying. Nor am I having a midlife crisis or finding Jesus. Your sister told me that you might think this was some sort of, how did she put it, 'old man reckoning' moment. That isn't why I'm here. I'm here to tell you that I'm sorry."

Hearing the actual words come out of my father's mouth was one of the most surreal experiences of my life. If you'd have told me that dogs could talk or that Mac could walk on water, I would have been less shocked. I scrubbed my hands over my face wearily before looking back at him.

"Sorry for what, dad?" Instead of answering right away he sat regarding me, with a forlorn expression I'd never seen on him before. When he finally spoke, there was a decidedly uncharacteristic warble of emotion in his voice.

"For my lack of support. I should have listened to you when you wanted to pursue woodworking. It's obvious that you have a great gift and I should have nurtured it. Instead, I tried to force you down a path of my choosing. Then there was my lack of support when Jessica and the baby died."

"Jack." My voice was ominous even to my own ears. "His name was Jack."

"Of course. Jack. When Jessica and Jack died, your mother and I weren't sure what to do. She wanted to stay and help you. I convinced her to let Tamryn handle things since the two of you are so close. To be honest, I was afraid. You were in so much pain…it was more than I could bear to watch-you suffering like that." Tears threatened to spill from his eyes and he blinked rapidly to keep them at bay.

I had no response. How do you reply to your father when he comes and apologies to you for being a dick? You can't yell, or walk away. So I sat there and stared at him. A minute passed, then five, then ten. I just sat there. It was like the flywheel inside my brain just refused to engage so my mind spun in neutral. In the end, it was my father that rose.

"I didn't mean to upset you, son. I know you have a lot on your plate with Molly and the twins. I just wanted you to know that your mother and I are here. We aren't going anywhere this time. If you need to talk, you can call me. Anytime, day or night." Pausing next to my chair, he faced away from me, staring out at the street with his hand on my shoulder.

"Son, one day, I hope you find it in your heart to forgive me. I'm not here to make excuses for what I have done beyond admitting that I've made mistakes. Soon enough you'll have your own children and then you'll start to understand how confusing and ridden with pitfalls parenting can be. However, you need to know that I love you. You're my son and I will spend the rest of my days trying to be the father I always should have been."

His hand slid from my shoulder and I made no motion to stop him as he walked away. I'm not really sure how long I sat there staring at my half eaten sandwich, but when I heard someone pull out the chair across from me, I looked up and Molly was sitting there.

"Molly?" She had a look on her face that was hard for me to identify. Reaching across the table she took one of my hands in hers.

"Hey there, big boy. You alright?" The gentle lilt of her voice anchored me to the present and I pushed away the mental fog I had been sitting in.

"Yeah. No. Hell..." Squeezing my hand she slipped around the table and taking the chair beside me, she snuggled up next to me. Having her pressed against me brought a simple peace to my troubled mind and I dipped my face down to kiss her forehead. "I just had one of the weirdest conversations of my life with my dad, of all people. The last person I would have expected to ever blink first. This must be what a pinball machine feels like when it gets tilted."

Smiling, Molly peered up at me from behind her long, beautiful lashes. Slipping my hand free from hers, I slid my arm around her and held her for a moment.

"So," she said finally. "Was it a good talk?"

"It wasn't a fight, so I guess it was. Normally my father and I end conversations by screaming at each other, at least for the last ten years or so."

Nodding, she stayed quiet as she nestled against me. It was a distinctly Molly move. Without my saying a word, she knew that I needed to talk and so she just listened. Moments like this made me realize how foolish I had been to think what Jess and I had was love. I often looked back on my interactions with Jess like an actor remembering a role from far back in the beginning of their career.

When I met Jess, she was, in my mind, the perfect girl. My

American dream, blonde, poised, together. I immediately saw a future with her the minute she told me her name. She fit the mold. She was like pure sunshine, and I even called her that. I was in love with the idea of us, and did all the things I thought I was supposed to do accordingly.

I did everything right. Everything by the book and look how that turned out,

When she was gone I fell into darkness. Then all of her lies began to unravel, and I was humiliated and devastated. It's like she'd been living two lives, and I realized I would never know what were lies and what were truths.

The only thing about our life together that I'd never questioned was Jack. I held that boy. I looked at his face. He was mine.

When I first encountered Molly last year, I existed in a fugue state of drinking, whoring, and working. You've heard of people having walking pneumonia? I was in a walking coma. Then she was there, and it was like I'd been struck by lightning. She shook me awake, and I promise you, it was nothing short of resuscitation.

Molly got me. We shared a long history. She knew what I was like before, and she put up with what I was now. She wasn't always happy with me, but she intuitively understood the important things about me. The rest of it would sort itself out, I believed that as sure as I knew the sun would rise in the east. Most importantly, I loved her. It's not a strong enough word to express what I feel, but it's all I have to work with. I wanted her to feel the same about me, that she could count on me. That she could tell me anything.

I knew she kept things back from me about Draven. The only reason I knew anything about their marriage was because Mason's wife is kind of a blabbermouth. And because I reacted so poorly, Molly kept her secrets locked inside. I couldn't help being overprotective of her. I'd been looking out for her since she was a kid and now she was mine.

How I felt with Molly was so intense that sometimes I felt compelled to pull away.

We sat and people watched until an audible growl came from Molly's stomach. Grinning at her, I sat up and motioned to the menu board behind the counter. I went and retrieved her requests and we moved inside. As she ate her lunch and I finished mine, we talked about simple things and enjoyed the brief window of calm. When the plates were empty and her "little stowaways" were satiated, Molly leaned against me again with a satisfied sigh.

"Joe?"

"Yeah little girl?" She smiled and wrapped her arms around my waist, resting her head against my arm.

"We don't have to force the issue of our families getting together. If it's going to stress you out maybe we could do it later."

I shook my head, "Tamryn would have my head if I threw a monkey wrench into her big event." Evil Joe threw a hellacious fit in the back of my psyche at this acquiescence. Unfortunately, we no longer had much of a choice. The sand in the hourglass was slipping away at an exponential pace. "We have to put them all in one room eventually. Better in a controlled environment than in the waiting room of a hospital."

I nuzzled my cheek against her fragrant hair and she turned up to face mine. She looked anxious and pensive, and I saw volumes of questions behind her eyes. Knowing I had few answers and the ones I did have she wouldn't want to hear, I gently pressed my mouth to hers. As I slipped my tongue between her lips, a gentle moan escaped her. Glancing up, I saw we were alone in the restaurant with the exception of two clerks at the counter. Both were too busy on their cell phones to even realize we were there. Helping Molly to her feet, I shot her an evil grin.

"Let's go back home, I have *something* I want to show you." She blushed at my double entendre and hurried out the door with me.

Nine

Molly

Pompeii

STRESS IS A MEGABITCH with dragon lady nails. If stress were embodied in a woman, she'd be an uncaring, prissy, skinny little plastic girl that revels in torturing kittens. Does she care that I can't drink anything without a bathroom trip in five minutes? No. How about that I can't sleep comfortably because I currently feel like I have a watermelon strapped to the front of my body? Nope. No personal fucking space because every Tom, Dick, and Mary put their hands on my stomach without asking? Uh huh. Or the endless stream of personal horror stories involving child birth from random strangers in the toilet paper aisle of the grocery store? Hell to the no.

Instead of cutting me some fucking slack, *she* (stress, that is) dropped napalm into the middle of a crowded room and then sat back to watch the place burn down. I really should have expected it. I should have known that things were going too well.

After deciding that we needed a break before the business trip to Galveston, Joe and I talked to our employees and delegated everything so we could have Monday off. For the first time in forever, we had some unscheduled time together. It was glorious to just lay around in bed until nearly noon, eating kolaches and drinking cocoa. We cuddled and argued about baby names. He refused to let me name our daughter Wednesday after the beloved Addams Family character, and I balked when he suggested Leonitus Maximus for our son. You might say we didn't make a lot of progress on that front, but it did make for lively conversation.

I had a growing feeling of foreboding as the holiday approached. The dreaded family gathering had morphed into a Jensen/Hildebrandt overnight Thanksgiving retreat at Tamryn and Robbie's 100 acre ranch. The ranch was just far enough outside of Driftwood to be considered a long drive. Tamryn planned to have plenty of booze flowing and insisted she had more than enough guest rooms for everyone. She demanded the kids bring their swimsuits and the guys bring their cowboy boots for a morning ride.

Once our bags were packed, I almost called her to cancel the entire thing. I had that feeling you get when you know you're forgetting something really important: like your coffee on the roof of the car or to put on deodorant before you leave for work. Then I decided it was just hormones messing with my mind. I couldn't have been more wrong. It was probably women's intuition.

We left town on Wednesday in the afternoon. We took the truck, and Joe drove slower than he normally did, almost as if he was unconsciously trying to delay our arrival. When we pulled into the ranch, Tressa and Jaimie were waiting on the stairs leading up to the rustic mansion. They dog-piled Joe when he stepped foot outside of the truck, and then peppered us both with questions about the babies. Tamryn rescued us and we all went around back to sit on the wrap around porch. As the girls splashed and frolicked with Joe and their father in the pool, Tamryn brought me some lemonade from the kitchen.

"So how have things been, Molly? You're not working too hard, are ya?

"Still working full time, but it's getting harder to put in my time in the truck. Frankly, my gut is getting too big for me to manouvre in such a confined space."

"Do you have enough coverage so you can quit working early?" She asked.

"We just finished training a couple of replacements. I'm watching them like a hawk for a while. Can't have quality compromised, ya know?"

She nodded. "What about Joe? I know last time he turned into a total workaholic. Is he getting any rest?"

I felt goose bumps break out at her mention of 'last time', but continued the conversation as if nothing was out of the ordinary. "I convinced him to push his workload off on Mac and his new employee Nick on Monday. The two of us actually got a moment's peace. Based on the stories my mother keeps telling me, we better sleep all we can before the twins arrive."

She laughed and nodded.

"Sleep deprivation. One of the many joys of parenthood. So how's the house hunting going?" Dread must have shown on my face because her expression sobered. "That bad?"

"Worse. Joe's started prescreening places. For every six he looks at, we might go see one. It's appalling what people want for houses with asbestos, black mold or structural damage."

"They can't all be wrecks and money pits. Are you two that far apart on what you want?" Maybe she was trying to be supportive but my anxiety purred like a well-tuned engine. Joe insisted she was being pushy with her suggestions and that made my temper flare. I bit back a comment about her living vicariously through us, but just barely.

"No, I'm sure we'll know it when we see it. We just haven't seen it yet." I decided to change the subject before my hormone-fueled madness won out. "So where are your parents? I thought they were staying here?"

"They *were* staying here..." She responded, her eyes shifting cautiously to Joe, who'd just climbed out of the pool and retrieved a towel from a neighboring chair. His hard body glistening in the last rays of the afternoon had me ready to retire to the room we'd claimed for the evening.

"Did you and dad get into it or something?" He asked, grinning slyly at his sister. "Did you finally tell him you voted for Obama?"

"No and no. They just found somewhere else to stay." She replied, toying absently with her dark braid. She suddenly seemed entirely too focused on her sweet tea.

"They got a hotel?" Joe dropped into the chair next to me, his face transformed with suspicion. "With all the guest rooms here at Palace de Robbie? What the hell, Tamz?"

"No, Joe." She snapped so suddenly that I actually jumped. "They bought a house, okay? Not everyone takes months to find one.

Joe looked completely stunned by her response and I felt my heart hammer. I was about to rip into Tamryn and tell her to get off Joe's back, when Jaimie ran up and squirted her in the face with a water gun. I nearly peed my pants trying to contain my laughter. Joe, on the other hand, cackled like a hyena.

Tamryn tore after her youngest daughter, letting loose with a stream of curse words. When her eldest daughter, Tressa, scolded her for her filthy language, Robbie, who was usually neutral, backed his daughter.

"Mom and Dad should be here in an hour." Tamryn continued our conversation as if things of this nature happened on a daily basis in her life. She wiped her running mascara onto a nearby towel as she turned her raccoon eyes on me. "What about your brothers and your mom?"

"Mason and his kids are waiting at Mac Jr.'s school so they can give bring him. Mac's closing up the shop and then riding his bike out. Mom and Granny should be here any minute. They're riding with Robin."

Tamryn smirked and took a drink. "I cannot wait to get my father and your grandmother in the same room. From the sound of things, that should be priceless."

"Like our own little Republican Convention. Someone call Rush Limbaugh," Joe joked, He leaned back in his chair and placed an ice cold hand on my shoulder. "Aren't you gonna get in the pool, baby girl?"

"It's November, Joe! It's too damn cold in there." I scoffed. "Our babies would be born with icicles hanging from their chins."

"It's heated." He replied, but I shook my head. The thought of anyone seeing me in a bathing suit was deplorable.

"I'm gonna go see what I can help with in the kitchen." I announced, starting to my feet. I was still moody from Tamryn's attack on Joe.

"Don't you dare! I hired caterers. You just sit there and re-lax." Tamryn ordered. I lowered myself carefully back down and chewed on the inside of my lip. I wanted to tell her that I did my best relaxing in the kitchen, but I figured from the loaded look Joe gave me I'd better just shut up and do what I was told.

I heard the familiar rumble or Mac's Harley, and rubbed my temples. I felt a headache coming on, one that the piddly Tylenol I was allowed to take couldn't touch.

"That's my brother." I said, pushing myself to standing. "I'll go let him in."

Mac had his hand raised to knock when I swung the front door open.

"Holy shit!" He blurted in a stage whisper, looking around

to be sure we were alone. "Tamryn did good. This place is a fucking castle."

"I know, right?" I asked, almost laughing at how Texan I sounded on the word 'right'. Being in the country was wearing me down already.

"You're moving on up, Short Shit. Out classing us, yet again." He mumbled, as his eyes swept the vaulted ceilings and marbled floors.

"Shut the hell up." I grumbled, rocking my shoulder into his.

"Where should I put my stuff?" He asked, taking off his do-rag and raking a hand through his near black hair.

"Come on. Let's go find you're room." I turned and Joe wandered into the room pulling a shirt on over his head and tragically hiding his six pack.

"Hey." Joe said, with a crooked smirk. "I see you found the place."

"It was kind of hard to miss." Mac deadpanned. "Do you *ever* miss an opportunity to take your shirt off you male model looking mother f—" Mac began in a mocking and accusatory tone, but cut himself off when the door swung open behind him and Joe's father and mother stepped across the threshold.

"Hi!" I chirped, elbowing Mac in the universal Hildebrandt shut-the-hell-up gesture.

"Molly!" Joe's tiny mother pushed his dad out of her path and made for me with outstretched hands. I braced for the impact of her hands on my belly, but instead she gave me a friendly hug.

"Ma'am." I replied, smiling. I'd only briefly met Joe's parents once before, but she'd hugged me that time, too. Joe's sister and mother were very touchy/feely types. Still, the familiar gesture took me by surprise.

"Please, call me Felicia. You look so lovely, pregnancy agrees with you." She grinned, and that was when her hand dropped to my baby bump.

"Mom." Joe's greeting sounded like a distant rumbled of thunder. Her eyes shot to his and she flounced in his direction and swooped into his arms.

"I cannot believe you didn't call me about this, Joseph." She scolded, but her tone resonated with unadulterated joy.

"And steal Tamryn's thunder? Not a chance." Joe replied lightly, but after a couple of beats too long. I was watching him carefully, when his father stole my attention away.

"Molly." Joe's father called out to me in greeting. He gave me a stilted smile and engaged me in a polite handshake. I could feel his eyes skimming my full sleeve of tattoos which had been demurely covered in a formal gown the first time we'd met. Okay, the long sleeve that covered them was about the only thing demure about that dress, but I think Daddy Jensen was getting a more accurate picture of just what type of girl his son was mixed up with. His sharp eyes ended their journey on my protruding stomach, and my chest tightened when they bulged in shock.

"My goodness! You look like you're due any day!" He exclaimed, and I wanted to vanish into my room with a box of tissues and a pint of Haagen-Dazs®. Ever supportive, my brother Mac snorted.

"James!" Joe's mother exclaimed, as if James Jensen had just slapped me across the face with a pair of leather gloves. "She's having twins. She's going to be twice as big!"

"Not helping, Mom." Joe murmured as I felt all the heat in my body rush to my face. I saw a storm front brewing behind Joe's green eyes, and tried to think of something funny to say that might lighten the mood.

"Hey, sis. Weren't you going to show me where I'm crashing?" Mac interrupted, and I wanted to kiss him.

"Oh. Yeah. Please excuse us." I practically curtseyed for them as I backed out of the room toward the north wing of the sprawling house.

"Jesus. Those two haven't changed a bit." Mac whispered

as I led him down the hall of guest rooms. "She's still June Cleaver and he still acts like he's running for re-election."

"What the hell are you talking about?" I asked, as I pulled open a bedroom door and saw our bags on the bed.

"He was a Representative when Joe was in elementary school."

I wrinkled my forehead, confused. "Of what?"

"Of the district, Molly. He was in the Texas House of Representatives."

"Oh, for fuck's sake." I rubbed my temples again. Just when I thought I'd made peace with our drastically different backgrounds, another whopper of a surprise popped out like a cobra from a woven basket.

"Is that your luggage?" Mac nodded to our bags, his pale eyes rolling to the ceiling. "If so, I want a room at the other end of the hall. I already have to work directly under your bedroom. I need a break from *that* disgustingness. Besides, tomorrow's the high holy day of pigging out and I won't have you two spoilin' my appetite."

It wasn't until dessert was served that I started to relax. After multiple awkward introductions, I was ready to no longer be the focus of attention. I could feel James' judging eyes on my body art, and it wasn't long before I borrowed a light sweater from Tamryn under the guise of being chilly. In reality, I was boiling, but I just wanted Joe's parents to like me and everyone to get along.

It turns out I had nothing to worry about on that front. Granny and James hit it off immediately. As soon as they were introduced, she beamed at him like a groupie, "James Jensen! I had no idea Joe was your son! I should have seen the resemblance. I voted for you. I probably would have anyhow, since you were a republican. But let me tell you somethin': you were the best looking one of the bunch!"

I blinked at Joe in horror, and he simply snorted. I glanced around and was relieved to see that his mother was nowhere to be seen. Fortunately, James seemed flattered by her proclamation and the two of them fell into conversation about foreign policy, immigration, and impeaching the president.

Thankfully, no one complained about dinner, even though Tamryn decided against a traditional Thanksgiving. Tamryn excelled at playing hostess, and she picked the perfect menu to please all ages and walks of life. What can I say? We're from the south and fried chicken done well is a crowd pleaser. Following it up with peach cobbler and real whipped cream was a slam dunk.

"Tamryn, you throw one mean party, sugar." Granny H. praised over her second helping of cobbler.

"Why thank you, Miss Elizabeth." Tamryn grinned, topping off Granny's cup of coffee.

"Joe, can you come help me with something in the study?" His mother called. Joe looked up from his conversation with my brother and nodded. He clapped Mason on the back, picked up his glass, and followed his mother out of the room. I noticed Tamryn dart out after them, and glanced at Robin. My sister in law's eyebrows smacked into her hairline so I knew I wasn't the only one who thought they were an odd bunch.

Curiosity gnawed at me, and after of few minutes I wandered in the direction of the study. I was a few feet away when Robbie intercepted me.

"Hey, Molly. Are you ready to run off to Galveston?" He asked, and I smiled.

"I really appreciate you helping me out, Robbie." I responded. His dimples appeared as he smiled shyly. "I'm pretty lucky to have an Intellectual Property Expert on speed dial."

"It's your concept and recipes they want." He shrugged. "You need to be compensated accordingly. You have one shot at this. It's vital that no matter what the offer is that you don't agree to anything before we talk. I want to make sure that we get the best deal we can."

"I'll call you if he makes an offer." I nodded. Normally, I'd have cringed at the thought of negotiating with Dan's brother, and taken any halfway decent proposal he made as long as he promised me quality control. I had a rep to protect, after all. But now I had my babies to think about. The phrase 'financial security' had a much louder ring to it these days.

"Be sure to email me any paperwork he asks you to sign. Make no promises until you hear back from me. Deal?" Robbie's voice was firm, and his eyes narrowed. It was a side of him I'd never witnessed, and I had mad respect for this bold new Robbie.

He pulled a bottle of wine from the massive wall rack housed in the entryway we were currently standing in. He held it up as if toasting me and I gave him a thumbs up. I turned back in the direction of the study just as the door swung open and Tamryn and her mother came out giggling. They both froze when they saw me, and exchanged a knowing glance. Joe appeared a few moments later, his face pasty and pale. When he saw me, he practically flinched. That was a bit of a blow to the ego.

"Baby?" I stammered, truly disturbed by the look he wore. I hadn't seen him look so troubled since the night he showed up on my doorstep the year before, covered in grass stains and damp with tears. "Are you alright?"

His only response was a curt nod. He looked nervous, and a little irritated. I reached out for him, but he didn't seem to notice as he headed back into the kitchen.

I trailed after him and he took a seat by Mason at the bar. All the kids had apparently sweet talked my mom, Robbie and Robin into taking them back out to swim some more, because the kitchen was blissfully quiet. I decided it was time to grab some dessert. I'd dished it up for all of the kids, but hadn't had a chance to taste it, and nothing relieves my tension like a bowl full of sugar.

"Careful of that sweet tooth, Molly." Granny called from her seat at the table. "You're already too big and you're only halfway into this business. It's not like Joe's got a ring on his finger. If you're not careful, you'll end up with a fat ass and lose that fine man. "

Mac's laughter rang across the room and Mason joined in. I felt the blood rush to my face as I fought back the words that wanted to spill out of my mouth. Fighting with Granny was a no win situation, a bit like pissing into an industrial fan. Ever since I was little, the only thing I had been able to hope for was to distract her. This was not the first time her well-meaning advice left me emotionally battered and bruised. But something had changed that she hadn't calculated into her lesson plans. Joe.

The sharp scrape of a bar stool on the hard wood floor sounded like fingernails down a chalkboard. It snapped everyone's attention to Joe, who rose to his feet. No, that's not quite right. He came up out of his seat like a monster stepping into the room. Somehow the anger radiating off of him made him seem bigger, almost superhuman. Red flushed his face, and when he spoke I expected to hear him yell. Angry Joe had a commanding presence that made even the strongest person present quail. When he opened his mouth though, the calm and measured delivery of his words was somehow far more frightening than if he had yelled.

"I'm sorry Elizabeth...what did you just say to Molly?" I had never heard Joe use Granny's given name. The wide eyed, startled way that she gawked at him would have been priceless in any other circumstance. Mac and Mason both rose reflexively and took a step to place themselves between Joe and Granny.

"Joe," I sat down my untouched bowl and started to tell him

to leave it alone, but he chopped his hand down in the air, as if directing a symphony. I felt my stomach give a flip flop as my jaw clicked shut. Joe had never made a gesture like that to me before, and it was as much out of surprise as the force of his gesture that made me slump back against the counter.

Well, you did say you wanted him to stop bottling things up.

Joe's fixed gaze never left Granny and I saw fire flash in her eyes.

"I told her that if she was *smart* she'd worry about marrying before those babies get here and less about dessert." Joe gave a humorless grin and shook his head.

"That's not quite right. I believe you said that if she wasn't careful her fat ass would cost her a fine man." Dead silence reigned as Granny squirmed under Joe's heated glare.

Tamryn looked from Joe to Granny and then reluctantly stepped forward.

"Joe, is this really the time? Molly's grandmother was just trying to help." Whipping his head around in her direction, Joe glared at Tamryn. She actually took a couple steps back from him.

"Really, Tamz?" His tone hadn't changed and the chillingly calm way that he was speaking made my skin crawl. It was like watching a volcano smoking silently right before it erupts. "Trying to help."

Each word was annunciated distinctly and Tamryn took another step back. Joe turned his entire body in her direction, and this maneuver had a decidedly aggressive feel to it. I felt my pulse racing, and couldn't decide what to do or say. He spoke again, and she actually shrank back at his words. "Kind of like *you've* been trying to help?"

"Joe," his father called from the far end of the room, his voice as commanding as his son's. "Can we step outside and talk?"

"Dad, you really don't want to join this conversation right

now. Things are about to get unpleasant. Shouldn't you and mom scurry off to Florida about now?" His parents both reacted like he'd just slapped them across the face. His mother had tears welling in her eyes, but Joe turned away from them as if they didn't exist.

"Joe, that's enough!" Tamryn had recovered her footing and crossed to him, standing directly in Joe's face. It was a comical sight, seeing her facing off against her gargantuan brother. Like a Chihuahua standing up to a St. Bernard. "I realize you're under a lot of stress with everything going on, but you are way out of line."

"Am I?" His head tilted slightly, and a malicious smile crept onto his face. "I can never tell. You know, with everyone giving me unsolicited advice on marriage, childbirth and how to run my life, I guess it's hard for me to figure out where the line is. After all, everyone else seems to be able to say whatever the hell they want. You lecture me on how I should have a house by now when it's about the biggest, most important purchase we'll ever make. Granny says all sorts of awful shit to my girl...her own flesh and blood. She should be supportive to her but instead she gives her nothing but hell. It's no wonder Molly ran off to school and didn't come back for a decade."

My mouth fell open and I gawked at Joe as if he'd just sprouted a tail. Evidently he'd bottled up his feelings for so long that the pressure had finally popped his cork.

"Now just a damn minute, boy!" Granny slowly rose from her chair and shook a gnarled, bony finger at Joe. "This little girl is the light of my life! I may not always do the best job of show-ing it, but the only reason I'm hard on her is that I want her to have a better time of it than I did." The admission shocked me as much as anyone in the room. I never thought that Granny hated me, but I never would have considered myself all that important to her.

"You do a piss *poor job* of showing it." Joe snapped. "I always envied my friends who got to know their grandparents. Now I think maybe I should count my blessings."

Gran flopped down in her chair as if he'd kicked her in the chest. Actual fucking tears were swimming in her eyes. Mason and Mac stepped forward like two sides of the same wind-up toy.

"Hey! You can't talk to Gran like that," Mason scoffed.

"Where the hell do you get off talking to Granny like that?" Mac rasped out at the same time, their words tumbling over each other. Joe turned on both of them, seemingly unimpressed. Both twins stopped mid step as he unflinchingly met their gaze.

"You," he spat, pointing to Mason's hat. "Either get hair plugs or shave your head. You look ridiculous. And you..."

He turned to Mac. "Shit or get off the pot. If you like that girl, you should tell her. God knows you aren't getting any younger. And like it or not, your Grandmother is talking shit to the woman I love. No one does that...*no one*, without answering to me. Got it?"

I was shocked when both of them looked at each other, then at Gran and nodded. They moved back toward Gran's chair but didn't move to comfort her. They just stood uncertainly. Men...

Tamryn shoved Joe hard and he took a small step back. "All right. That's it. Get out front. The girls are out back swimming and I don't want them exposed to you right now. Are you drunk?"

Joe shook his head and gave a humorless laugh. "I haven't touched a drop. Maybe if I was, I would be able to put up with all of this better."

Tamryn shot him a withering look that made me cringe. It seemed to roll off of him like water.

"Oh, because it is just so damn taxing to get together and spend time with family. Jesus wept, Joe. What exactly is your damn problem?"

"You want just the highlights? Hmm....let's see. For starters, you regularly wake me up at 3 A.M. with a fucking text about the ideal house for us, all under the guise of 'helping'. Then mom and dad show up to play the perfect parents and expect me to totally disregard the shit shaft they have given me over the last few years." His voice caught just a tad and he took a deep breath before continuing. "Like they didn't abandon me when I needed them the most. And on top of all that I've got this beautiful pain in the ass who's the love of my life. She helped pull me out of hell and just when it looks like we might get to be happy, we accidentally get pregnant and she doesn't want to marry me. She's high risk and I'm terrified that I am going to lose her one way or another."

It was more truth than I had heard out of Joe in months. His raw honesty was one of the things I loved most about the man. Seeing the pain flash across his face as he spoke nearly brought me to my knees. It was obvious to me that this was what he'd been holding in since we found out we were pregnant. I hadn't realized how much my response had wounded him, even though I stood behind my rationale for not jumping into a wedding on the heels of the babies.

Pushing myself away from the counter, I crossed the room and put my hand on his shoulder. Turning him toward me, I cupped his jaw in my hand, forcing him to look into my eyes. For the first time since his tirade began, I saw him look unsure...hesitant.

I pulled him into a hug and held him. I felt his tension melting, and his musky scent fired my imagination. I was tempted to ditch them all and drag him away to bed. An urgent need simmered within me, spurred on by the decisive way he'd stepped forward in my defense. But now wasn't the time. Instead we needed to deal with the elephant my lovely man had just dropped into the center of the room. Intertwining my fingers with Joe's, I turned to face our combined family. Before I could say a word, Joe stepped in front of me and spoke once more.

"Molly's mine. I don't care if we're married or not. She's

mine and I'm hers. I will not stand for anything less than each of you being respectful to her. Now y'all can be as pissed at me as you want. I can take it. But each and every one of you is going to make sure this little girl has the least amount of stress possible for the next few months. Or you can say goodbye until after the babies are born. Any questions?"

CHAPTER Ten

Joe

Alone Time

I WATCHED AS Molly waddled back and forth between our bedroom closet and the bed, quickly filling a large suitcase. We'd been arguing for hours, and I felt defeated and powerless. The air in my lungs burned as I finally managed to take in a breath. The situation had spun out of control and it looked like she was serious about leaving.

"Baby girl, please. Can we just sit down and talk?" My voice was strained from all the arguing and came out as a rough rasp.

"No. The last thing we need to do is talk more. All we've done since Friday is talk talk talk. I'm fed up with talking. It's stressing me out. The sooner I get out of town the better."

I froze at that, paralyzed with uncertainty. "Molly. Don't do this."

I tried to put a hand on her shoulder, but she brushed it away. Acid churned in my stomach at her words. She went back into the bathroom and when she came out, she dropped a second bag of makeup and toiletries onto our bed. Giving a last look around, she nodded and then turned her eyes on me. Her confident and determined look wavered for a moment, and then she blew out a ragged breathe.

"Joe…look…I know that you don't understand why you can't come. You've made that pretty clear. And I know it's driving you insane that I'm going without you. But I think once you have a little distance you'll see that you need some down time and so do I."

"I don't want you driving all the way to Gal Island alone. Houston traffic sucks." I tried a last ditch argument regarding the practicality of her going without me. She hated going out in the madhouse traffic of a major city, and Houston was legendarily awful. Maybe she'd rethink things.

"Luckily that is not even an issue. I'm not driving. Sanchez is taking me to the airport and David is flying us down on his private plane." She replied, zipping a few plastic baggies into the outer pocket of her suitcase.

"Sanchez!" I exclaimed. "Why does he get to go?"

"What are you, five?" She graced me with a gentle smile. "He's my sous chef, darlin'. If we sign a deal, he'll do the demonstrations for David's staff. I'm being practical. I'll be banned from travelin' soon, so I'll have to work the truck and send Dirty S. down south. I want them to see us as a united front. Introduce him out of the gate as my right hand. I thought you'd appreciate me being responsible…you know, thinkin' ahead."

I dropped onto the bed and put my head in my hands. I probably should have gone to take a couple of the Xanax that Dr. Greene had prescribed for me for situations like these. My legs felt like jelly and I had serious doubts about my ability to make the seven foot journey into the bathroom. What she was saying sounded completely logical. The doc said it was safe for her to travel for at least another month, but after that we'd have to reassess week to week.

She was right to try to take care of the preliminaries of the deal all in one trip. But none of that logic and reason did anything to calm the monster in my head. And right now he was warning that if I wasn't there to protect her anything could happen. When I thought about her driving around a city without me, the specter from my past laughed at me chillingly. It made me start to wonder if it was us tempting fate. Logical? I don't think I could even define the word right now.

I felt the bed dip and she was beside me, wrapping her arms around my waist and nuzzling her head against my upper arm.

"Baby." She cooed, commanding me to look in her direction. "You cannot control every situation. We can't be together every second of every day. I wish we could, but it's not sustainable. I *love* that you want to be with me, but you really *need* to decompress. Go have a drink with the twins. They're probably getting a complex from you bitching them out. Play some golf, darts, Xbox… whatever you used to do for fun before I moved in with you. Pretty soon we'll have two little ones demanding every waking second of our time and you'll have no time for *you*, let alone me."

I didn't think it would be a good idea to mention that before she moved in, all I did was get drunk and troll Sixth Street looking for an easy lay. Not that that appealed to me anymore. Dropping my gaze, I let out a breath and tried to get it together. She stood and wrapped her arms around my neck so that we were practically eye to eye. I asked the questions that loomed in the forefront of my mind. "What if something happens with the babies? What if you need me?"

"I'm twenty weeks along, Joe. If something goes wrong, there's not a whole lot they can do." She must have seen how deeply disturbed that statement made me, because her eyes softened and she kissed me delicately.

"I checked with Dr. Myers. There are a couple of hospitals on the island. And there is a center for women's health. She gave me all the contact information and she even gave me a copy of my chart. I'll take care of our precious cargo. Don't you trust me?"

"Of course I do." I replied, realizing as I said it how true the statement was. It was my luck, fate, God, and the universe at large I didn't trust. All the things that collectively enjoyed seeing me in agony.

"Good." She kissed the tip of my nose and her finger tickled the back of my neck, which caused me to shove her suitcases aside and sweep her onto the bed. I captured her lips with mine and proceeded to kiss her with everything I had, as if it was the last time I'd see her. I knew it sounded irrational, but I worried that something would happen when she was out of my line of sight.

"I miss you already." I mumbled against the hollow of her neck as I trailed kisses over her collar bone and down the exposed flesh of her chest.

"I'll miss you, too." She sighed. "Please try to relax. Get your head together. Enjoy some alone time."

"How long do we have till he gets here?" I asked, pressing my hard on against her thigh.

"About an hour." She sighed breathlessly, scraping her fingernails across my shoulders.

"Good. I have a going away present for you." I drawled, pulling her to me I lost myself in the heat of our embrace.

Molly had only been gone for a few hours and I was practically bouncing off the walls. I watched a movie she'd recorded for me, but I'd be hard pressed to tell you the plot. I kept checking my phone compulsively. Finally, she texted me to say that they'd landed in Galveston. Dan picked them at the airport and they were on their way to his house. Relief washed over me and the knots in my chest loosened. My entire body felt like I had been tensing for an expected blow. There was no way in hell I was going to be able to sit at home. Suddenly, the idea of going out with Mac and Mason sounded like a lot more fun. I decided to call them and see if either of them would answer when they saw the caller ID.

Mason's phone rang until it flipped over to voicemail. I pursed my lips and tried to ignore the sting. Mason had always been my best friend, even the best man at my wedding to Jessica, but lately we'd had a Molly-shaped wedge between us. He'd totally lost it when he found out I was seeing his sister and though that had blown over, things had never quite gotten back to normal.

With Mac now working for me and far more philosophical in his approach to me dating Molly, we'd actually formed a tighter friendship. I had mixed feelings about this development, mourning my best bud, but none-the-less enjoying Mac's no nonsense approach to things. I punched the call button beside Mac's name and waited.

"Hey." Mac said, his tone neutral as he picked up on the second ring. "What's up?"

"Thought I might take you out for a drink and darts. You know, an 'I fucked up and I'm buying the first three rounds' kinda night. Unless you're busy or have Mac Jr."

"No. I'm free." He exhaled, and I could tell he was smoking again. "Malcolm's back with his mom. She and her new boyfriend took him to LEGOLAND or some shit. Do you want to meet somewhere or should I pick you up?"

"Let's cab it." I replied. "It sucks to have to sober up before you can go home. This is the kind of night that needs lots and lots of beer. I tried to call Mason."

"I think they had a soccer tournament tonight...or was it a dance recital? Who the fuck can keep all that shit straight? That's why I only had one kid." Mac declared.

"Yeah...that's why." I mused sardonically.

"Well *that* and his mother was a drunken whore." He snickered in agreement. "Mason should be done by now, though. I'll try to get ahold of him."

We agreed to meet at a place on Rainey Street called Banger's. I started to object when Mac suggested it, but he assured me it wasn't a strip club.

As it turns out, Banger's was a converted bungalow with a sprawling beer garden in the back. Long strands of white lights illuminated a decent sized stage and crowded community style tables outside. I paid the cabbie and stepped forward to read the sign. Bangers's Sausage and Beer Garden.

What a relief. The last thing I needed was for Molly to hear that our first night apart I ran out to get a lap dance. I leaned against the wall outside and waited for Mac, who'd texted me that he got ahold of Mason and he was coming along. Live music from the beer garden around back reached my ears, I started to get nervous about seeing the Hildebrandt boys. Things with the families had still been very up in the air when Molly and I left Tamryn's the morning after my freak out. Since the shop was closed until tomorrow, I hadn't spoken to anyone since.

Right after I issued my ultimatum to the families, the back door swung open and the kids trailed in like frozen drowned rats. Robin, Robbie, and Betty struggled to coral them so that they didn't drip all over the kitchen. No one who'd been present during my tirade spoke, and Robin took one look at Mason's stricken face and said "What did I miss? Damn kids! I always miss everything."

"Joe and I were just heading off to bed. I'm exhausted." Molly lied, grabbing my arm in both of her hands and trying to tug me out of the room. I was too fired up to go along with her excuse. Just before Granny insulted Molly, my mom had cornered me in the study and the combination of those two events finally pushed me beyond my breaking point.

When mom took me into Robbie's study, I expected a sequel to the conversation I'd had with my father. Imagine my shock when she presented me with my Grandmother's diamond ring.

"It's perfect, don't you think? Your grandmother always had such peculiar tastes. It really isn't my style, but I think Molly would really like it." I frowned at what sounded like a back handed insult at Molly, and I opened my mouth to begin a long overdue discussion about my mother's jarring absence in my life when Tamryn burst into the study and interrupted us.

"Is that a ring? Let me see!" She rushed forward and gaped at it. "Ooooo...black gold. How unusual! That vintage setting is perfect for her, Joe!"

At first I simply stared at them, wondering if they were conspiring. Tamryn frowned at my suspicious pause. "What?"

"You aren't in on this?" I demanded and Tamryn folded her arms defensively.

"What the hell are you taking about?" She snapped.

"Joe didn't buy the ring." My mother confessed, explaining the ring's history to my sister.

"I stand by what I said, Joe. If you do propose, this is the one." Tamryn lifted her eyes from the diamond that had to be at least a carrot. The corner of my mother's mouth inched toward the ceiling. Now they were ganging up on me, and they were about as subtle as a heart attack. I glanced down at the ring my mother still displayed for me and saw my hand reach out for it. I didn't know shit about jewelry, but something told me Molly would love it. It was non-conventionally beautiful and eye catching.

Simply put, it was *made* for Molly.

"Molly said no, y'all." I explained, turning the ring from side to side, imagining it on her finger. I hated saying that phrase out loud, but they needed to know the score. "She doesn't want to marry me."

"What do you mean she said no?" Tamryn demanded, her hand shooting to her hip. "When did you ask her?"

I paused. "The day we found out she was pregnant."

They both rolled their eyes spectacularly and for a moment, they could have been sisters rather than mother and daughter.

"Well of course she turned you down, Joe! You can't ask a girl to marry you two seconds after she finds out she's pregnant. How the hell do you think that made her feel? Like some consolation prize at the county fair." Tamryn snapped.

My mother nodded in agreement. "Tell me you gave her flowers at least? What did you say? Did you take her someplace nice...try to make it romantic?"

I thought back to Molly, overwhelmed in the bath tub and me blurting something like 'let's get married'. The questions made me realize what an utter ass I had been.

"I don't even think I asked her. I think I might have suggested it." I admitted, putting a palm over my eyes.

"Dear God, Joe!" My mother finally murmured. "You need to do a whole lot better next time around."

Needless to say, I accepted the ring that my mother thrust at me, stuffing the small box into my front pocket. I made both of them swear not to breathe a word about it to anyone, and then proceeded to return to the kitchen where I chewed out almost everyone in our families. Good times.

"You may as well know." I directed my words to the three adults who'd been outside supervising the kids. "I've made a spectacle of myself. Molly and I are leaving now. She doesn't need the stress and I can't keep my mouth shut about things."

Robbie and Betty gaped at me, but Robin simply looked intrigued.

"You can't leave, Joe. You're the guests of honor." Tamryn shot back, and the kids stopped chattering and stared at her. When it was clear that I wasn't about to budge an inch, she turned her eyes on Molly. "Molly..."

"Back off Tamryn. She doesn't need you trying to guilt her into staying." I spat, raising my voice for the first time. Molly placed a gentle hand on my arm.

"Okay. We all need to calm down. The kids don't need a show. Joe, I'm grateful for the assist but I can speak for myself, baby." She interjected quietly, pinning my gaze. Her eyes were insistent before she turned back to my sister. "We're gonna go ahead and go to bed. It's been a long week and I'm wiped out. There's no need to upset the kids. Everyone's already said their piece. I'm an early riser, so I'll make y'all brunch in the morning."

"Chocolate chip pancakes?" Her little nephew cheered, his gap toothed smile nearly making me laugh in spite of everything.

"Of course, hon. What's brunch without chocolate chip pancakes." Molly ruffled his hair and this time when she took my arm I let her lead me away to our room. She didn't try to launch into conversation, she just got ready for bed. I wasn't in the mood to talk about things. I'd already said what I had to say. Molly seemed to understand that and when she came back out of the bathroom she just crawled into bed and cuddled up to me, I thought about how she'd diffused things with Tamryn and how she'd handled her nephew. She was mom material, that's for sure. I wondered what kind of a dad I'd make. Molly's wandering hands soon took my mind off of things.

"I thought you were tired?" She nipped my ear and pinned me down on the bed.

"Do you know how hot you are when you get all protective? You inspired me to take a midnight ride, cowboy." I glanced at the wall, wondering who our neighbors were.

"Aren't you afraid someone will hear us?" She gave me a

lecherous grin, then kissed me hard.

"Guess you will have to be quiet then. Doesn't that make it hotter?"

She practically ripped my clothes off and had her way with me, our vigorous lovemaking session helped me wind down enough to fall asleep. Brunch the following morning was quiet and overly polite. Everyone gave controversial subjects a wide berth and focused on the kids and the weather, which had snapped cold. Molly and I did get a few questions, mostly initiated by the children, regarding baby names. We admitted we had a long list of ones we wouldn't name the babies, but that was as far as we'd gotten.

My awareness was pulled back to the present by a yellow cab slammed on its breaks right in front of Banger's. The screech of the tires pulled me out of my review of the debacle at Tamryn's. Mac and Mason hopped out of the back and Mason snorted.

"You do realize you literally brought me to a sausage factory, right?" He said to Mac.

"I figured it was long past time you came out of the closet." Mac replied so smoothly it sounded rehearsed.

"Hey." I called, stepping out of the shadows. Mason eyes shot to me and I could tell that Mac had neglected to tell him I was joining them.

"Hey…Joe…" Mason dragged out the response. Mac trotted ahead and yanked the door open, waving us both inside before we had to come up with anything else to say. It was a strange dynamic shift, Mac being the peacemaker and Mason and I being at odds.

Since most of the action was outside, we quickly found a seat indoors and were greeted by an overly friendly waitress. Mac flirted with her a little, but it was a pretty lame attempt. When she walked away, Mason turned to him.

"Mac, was it insensitive for me to make that sausage factory comment earlier?" Mac looked at him in confusion.

"What the hell are you talking about?" Mason had an innocent look on his face that he normally only wore when he was getting ready to fuck with someone.

"Well...are you batting for the other team now?" Mac looked like he didn't know whether to smack Mason or laugh at him.

"Why the hell would you say that?" Mason leaned back and gestured absently at the waitress on the other side of the room.

"Based on your half assed flirting with our waitress I just figured you might have decided to give up on women." I choked on a mouthful of beer at the look on Mac's face.

"Dude. I'm just not feeling it." Mac grumbled, kicking back in his seat.

"No shit, your aren't feeling it. You've got no game. None. That was like whiffing when batting in tee-ball. That girls was practically in your lap." Mason exclaimed. "No wonder they call this place Bangers."

"Quit trying to live vicariously through your single brother, Mason." I interjected, suspicious that I understood why Mac wasn't on the hunt. "His hearts not in it."

"Normally his heart isn't the one in charge." Mason sipped his beer and smacked his lips together in approval.

I nodded my head in Mac's direction. "He's sweet on Kelly."

He nodded and took another long swig of his drink. "Yeah...I don't see anything coming of it."

"What happened? She seemed pretty into you at the race. "I sipped my beer and watched him for visual clues. Mac looked pretty broken up about this turn of events, so I wondered what had changed Kelly's mind about him. "What did you do to screw it up?"

"Are we talking about *Francis'* daughter, Kelly? Jesus, you two need to look up the definition of boundaries." Mason shook his head and adjusted his cowboy hat. I noticed he hadn't taken my advice on the head shave, and I wondered if he'd called The Hair Club for Men.

"Says the guy who married his *nurse.*" I raised my eyebrows at him in a challenging manner.

"Touché." He nodded, as if we'd just finished a duel that ended in a draw. He turned back to Mac. "So how did you fuck things up with Kelly?'

"Things were going good. I asked her out and she said yes. We went on one date that lasted all of twenty minutes." I couldn't help it, the smart ass in me just couldn't resist a right cross.

"Mac, how many times have we told you to think about baseball?" He flipped me off and Mason laughed. Mac wiped his face and shrugged.

"I figured we would go out, have a good time and within a few dates end up back at her place. I mean, that ass of hers is smoking hot in tight jeans. Or shorts. She looks pretty good in skirts too. Milk did her body good. She's gorgeous."

"Yeah yeah…spare us the blow by blow, this isn't Penthouse." I rolled my eyes, but Mason shot me a dirty look for interrupting.

"Anyway, I wanted to take to her somewhere we could talk, so I figured the movies was out. I wanted something fun and casual…not too serious." Mac proceeded, looking a little embarrassed. I'd never seen him seem remotely serious about anyone, not even his ex-wife, so I leaned forward to make sure I heard the details.

"Good idea. Casual for drinks and conversation. Seems reasonable." I tried to think of something supportive to say.

"Says the guy who snuck around all over town with our sister." Mason snickered, and I actually laughed when I saw how casually he joked about what had once been a huge issue.

"I didn't sneak. I just didn't come to your house and ask your permission to see your 27 year old sister."

Mac didn't seem to hear the exchange, and continued to stare into space.

"So I took her to Ginny's." He continued, and finished off his beer in near record time. He waved to the waitress, who came to take the glass away. "I'll have another, thanks."

I figured he meant Ginny's Little Longhorn Saloon, which was a tiny little honkey tonk with live music.

"Was there a band playing?" I asked. "If so, it's not really the best for getting to know each other...having to shouting over tunes."

Mac shook his head, his cheeks flushed with alcohol and embarrassment. "It was Sunday. We went for Chicken Shit Bingo."

My eyes bulged out of their sockets. Mason and I burst into laughter, exchanged disbelieving looks, and shook our heads. All of us had spent time at Ginny's, especially since Austin legend Dale Watson played there. Hell, the place was a local institution. Beyond the music there was another big draw to Ginny's and that was on Sunday when a chicken named Sissy was set loose in a cage atop a grid lined board below. You bought a card and took your chances. When the bird shits, you could be a winner. The place could be a lot of fun, but it was pretty far down on my list of first date locations.

One look across the table at Mason and I knew he was thinking the same thing. Mac looked more miserable than I had seen him in a long time.

Damn, he must really have it bad for that girl.

"Mac. What the fuck is wrong with you? Did you fall off that new hog of yours and land on your head?" Mason asked, and I raised my pilsners to his. We clinked glasses in a show of solidarity.

"You don't take a date to Chicken Shit Bingo, bro." I agreed, polishing off my beer and nodding at the waitress when she appeared out of thin air, asking if I wanted another. "Not if you want *another* date."

"And not if you want to get laid. Unless you plan on climbing up the chicken's ass..." Mason was interrupted by the waitress arriving with a huge plate of sausages.

"We weren't there for a half hour and the last ten minutes of that she spent in the bathroom. She came out and said she had a headache and took off out the door. I went out after her and saw her hop into a cab waiting outside." Mac said, not even touching his food.

"She must have called them from the bathroom." Mason laughed, but it sounded more astonished than amused.

"No. There's an app." I replied, talking with a mouthful of fantastic food. I made a mental note to bring Molly here as soon as she could drink again. Otherwise, the sight of 150 beers on tap would just piss her off. "You don't even have to call them anymore. Just select your location and someone shows up. It even shows you when they arrive."

"Shit. I didn't even think of that." Mac muttered, looking depressed.

"Ask her for a do-over. One that doesn't involve animal excrement." Mason suggested as he dabbed his face with a napkin.

"This time take her someplace a little more upscale to show you have it in you." As the words came out of my mouth, I thought about my mother and sister's reaction to my would-be proposal to Molly. They'd been far kinder to me than I'd been to Mac, considering what a blunder it had been.

"So..." Mason began, seemingly eager to change the subject. "How are things with you, Joe? Reamed anyone's ass lately?"

I sighed, took another bite, and chewed.

"Not that Granny didn't have it coming..." He added quickly as if concerned he was about to get a repeat performance out of me.

"Molly wants me to be more open about my feelings." I

said, without a hint of sarcasm or apology. "My shrink agrees. Sorry about the cheap shots…but I have to admit, it felt pretty good."

Mac and Mason looked at each other and did that annoying 'twin thing' where they have an entire silent conversation in seconds.

Mason looked back at me and grinned. "You're just jealous that I look good in a hat."

Mac laughed, and the tension I felt building inside me dissipated. I'd begun to fear that I had irreparably broken something between us. But it seemed like despite my reading the riot act to Granny, we were all still friends.

"I don't think I have ever seen the old bird at a loss for words," Mac said with a snort.

Mason shot beer out his nose and started coughing as he tried to laugh and swallow at the same time. Once he got his wind back he waved the waitress over and ordered a few pitchers. Over the next few hours we ate meat, drank beer and talked sports. In short, we forgot that any women existed in the world with the exception of our waitress. And her sole purpose was to bring us more beer. Things were going my way, which only means I should have been on my guard.

Through beer addled eyes I saw someone swaggering toward the table. The swagger should have been my first warning and had I not been so hammered I might have been able to avoid the trouble headed my way. Or not. Karma can be a real bitch and sometimes she comes in the form of an actual bitch.

Five and a half feet of over-made up woman came to a stop in front of our table. Mason flicked his eyes up and then ignored her. Mac looked and raised a glass in her direction. She nodded at him and then turned her attention on me.

"Well hello there, Joe. Out for a little fun?"

Part of my brain, that low level Neanderthal that warns you that fire is hot and a charging rhino is dangerous set an alarm ringing. But in my defense I was floating on a beautiful ocean of barley and hops and could not be bothered to answer some pesky warning bell.

"Sort of. Can we get another pitcher?" The smile on her face transformed before my eyes to the hellish grimace of a monstrous she bitch. Before I realized what was happening she had slapped me across the face. It was a pretty good hit. I almost felt it through the beer.

"I am not your waitress, you fucking pig! You don't even remember my name do you? Am I so utterly forgettable?"

Ah. So that was what the little alarm bell had been for. I recognized her now. Julie Madison. The woman single handedly responsible for four of my rules. Don't ever sleep with the same girl twice. Don't forget anything when you leave. Don't let them get ahold of your phone. Take the stairs. The last time I had seen her she was screaming obscenities at me, in the elevator I had just left, on the ground floor of a fairly nice hotel. Wrapped only in a bed sheet. Not my finest hour. It was the third time we slept together and she somehow got it into her head that we were in a relationship. Total psycho hosebeast. Fuck my life.

"What the hell is your problem, bitch?" Mac had leapt up from the table when she hit me and gave her a shove back.

"Don't touch me you fucking prick or I will call a cop!" She glared at him with her fists bunched at her sides and I could see we were attracting attention.

"Mac, let's just go. It isn't worth it." I tried to rise and she darted around Mac and attempted to claw my eyes. I'm not sure what I would have done if Mason had not grabbed what was left of our pitcher of beer and thrown it in her face. She recoiled like he had doused her with acid and started making this high pitched keening.

Like they were following a sirens call a bunch of over co-logned, muscled young punks rushed to her side. I didn't like the odds. There were about ten of them and three of us.

"Come on guys. Let's head out." Mason nodded and Mac seemed to realize that we might be in trouble and started backing away as well.

"No!" Julie pushed her way out of the group of young men around her and pointed a finger at me. "You don't just get to run away after how you treated me. These men know how to treat a lady."

Damn. She'd played the lady card, as tattered as her's might be. She'd appealed to the chivalrous nature of the inebriated men surrounding her and I could see they were buying into it. Disgust showed on their faces as they imagined what horrible things I had done to this woman. It never seemed to occur to them we were all in a crowded room and there wasn't a lot I could have done. Only a few of them had seen her slap me and none of them were close enough to hear what she said. I saw the bartender on the phone, likely calling the cops and I nodded to the door behind me.

"Mac, Mason, let's go." Mason started toward the door and three of the guys moved to block his path.

"Damn it, Joe," Mason said with exasperation. "How the fuck is it that I am a grown man with kids and your dick is still getting me into fistfights?"

I didn't have a chance to answer as the nearest guy charged and threw a wild right at my head. The thing about bar fighting is that things are a lot different than they are in the movies. There is no order, no beer bottles over the head or chairs broken over backs. They're brutal, bloody and don't take long. By the time the cops arrived, half the guys had lost their taste for the fight and Julie had disappeared.

When the officers entered the joint, my stomach sank. They were two of my all-time favorites, which I'd nicknamed Tweedle Dee and Tweedle Dumb. The fact that I'd done this aloud in the back of their squad car might be why they took one look at the place and cuffed me. Mac and Mason got cuffed as well. I could only imagine the hell I was going to catch from their mother for this.

Luckily, the bartender caught up to the cops before they got us into the car and explained that we were actually the victims. After some posturing, the cops let us go. They insisted we get in a cab and head home, which we were more than ready to do.

Once we were underway Mac pulled out his phone and started fiddling with it. Mason glanced at the screen and pulled it out of his hand and tossed it to me.

"Hey! Give that back," Mac grabbed for the phone and I held it out of reach. Kelly's picture was on the screen and it looked like he had just started a text to her.

"Oh hell no," I shook my head and tossed the phone in my pocket. "You are not drunk texting her and ruining what little chance you have left. You can have you phone back tomorrow when you are sober."

Mac grunted in annoyance and then pretended he didn't care. Glancing at his brother I noticed Mason's left eye was red and puffy.

"Your wife is going to ground you when she sees that eye." I razzed Mason, who grinned and then winced. "She'll never let you out of the house with me again."

"She's picking her battles a lot more carefully these days." He replied, and I saw Mac cock a confused eyebrow at his brother.

"You two have been pretty antisocial lately. Is everything alright?" All trace of the grin evaporated from Mason's face, and I felt my ears perk up.

"We had a recent scare. She found a lump." I felt instantly sick and turned to him in horror. "It scared the shit out of us, but it turned out to be nothing. I guess it made us prioritize things."

"What the hell? Why didn't you say something?" I asked when I was able to gather my wits.

"I was too freaked out that I was going to lose her and have to raise three kids alone." I saw his eyes misting, and for a moment, I thought I might start bawling. He was my best friend and I'd had no clue he'd been suffering through something like this. As if he read my mind, he turned to me with the gravest expression set on his face. "I couldn't tell you, Joe. I think you can understand why. Plus Robin made me promise not to. She was afraid of stressing Molly out. We decided to wait until we were sure we had something to worry about."

I still felt nauseous thinking about Mason and what he'd been going through alone. I realized what a shitty friend I'd been to him and how self-absorbed I was.

"Why didn't you tell me, asshole?" Mac demanded.

"Cause you can't keep your fucking mouth shut." Mason shot back. Mac glanced at me in outrage and I cocked my head at him then nodded in agreement.

They dropped me at my place and I carefully made my way upstairs. I took a hot shower and drank a ton of water before I went to bed. When the cruel spears of sunlight pierced my eyes in the morning, I realized I had drank far too much beer. My flimsy back end measures, namely the shower and water guzzling the night before, did nothing to counteract the consequences. Perhaps they saved my head from exploding. My hangover made me feel like I was twenty years older.

The trip down the block to the bakery was brutal. The wind whipped at me, and it felt like winter was truly upon us. I ordered a box of assorted crap and two giant to go coffee containers. Mac was in the shop with his head on the counter when I came in. He looked up at me with bleary eyes.

"I didn't see your bike outside. Did you cab it?" Mac nodded then winced in pain. I could relate. My head felt like it was going to split in half.

"Yes. Quit shouting. I still can't focus my eyes. Is that coffee? Tell me that you brought coffee and I will forgive the yelling."

"Yes, Mac, it's coffee and I'm not yelling. Get the sand out of your vagina." He flipped me off half-heartedly and carefully poured a large cup of coffee.

We sat in blissful silence nursing our java until Nick came in, trudging loudly in his unlaced boots that looked like they'd been purchased from a military surplus store. I had the urge to grab him and drop him in the dumpster outside. Seeing the expression on my face, Mac immediately banished him down the street to gather hang over cure supplies from Whole Foods. We'd finished the second container of coffee and I felt less homicidal by the time he returned.

Mac set about mixing up a noxious concoction of liquids that he tried to convince me to drink. When he ran to the bathroom ten minutes later, I was glad that I had declined. I wanted no part of the sounds coming out of that bathroom. Nick flopped down at the workstation across from me and I waved him off.

"No building today, Nick. We're taking a hangover holiday. If you want to, help Francis around the shop. I think Mac and I need to take off early." Nick nodded sagely.

"Hey, that's cool, boss man. What good is being the man in the big seat if you can't take off when you want? Look, I don't want to add to your stress, man, and it's probably none of my business, but I told Pops I'd pass along that he has a house for sale. It was my Gran's, but she broke her hip a few months ago and decided to move into assisted living. He had to redo it before he could put it on the market. I guess Graham told him you were having trouble finding a place. If you want to stop by and take a look, here's the address. It isn't listed yet. Maybe he will cut you a deal. He has a lot of crap going on right now and I don't think he wants to fool with it."

It was the longest conversation I had with the boy since I hired him. If it wasn't for the hammers banging on the inside of my head, I would have thanked him. Instead he got a grunt of acknowledgement. It seemed to be enough because he headed to the other side of the shop. I cracked the door to the bathroom long enough to tell Mac to go home and went back upstairs to bed.

The afternoon sun was high in the sky by the time I woke up. My stomach woke me up, complaining about its cavernous empty state. Once I rinsed the kitty litter out of my mouth, I jumped in the shower and turned it up as hot as I could stand. The business card with the address Nick had given me was sitting on the table with my keys. It wasn't far and there were a few restaurants between it and me that sounded good. Ten minutes later, I was on the road.

I took my time eating, figuring the house would be another lemon. The food was alright, but after Molly's cooking, most food tasted substandard. My girl had spoiled me for other chefs. I left a decent tip and jumped in the truck. The house was in a great neighborhood smack dab in the middle of an area Molly called 'charming'. My plan had been a quick drive by, but that went out the window when I spotted Graham standing in front of the place talking to someone.

Parking the truck, I walked up the sidewalk and recognized Jeff, Nick's father, standing with Graham. He shot me a surprised grin and stuck his hand out and I shook it.

"Well Joe, were your ears burning?" Jeff said with a laugh. "Graham and I were just talking about you." I turned to Graham, who nodded.

"I told him you and your lady are looking for a house but just hadn't been able to find anything worth buying. This place might just be the thing for you."

"Well, Nick mentioned that you were getting it ready for sale. Molly's out of town but I figured I would stop and take a look."

Jeff laughed and chided, "Trying to see if it is worth showing the little lady?" I winced.

He chuckled at my reaction. "We have all been there. A

happy wife makes a happy life."

"We aren't married," I said, sliding a glance sideways at Graham. We had yet to have an in depth conversation about Molly's pregnancy, but I'd given him the broad strokes. I grated on my nerves to have to correct Jeff on our marital status.

Graham waved his hand dismissively. "It's the sentiment that matters. In your case it might be better to say if mama's not happy then no one is happy."

One of my favorite things about Graham: no judgment. He was willing to take people as they were. That didn't stop him from trying to get me to come to church, but he never pushed it.

The two of them ushered me inside and gave me the grand tour. The place was amazing. Jeff explained that they had gutted the whole house, setting aside what they could for reuse. There had been asbestos and lead in the house, so they had an abatement company sanitize the structure before building it back up. They'd been able to save a ton of the stuff that made these older homes cool: architectural features like the subway tile backsplash, lead glass windows with arts and crafts frames, arched doorways and vintage cupboards and built-ins.

It had a five hundred square foot basement which made it unusual for the area. The kitchen had been demo'd but hadn't been remodeled yet. It was a blank canvas just ready for a chef to design, and the backyard looked like something out of a Norman Rockwell painting. A huge tree had a tire swing hanging from it and a meticulously laid out garden ringed thick green grass. Privacy fencing made it seem like a secret oasis.

Some of the woodwork had damage. Jeff sheepishly told me he was responsible for some of the carnage, in his childhood. He'd just begun to sand it along with the floors Most of it I could replace easily. By the time he finished telling me what all they had done on the place, I couldn't wait to bring Molly to show her.

Jeff headed back into the house to lock up, leaving Graham

and I out in front.

"It's a heck of a place, Joe. I know every tradesman who's worked on it. Hell, I even know the inspector. It's in impressive shape and the parts that weren't have been completely redone. You think Molly will like it?" I looked back at the house and nodded.

Doubt must have showed on my face because Graham put his hand on my shoulder.

"What is it, son?" He motioned to the tailgate of my truck and we sat down.

"I just haven't handled things well with Molly. To be honest, I didn't even ask her to marry me. I just told her we should get married." Graham gave me a knowing look and nodded.

"Don't be too hard on yourself Joe. Things have been flying at you pretty fast. It wasn't that long ago that I worried we were going to lose you, or more accurately that you'd lost yourself. Now look at you. Finally healing and about to be a father. Don't beat yourself up for every little misstep."

"I've given myself a break about a lot of things but when it comes Molly...not giving her everything that she should have..." I broke off as a lump formed in my throat. We sat in silence for a few moments before Graham spoke.

"To be fair, no one can tell you what Molly needs except Molly. And every man has to find his own way to ask the woman he loves to spend the rest of her life with him. You'll get no shortage of advice on it, a lot of it bad, but it all amounts to the same thing. What a woman wants is for the man to make a gesture that not only shows how much he loves her, it shows how well he knows her."

The simple wisdom struck a chord deep within me and I found myself nodding. Graham stood and clapped me on the shoulder.

"Take some time and think about it, Joe. The answer will come to you." Waving goodbye, he headed over to his truck and then drove away. All the way back to the apartment I thought about Molly. Then I went up and sat on the roof in the outdoor space I had fixed up for her. I watched the stars and contemplated how she'd turned my life upside down. My phone rang, and it was her picture that lit up the screen.

"Hey, baby girl." I murmured, realizing that my ears were stinging from the biting night air.

"Hi." She sounded breathy, but so close it was impossible to believe I couldn't reach out and touch her. "I know I said I wouldn't call..."

"I'm glad you changed your mind. I miss you." I replied. "I have a surprise for you."

"I bet you do." She responded coyly, and I bit my lip in frustration.

We talked for about fifteen minutes. She said she'd been offered a deal and Robbie was looking over the paperwork. I told her I had a lead on a house, but begged her not to get her hopes up.

When she finally said good night and hung up, I sat and watched the traffic meandering in the distance. Suddenly it felt much colder on the roof and I decided I needed to do something to take my mind off of Molly, otherwise I would end up brooding about how much I missed her all night long. I took the stairs down to the workshop and turned on the lights in the back. Grabbing the bin of scrap wood I dumped it onto my workbench and stared at it.

One of the things that I hadn't told anyone, not even Molly and Dr. Greene, was how badly losing my ability to carve had wounded me. At the time, it was buried beneath the weight of crushing grief. But as the days dragged on, the absence of my gift was almost as bad. That part of me that could create was crippled. Deep down, I thought it might be gone for good. Now every time I reached for it, I worried that it might not be there. But this time, like each time since it had come back, the intuitive knowledge flowed back into me.

It was hard to explain to other people what it was like to carve. My mind didn't so much disconnect as it went into a different gear. Suddenly, there was clarity of action. My hands flowed through the motions necessary to create the vision in front of me. A profound sense of peace settled over me whenever the tools were in my hand. It transcended almost anything else. I felt it most deeply when I wasn't making something specific, but when I was creating. Like the day that I built Molly her spice box.

Now, as I sat at the workbench and began shaping the wood in front of me, I cleared my mind of what I was doing and let my hands work. Woodcarving isn't a speed activity and the time it took to slice away the unnecessary bits of material left me time to consider my current state of affairs.

I hope the reason Molly said no to marrying me is because I screwed up how I brought it up. Tamz and mom were right. I really fucked up. That ring...it's perfect. As much as I hate to admit it, I think mom actually scored some points with me this time. If Molly likes the house, we could have almost everything we need for our new family except Stow and Go seating. If she says yes...we could actually be a real family.

Tears blurred my vision and my work ground to an instant halt. It was hard to think about Molly this way. The intensity of my love for her burned like molten metal in my heart. She'd brought me out of darkness like a torch left burning in the night. I hated to admit it, even to myself, but before her...I *had* given up. I was marking off days until life ended with no other concern than making sure I didn't make myself a burden. She'd changed all of that. My life was forever altered because of her love, and I shuddered in horror at the thought of losing her. Unbidden, Molly's voice rolled through my head.

Joe...you can't control everything. If something goes wrong there's not a lot you can do.

I sat in the chair silently and after a few minutes my hands started working again. As calm returned, I rolled her words around in my head. The simple truth of the matter was that she was right. No matter how much I tried to protect her, there were no guarantees that I would be able. I hadn't been able to the first time. It didn't stop me from torturing myself with the lie.

Jessica and Jack.

The names still tore through my heart. But they lacked the full force that they once had. It wasn't that I was getting over their deaths. I don't think the pain of loss that deep ever really goes away. The pain was still there, but I no longer let it control me. Instead, being with Molly was showing me how I could keep living. The undeniable truth was that I wanted to be with Molly. To live our life together and give her every part of me. Setting my things down on the table, I grabbed my keys and headed out to my truck.

I was going to give Molly what she wanted: my whole heart. In order to do that, I had to do something for myself first. I had to move on, leave the past where it belonged.

The drive across town took less time than normal with most travelers already home for the evening. The cemetery was locked when I arrived, so I drove around and parked near a side gate. It wasn't open but there were two loose bars near it that I could just slip through. I'd found this security flaw shortly after the funeral. It's amazing what you discover when you wander outside a locked cemetery for five hours.

It was pitch black inside, but I had a small flashlight with me. I kept it low to the ground to keep from attracting attention from anyone passing by. I could have found the graves in total darkness. In no time, I was standing in front of them and I sank down into the cold wet grass above them.

"Hey, Jess, hey, Jack. Sorry to bother you guys so late, but I need to talk." Realizing how ridiculous it was to apologize for the time in a cemetery, I paused. Their constant presence had always felt very real to me, and I took a moment to gather myself.

"Jack, I miss you, boy. There isn't a day that goes by that I don't wish that we could have traded places. You had all that unlimited potential. It isn't fair that you didn't get a chance to experience everything that life has to offer. I want you to know that I'll never forget you. I will always love you. I may not get out here to visit you as much as I have in the past, but I want you to know that isn't because you mean any less to me. I have to start taking care of myself and those around me now. I hope you understand, son."

Tears were flowing down my face and I let them fall. There was nothing that would stop me from coming to visit him, but I was finally truly saying goodbye to him. I heard a sob and realized it was coming from me. I was finally ready to let him go. They'd buried my boy years ago, but I had carried him with me every day since. Now I felt ready to lay him to rest.

Laying my hands on his tombstone, I leaned into the heavy marble and locked my arms around it in a crushing embrace. The stone seeped the warmth from my body, but I held onto it until my shivering made it to difficult. Rising, I walked around rubbing my hands to get the blood flowing again. When I was warmer I turned to look at Jess's tombstone.

"I haven't really been fair to you." The words tumbled out of my lips before I even had a chance to think. Taking a deep breath, I fought against the rage inside and tried to get out what I needed to say. "Bethany defended you more than once and I was just too damn stubborn… full of too much anger and pain to listen. It was easier for me to build you up like some monster that killed our baby. But that isn't fair…and it isn't true. I can see that now. You were sick, and needed my help and support. But you were too scared of me judging you to ask me. I have hated you for what you did, but I was also hating myself."

Reaching down I picked some leaves from the top of her

headstone and tossed them aside. From inside my pocket I took my wedding ring. Twisting it around in my fingers I stared at it for a while.

"I remember everything, Jess. The good memories along with the bad. I can say that now. It isn't just the accident and the aftermath. I remember how excited you were when we found out we were pregnant. How angry you were when I showed up late for our wedding. The pizza nights when we would skinny dip in the pool behind your parents' house. It wasn't all good but it wasn't all bad either. I loved you…and I think you loved me. What happened to you wasn't fair. My hatred of you wasn't fair either. It was an accident. You didn't do it on purpose. I know you would never have left me or harmed our baby. I'm sorry, Jess. I hope that wherever you are you can find it in your heart to forgive me."

Digging my hand into the turf I made a hole about six inches deep and dropped my wedding ring into it. Tamping the divot back in place, I stood and let the tears flowing down my cheeks fall onto the graves. Standing there, I felt a warm wind blow away the cold for just a moment, or maybe it was my imagination.

CHAPTER

Eleven

Molly

Surf and Turf

I CALLED SHOTGUN in the six seater Cessna, but was only awarded the seat when I threatened to puke all over the plane. I'd never flown in a small plane before, and I found the entire experience exhilarating. Though the pilot insisted he needed the legroom, Sanchez had to fold his giant frame into the back. He didn't complain, but he never complained...ever...so I had no idea if he was upset or not. I figured that my lack of upchucking made it a win for everyone.

Though David had sent a limo driver to pick us up, we blew him off when we spotted Dan waiting just on the other side of the security doors. Looking casually elegant as always, Dan breezed forward all smiles and hugs. He positively fussed over my belly and was the first person besides Joe that touched my stomach without me feeling violated.

"Well? What's the verdict? Pink or blue?" He asked, his eyes dancing spritely.

I grinned at his contagious excitement. "Both!"

"Oh my God!" He cried, as if ready to burst. "I can't believe it."

I quickly introduced him to Sanchez, and both men refused to let me carry anything but my purse.

I texted Joe that we'd landed, knowing he'd be anxious if he didn't hear from me. As Dan pulled out of short term parking and onto the road, he gushed. "A boy and a girl. Oh, Molly. You're so lucky!"

It was the first time anyone had framed the situation in that manner, and it gave me pause. I remembered Dan saying more than once that sometimes he wished he'd played it straight long enough to have children. That realization sobered me up. I spent a great deal of time thinking of our accidental pregnancy as a curse, when it would be the biggest blessing imaginable to many couples.

"Thank you." I replied quietly.

He frowned and gave me an admonishing side glance. "What are you thanking me for?"

"No, really, Dan. I needed a wakeup call." He blinked at me in surprise, and I turned to look out at the scenery. Seeing the swaying palm trees and historic architecture, invigorated me, and I suddenly had my second wind.

"I'm starving. Where are we going to eat?" I asked.

"You mean you aren't cooking for me? What the hell good is it to have two chefs as houseguests if they won't take it out in trade?" Dan joked.

"Tomorrow night." I shot back. "Tonight, I want to be wait-ed on. What about you, Dirty S?'"

He nodded.

"I'm sorry...did you just called him Dirty S? As in Dirty Sanchez?" Dan's eyes flew wide and his lips curled up in a

Grinch-like smile. "You tolerate that from this little monstrosity?"

"She's the boss." Sanch replied, but with an unmistakable smart ass twinge in his voice.

"You might have a lawsuit on your hands." Dan drawled.

"I record all of our conversations." Sanchez volleyed his response like an ace serve.

"Oh, I like him." Dan quipped, making an abrupt U-turn. "I know exactly where to take y'all to get your wine and dine on. Or in your case Molly...just your dine."

"Go ahead and rub it in, why don't you?" I shot back.

"We're drinking wine tonight, sweetie. You won't miss it, being a Shiner girl." Dan loved teasing me about my penchant for simple beer over his pretentious vintages. I would've chugged Boone's Farm if it would alleviate my lower back ache, but my doctor said the safest course of action was absolutely no alcohol during pregnancy.

I sulked, and threatened to take video of them acting idiotic if they had too much fun. The moment we got out of the car, I took his keys, planning to be the designated driver for the remainder of the evening. Sanchez had only been of legal age to drink for a few months, so the novelty hadn't worn off yet, and Dan was a notorious lush.

Dan had parked in the lovely Strand Historic District right down the street from the Opera House. Sanchez snapped a few pictures of the buildings as we wandered down to a restaurant called Rudy and Paco's. I was in love the minute we stepped inside and I smelled the delectable scents wafting in our direction. We were seated quickly by a host that recognized Dan as a big deal on the Galveston food scene, and he explained Rudy and Paco's specialized in seafood and South and Central American cuisine.

The ambiance was fantastic. It somehow straddled the line of whimsical and elegant, and the entire time we were there, I really wished I'd brought Joe along. I felt the unfamiliar ache of longing I used to have when I was a girl and hadn't seen him in a while. Back then, it would have been impossible to believe I'd ever want to spend a night away from him. I still didn't, but I understood the importance of our time apart, and moped into my iced tea as I watched Dan give Sanch a mini wine lesson.

I wasn't mad at all about Joe's outburst at Tamryn's. Far from it. The word relieved might have captured my reaction much more accurately. Honestly, everyone there had the ass chewing coming, including me.

Joe had been wound so tight that he simply snapped back like a rubber band, but instead of lashing out and hurting me like Draven would have, Joe's thoughtful and controlled chastisement reminded me of what he'd been like before. Confident, honest, strong. It was like for a few precious minutes he'd forgotten that he'd once been defeated by life. Like he was ready to just hop on a board and ride a monster wave. I wanted him to have time to reflect on what that moment had felt like. I also needed him to see that I could be out of his sight without some handlebar mustache-twirling villain tying me to the nearest railroad tracks.

"So…what are we naming these babies?" Dan asked, and Sanchez leaned in to hear my response.

"Well, for a girl I want to name her Lola…but Joe said it reminds him of the song and he thinks that his daughter being named after a transsexual would be a bit awkward".

Dan sighed. "You need to bring him down for Mardi Gras. We'll tie him up to the drag queen float and brainwash him into seeing things your way."

Sanchez sniffed, and when I glanced his way, he was smiling.

"He liked Henry for a boy. But I told him it was as "little old man" as that truck he drives. So I think we've decided that he gets to pick our daughter's name and I get to pick our son's."

"I'm so scared for your children." Sanchez remarked, and I blew my straw wrapper directly at him.

"Now, kids. This is why we can't have nice things." Dan scolded us. "It's all fun and games until someone gets an eye poked out."

"That's what *she* said." Sanchez replied just as I took a long gulp of my drink, and I nearly shot iced tea out of my nose. Dan and I both giggled and Dirty S. turned beet red.

"I believe Stacy's rubbing off on you." I smiled and then my eyes shot wide at how bad it sounded.

"Dirty!" Dan critiqued, and I laughed a little. I noticed a slight headache forming behind my eyes. I figured it was mostly likely from the motion sickness and cabin pressure shifting on the plane. Since having a nice drink like a civilized adult was out of the question, I dug in my purse for some Tylenol.

The dull throb eased up by the time our food arrived. I ate every single morsel of my pan seared potato encrusted trout with lemon sauce and fought back the urge to lick my plate. By the time we shambled back to Dan's car and I drove the men down Seawall Boulevard to the high rise building, I was ready for bed.

"Holy shit, Dan!" I murmured as I parked in the massive garage. As we walked through the impressive lobby and made our way up to his apartment on the eleventh floor, I grew more and more astonished.

"Home sweet hovel." Dan called as we wandered into his impressive condo. Though it was pitch black outside, I could tell that the panoramic view from his balcony would make me green with envy once the sun rose.

I put my hands on my hips. "How the hell can you afford this?"

"I'm in high demand. David knows he has to take care of me." He referred to his restaurateur brother as if he were a sugar daddy.

"Thanks for the tip. I'll file that away for tomorrow." I

quipped, referring to our business negotiations.

"It helps that the Emerald by the Sea has a wine room." He explained, referring to his high rise building respectfully by her given name. "I do a few hours of selecting and ordering a week and offer a couple of classes every month to offset some of the fees."

"Snow birds like to drink." I nodded sagely.

"Everyone likes to drink." Dirty S. added, reappearing from the back hall. "I put your bags in the guest room closest to the bathroom."

"You're a golden god. Thank you." I replied with a joint stretching yawn. "I have got to get some sleep, y'all. My entire body hurts."

That night, I was sure I'd pass out the minute my head hit the pillow, but I wasn't used to sleeping without Joe. The bed felt clinical and cold, and I tossed and turned a while, eventually digging an extra pillow out of the closet to cuddle up with. Finally, I drifted off to sleep, missing my man and hoping he was getting more rest than I was.

By the time I finally pulled myself out of bed the following morning, the sun was high in the sky. Feeling a lurch of panic, I hurried out to the open concept living room/kitchen/dining room and was momentarily distracted by Dan's jaw dropping view.

"Morning, sleepy head." Dan called from the living room chaise, a coffee mug clutched in his hand.

"Shit! Why'd you let me sleep so long, Dan!" I cried, hurrying into the kitchen for a cup of his famous gourmet bean juice. Even if it meant it was the only caffeine I got all day, I needed it for medicinal purposes.

"Relax, sweetie. David texted me this morning and said he wants to do a lunch meeting at Madeline's. I figured y'all would get up when you were ready."

Sanchez stumbled out of the hallway, grabbed a pop tart from the counter without toasting it, and collapsed into a seat at the table.

"Ya alright?" I asked, eyeing him curiously.

"Yeah. I haven't really drank much since the honeymoon. Out of practice." He croaked.

"Do you have eggs?" I called to Dan, wandering into the kitchen.

"Of course. What do you think this is? Lithuania?" Dan drawled, scrolling on his phone. I quickly whipped up some scrambled eggs and toast and I wandered out onto his wrap around deck. The wind coming off the water was a tad cold, but still far warmer than Austin. The view of the bay and the gulf was well worth the staggering price he'd paid for the place. Again, I pined for Joe, wishing he was here to see it with me. Dan appeared at the sliding glass door and let himself out to join me.

"Sanchez went to jump in the shower. I swear, if that boy weren't married..."

I raised my eyebrows. "He's a wee bit young for you, don't you think?"

Dan laughed and batted his hand at me playfully.

"I'm twenty-nine, sugar. Don't you remember?" He grinned, his tanned face contrasting fantastically with his whitened teeth.

"For the twelfth year in a row." I nodded. We sat quietly for a moment.

"How are you, really?" His sweet eyes weighed heavily on me. "Have you heard anything about Draven's hearing?"

"I got an email a couple of weeks ago from Elaine." I said, dropping my toast on the plate. The mere mention of my ex-husband's name chased away my appetite. "He was denied parole."

"That's great news."

"For now." I agreed.

"Afraid he'll turn up on your doorstep again?" Dan asked,

his expression telling me he most certainly was.

"I feel like Draven has a lot more to worry about than me these days." I sighed, sipping my coffee, which was sadly luke-warm. "I'm a lot more concerned about the other man in my life."

"Last time we talked, you mentioned that the two of you were going to see his psychiatrist..." Dan began, sitting his cup down on the small bistro table between us.

I nodded, pulling my hoody around me. "It was enlighten-ing. He said Joe has made great strides since we got together, but he has classic signs of survivor's guilt or post-traumatic stress. Abandonment issues, trust issues...it goes on and on."

"Does any of that surprise you?" Dan asked. I shook my head.

"No." I admitted. "I'd be surprised if he didn't. "

"So talk to me, sweetie. Why do you look so blue?" Dan's companionable tone eroded my walls enough to let him slip in sideways.

"For as long as I'd known him, Joe's always had luck on his side. Things just kind of went his way." I began, sitting down my fork and meeting Dan's gaze.

"Alright. Go on." He replied.

"His parents cut him off, but he grew up with money. Like...serious money. They lived in a house in Pemberton Heights, which is one of the richest neighborhoods in the city...maybe even the country. I've listened to him with Tamryn, talkin' about some of their family vacations to Europe. You wouldn't believe the places he's been. He had a private educa-tion for most of his childhood. Even when he had his big falling out with his dad, he still had his craft to fall back on."

I thought about how quickly Joe's business started turning a profit and how remarkable his carpentry skills were and shook my head. "Mac has always claimed Joe was a natural carpenter. I know you've seen the website so I don't need to explain. He's so damn talented. And the way women flock to him? Please. Knowing Joe, he probably didn't have to chase Jessica down to get her number."

Dan's expression was mildly lascivious. "Yeah. I doubt that."

"So...what I think I'm getting at is...Joe led a pretty charmed life, at least until the night of the accident. It fucking kills me to imagine how it undid him. Losing everything at once like he did...I don't know, Dan. I wasn't there. I've only seen the aftermath." I raked both hands through my hair at my temples, looking up at the pale sky as if it would have the answers, like some giant Magic 8 ball. "I just hope I can be what he needs. If not, I guess we'll always have the unbreakable bond of our children."

Dan looked devastated at my words and my throat narrowed as I said them aloud. I always got very emotional thinking about Joe during that dark time in his past. I missed it all, and I couldn't imagine the incredible blow that it had been to his spirit. I often worried that I wasn't capable of helping him the way he needed helping.

"But..." Dan started, uncrossing his legs and sitting forward with his hands folded on the table. "He's shopping for houses with you. He wants to marry you."

"No. He feels *obligated* to do those things." I could tell I was going to get weepy and it pissed me off. I didn't need my hormones giving Dan the wrong impression. I wasn't feeling sorry for myself. I was simply stating the facts. Biology had forced Joe's hand, and in typical Joe fashion, he was being a man about it. It was his nature to do 'the right thing', but I wanted him to do the right thing for himself.

"Molly..." Dan responded, disbelief splashed all over his face. "You don't know that."

"Fair enough. But I don't know that it's *not* true. We weren't ready for any of this. Goddamn fucking broken condom!

I should have just left him the hell alone, but I was too damn selfish. I just loved him too much to leave him be and let him heal, and now we're all twisted up in this mess."

"*Now* who has post-traumatic stress?" Dan chuckled, and I felt my anger surge. I was bearing my fucking soul to my dearest friend and my face lit on fire at his condescending tone. "Molly, you were terrorized by your husband. Someone who should have been your protector turned out to be a monster. You blame yourself for not seeing the psycho behind the pretty boy mask but he was damn good at pretending and he fooled us all. You kept that disastrous marriage together because you made promises that everyone else in the world breaks without an afterthought. Now, I've met Joe. I've seen the way he looks at you. Molly, he adores you. And you *love* him. He wants to rebuild his life with you by his side and you're actively keeping him at arm's length. Why?"

"I told you why." I shot back, but Dan shook his head.

"I think you're scared, and afraid to believe in him, to take what Joe says at face value and the challenge of an equal partner, because you'll be vulnerable again. It's easier to play the strong, independent woman than to put yourself out there. Be pissed at me all you want, sweetie. But I'm calling it like I see it."

Unable to string a simple phrase together, I sat and let his wisdom wash over me like high tide. The communication breakdown between Joe and I had maybe been fifty percent Joe. Maybe less than that. With bold eyes, I reexamined "us" and it was startling for me to recognize that I'd been pushing him away since before we knew about the babies. It had been exhausting, but the thought of letting him take care of me on any level made me want to jump in my car and drive until I ran out of gas. Soon I was crying, and Dan ran into the house for a box of tissues.

It was a couple of minutes before I pulled myself together enough to speak. "What if he changes his mind, Dan?"

He frowned, and for the first time since we'd arrived in Galveston, he truly looked his age. "What if he's being one hundred percent honest and you push him so far away that he decides to stay there? Then who wins?"

Dan's brother David was smooth. Like 'find a reason to check the time so I can display my Rolex' smooth. He had a totally approachable and welcoming demeanor, but it contrasted dramatically with his Armani suit and his perfectly manicured hands. In a moment of introspection, I realized that my immediate distrust of him was a direct result of knowing Draven Cirone. I was moody after my discussion with Dan about Joe, and the babies were kicking the hell out of my bladder, so I tried very hard to push my snap judgments aside.

He and Dan were half-brothers, so when Dan introduced the thin, well dressed black man to Sanchez, Dirty S. reacted in thinly masked surprised just like I had the first time we'd met.

"Molly. So nice to see you again." David reached out to shake my hand and his eyes dropped to my mid-section. Pregnancy was a never ending series of odd experiences, and this business meeting was no exception. I found it awkward to have public evidence of my sex life on display for the entire world. Thankfully, he made eye contact again, his professional mask firmly in place. "Thank you for coming all this way to meet with me."

"Please. Like it's a hardship to come down to the Gulf! I love it here. I *am* missing the margaritas this time around, though."

He chuckled politely. "When are you due?"

"April 4th." He reacted in open surprised. "I'm having twins."

"Congratulations." He pulled out my chair, and I gave him a gracious smile.

"You've got quite the place here, David." I tried to act disinterested in Madeline's, but I had been offered the head chef position when he was opening the place, and I was guilty of imagining how different my life might have been if I'd entertained his offer. All dark woods and dim lighting, the ambiance oozed sexy elegance. Water walls, ran the length of the front wall, and a long and impressive bar separated the kitchen from the front of the house. The bank of windows facing the gulf were naturally highlighted as they were the primary source of light in the place during daylight hours. I was very curious about the menu, and what the place looked like at night.

"Thank you, Molly. It could have been yours." He chided lightly.

"I know, I know." I sighed dramatically, putting a hand to my belly. I decided to play along, since people who took themselves too seriously always made me mischievous. "I'm sure we would have made wonderful gourmet babies together."

He laughed and toasted me with his glass of iced tea. "We would have made swimming pools full of money together. We still can."

Thus he launched into his well-rehearsed pitch, using pie charts and graphs that would likely have had a Wall Street investment firm hanging on his every word. It was largely lost on me and I spent most of the time focusing on the plate of perfect croissant sandwiches and crème brûlée. They were divine. David's smooth exterior became more ruffled as his presentation went on and he finally sputtered to a stop.

"I don't mean to be rude, Molly, but is this all going over your head or am I just boring you?" The slight sharpness in his tone made me smile as it reflected the familial similarity that I had often looked for between him and Dan. Setting down my spoon, I turned and gave him my full attention.

"David, I am far too pregnant to waste your time or mine. Why don't we just skip through the courtship and get down to brass tacks, shall we? Tell me what you want from me and tell me what you plan to give me for it."

Dan gave a giggle that he quickly stifled at a sharp look from David. Sanchez put his hand to his mouth and acted like I had just kicked a cop in the junk. I patted his hand and smiled calmly. Dan shrugged at David and made a "what can you do" gesture before folding his hands back into his lap. David fixed him with an authoritative glare for just a moment before a smile twitched on his lips.

"Very well." He laced his fingers together and sat back. "Dan warned me that the flowers and candy approach wouldn't help me, so let me speak plainly. I have a bar that needs food. A new product that is different from everything happening on the island. Your trucks in Austin are the perfect gimmick, and from what I hear the one parked at Cas's turns a great profit." For a moment I wondered how he'd come by that bit of information, but he pressed on and I was once again forced to focus on his presentation. "So, simply put, I want to franchise your food truck. In essence, I want you to open a third truck that is permanently parked here at my new bar, which will also be called Wrapgasmic. The vintage food truck theme will carry into the bar. All your recipes, with a staff approved by you. You'll have total autonomy for the menu, and Dan has helped me design some themed cocktails to go along with your food. In return, I would own 50% of the new truck. We would split all the food proceeds between us after expenses on the truck were recouped."

I looked at Sanchez, who had an unmistakable glow of excitement behind his dark eyes. Finding no immediate objections, I asked to see the location. We all left Madeline's and David insisted I ride with him in his shock white Audi convertible. I wasn't sure if it was another attempt to show off his success or to separate the weak one from the pack, but I really didn't care either way. I reached over and switched on his stereo, blasting Ke$ha on full volume just to see how he'd respond. When he chuckled and sang along with me to the chorus, I decided we might be able to do business with the guy.

He cut down a side street and parked behind a bold red building. As we walked to the side of the building where Dan and Sanchez had parked, I gaped at the candy apple red food truck parked where those driving down the boulevard wouldn't be able to miss it.

"Pretty sure of yourself, aren't you?" I asked, my eyes sweeping the expensive wrap that spanned the entire length of the truck. It was unsettling to see the ultra-professional version of Mason's paint job, and they'd even included a slightly modified version of our logo. It was crisp and clean and streamlined.

David didn't even blink at my smart ass remark, and his poker face was nearly impenetrable. "It's a wrap. It can be changed easily enough."

Sanchez gushed and carried on about how amazing the new, custom truck was. David launched into the specs and proceeded to explain how the kitchen was 'top of the line'. He went on to say that the entire side space where Dan had parked would be turned into an outdoor seating area for customers with children who didn't want to come inside the bar. He went on and on, but I couldn't stop looking in the direction of The Pleasure Pier, Galveston's answer to Navy Pier in Chicago. The carousel, roller coaster, and other motion sickness inducing attractions were just on the opposite side of the highway.

"See, Molly? It's a prime location. The Pier is an easy stroll from here."

"That can be a blessing or a curse, though." I replied, wrinkling my brow. "Won't you have to compete with everyone on The Pier?"

I spotted the Bubba Gump sign wedged between two buildings on the pier and shook my head doubtfully.

"Galveston needs variety, sweetie. This is a vacation destination." Dan's soothing tone made the obvious statement seem like an ad for the Galveston Tourism website.

"Look, Little Mama! They have a flat screen built into the side of the truck!" Sanchez called like a preschooler at the top of an especially cool slide on the playground. "And a Karaoke machine!"

I shot David an uncertain look.

"People have to have something to do while they wait." His humble shrug was unbecoming, but I had to admit, the idea suited the good time atmosphere we'd tried hard to market in Austin.

"They'll need a gong." I joked. "We could mount it just outside the window. That way the staff can shut up anyone bad enough to chase away customers."

I was kidding, but the three men with me laughed and nodded as if I was a genius.

"Come on." David said, placing a hand on my shoulder, "Let's go look at the bar."

As we stepped into the entryway, I stopped short and my jaw dropped to the floor. I was staring up at a floor to ceiling image of myself. Somehow, David had acquired a copy of the Austin Chronicle photo of me that caused such a giant influx of attention for the trucks.

In a moment of utter naiveté, I'd allowed the photographer, a shifty little bastard, to shoot a playfully suggestive picture of me draped over the hood of my food truck holding one of my strappin' wraps. He'd asked for my phone number after the shoot, and I've never been so happy to turn someone down in my life. The photographer had kept repositioning the wrap and shouting "lean closer". In the end, he'd had me lean way too far forward for the plunging neckline of my tank top.

Here right inside the front door, David had elected to display a boldly lit black and white version of the photo to greet bar customers. In the photo, my boobs were at eye level and blown up bigger than Sanchez. I looked a lot like a pin-up from the old days, and the wrap looked a lot like a giant phallus. Mortified, I consciously crossed my arms over my cleavage.

"Oh, hell no!" I complained, shaking my head and feeling all of the blood in my body rise to my cheeks.

"Oh, yes." Dan replied sternly. "What is it you always say, sweetie? What sells?"

"Sex sells." Sanchez smiled at me in a way that seemed to say 'take what you dish out'.

All of the upholstered booths were white and patterned with red cherries, and there was all manner of vintage neon from places around Texas. A plethora of other cool rockabilly themed memorabilia was strategically scattered on all the walls. The bar itself looked a lot like a dimly lit diner counter. Chrome accents were a theme throughout, from the counter, to the clocks, to the bar stools. A giant vintage jukebox sat as a focal point in the far corner, obviously for show. The area centered around my distracting picture had seats that were mounted to the walls. They looked like the tailgates of old style red and white trucks, complete with functioning tail lights.

I was so enraptured by the eye candy, that I barely registered Sanchez's flash going off. When I looked over at him, I realized he'd just snapped a picture of me standing next to my obnoxious portrait.

"Sometimes I want to hurt you." I admitted, and he smirked in an evil manner.

"So *I* shouldn't have posted that to Facebook?" He blinked innocently, and continued snapping pictures all throughout the bar. David led us to the bar itself, showing us the giant margarita machines which were a must for the Texas heat and an oceanside setting. He'd had collectable glasses made, margarita style, shot glasses, and pilsners. Red and white t-shirts like my staff wore on the Austin trucks were for sale, as well as a black and white version. They hung behind glass above the hostess station, with a few new editions, including white ones screen printed with my boobalicious image.

"I'll be contractually obligated to give you 25% of the profit from the merchandise as well, of course." David explained.

"This is the coolest thing ever. I want one of the Molly shirts! Does it come in triple X?" Sanchez inquired, and I reached my hands out as if I were about to choke him.

"It's practically triple X all on its own." Dan giggled.

"So?" David asked, looking at me expectantly. He was waiting for an answer to the biggest question of all.

"Well, I guess I'd be a giant asshole if I said no now with all you've invested." I replied, scanning the room with a leery expression. As annoying as it was that he'd gone so far without my permission, the truth was I could see the place making money. Also, I really liked the idea of writing off countless family vacations to the beach as business trips. "I need to run this all by my lawyer."

"Of course." David nodded, but I could tell he was jumping up and down on the inside. If he knew who my lawyer was and what he specialized in, he might have been a lot less enthusiastic. "Can I bring the wife by tonight? Dan says that you and Sanchez are cooking. I thought it might be nice to show her what we've invested in."

"I'd love to meet her." I replied, trying not to panic that we'd just been put on the spot. Sanchez nodded in agreement. By the time we parted ways, we learned we were cooking for a party of fifteen. David wanted to bring his business partner from Madeline's and his wife, and a few employees who he planned to move from Madeline's to Wrapgasmic once he was ready to staff it. Dan said he'd reserved a party room in his building, and they were equipped with full kitchens. We made a couple of stops on the way back to The Emerald by the Sea to gather supplies for the wraps we agreed to make. Since some of our concoctions required hours of prep, we modified a couple of them and cut the rest from the evening's menu.

Dan busied himself preparing his secret recipe for Sangria

and Wine Spritzers to go along with our casual menu, while I went upstairs to shower and change. By the time the guests arrived, Sanchez and I were practically twiddling our thumbs. We were used to a much larger prep and a much more hurried crowd. Dan had outdone himself, setting a lovely table which included a colorful tablescape.

I did my best to play polite hostess, but exhaustion won out, and left me with no choice but to sit. People couldn't stop talking about the wraps, and everyone already had their favorite. We warned them that a few of our die hard best were still yet to come, like the Gangsta Wrap and The Sunday Brunch. Both took over 24 hours to prep. David informed me he'd already emailed me the proposal, and I immediately hopped onto my phone and forwarded it to Robbie.

"How do I get in on this project?" David's business partner, Emmanuel, asked, after polishing off the final bite of his Cranky Carpenter Wrap.

"Join me for a cigar?" David replied. He stood and led the older gentleman out onto the balcony overlooking the infinity pool. A few minutes later, I saw David wave Sanchez out onto the patio. A silent alarm triggered in the back of my mind, and I was about to go out after him when I felt a tight pain in my side. I inhaled sharply and after a few short seconds, it vanished. I relaxed, exhaling in relief.

"Was that a Braxton-Hicks?" David's wife asked, plopping down next to me with a long sip of sangria.

"Huh?" I asked, so tired I was having trouble focusing.

"You looked like you were having a contraction." She smiled, and her white straight smile contrasted beautifully with her mahogany skin. "You're probably a little dehydrated. Hold on, I'll get you a big glass of water."

"No...I'm okay." I replied, but she simply shook her long mane of cornrows and in seconds she returned with an ice cold bottle of water. She nodded at it encouragingly.

"Trust me. I've been through this a couple of times." She looked serene as she discussed childbirth, and I did as she demanded. She regaled me with stories of her two year old and six month old. She beamed when she heard I was having a boy and a girl, and proclaimed she was jealous, since both of hers were sons. Minutes later, I felt considerably better, though still ready for bed.

"I'm so sorry to be a poor hostess, but I really need to go lie down." I stood on wobbly legs, and she nodded. "Could you make my apologies to David and the others?"

"Of course. Don't give it a second thought." She replied.

Dan sent me off with his spare key and I staggered into the elevator. As soon as I stepped inside the apartment, I went directly into the bedroom and crawled clumsily onto my bed.

I fished in my purse for my phone and selected Joe's number.

"Hey, baby girl." The rumble of his deep voice left me breathless

"Hi. I know I said I wouldn't call…"I trailed off, feeling juvenile, reneging on my self-imposed exile in just over twenty-four hours.

"I'm glad you changed your mind. I miss you." His words were like a security blanket, and I felt all the tension of my day drain away. "I have a surprise for you."

"I bet you do." I felt my lip curl, and I sighed. "So he offered me a deal. Robbie just texted me that he's looking over the paperwork. It's going to make a lot of money, Joe. We should be alright if I can't work for a while."

"Just put any money worries right out of that pretty head of yours. I've got this." He assured me, and I closed my eyes, imagining him sitting on our bed. I wanted so badly to me home with him that I could taste it. "I looked at another house today."

"Yeah?" I yawned. "Black mold, or Brady Bunch wall paper?"

"This one's good." I could tell by the undercurrent in his tone that he was onto something. "It passed my tests. Just don't get your hopes up until you see it, alright?"

"Too late. I'm already redecorating it and I haven't seen it yet." I joked.

"Molly." His firm scolding tone sent a delicious shiver down my spine.

"I can't help it, Joe. I'm anxious for us to find our home."

"My home is wherever you are, little girl." He said it so easily, with no premeditation. I felt my heart skip a beat.

"I miss you." I whined, rolling onto my side and sitting up. I felt a strong kick from one of the babies. "The babies miss you too. We can't wait to come home."

Chapter

Twelve

Joe

Treats and Treaties

THE SECOND I saw Sanchez's car turn onto our street, I rushed down the stairs and out onto the sidewalk. Molly was typing on her phone, but she glanced out the passenger window as Sanchez parallel parked, and the smile that blossomed on her was a sight for sore eyes.

"I was just texting you." She laughed, as she swung her door open. I offered her my hand and helped her to her feet. Her arms came around me and I swear I could feel the thumping of tiny baby feet or fists against me as she held me tightly, but it was probably my imagination.

"Welcome home." I whispered, planting a quick kiss on her forehead and locking eyes with her. I heard Sanchez clear his throat, and quickly claimed Molly's bags from him. With a silent wave, he took off, obviously anxious to get home to his wife.

Molly was halfway up the stairs when I came in the door, but she'd paused and was holding her side.

"Molly?" I didn't like the alarm I heard resonate from my own vocal chords. She squared her shoulders without looking back at me and proceeded up to the landing.

"I've had a couple of contractions since we landed." She explained, as she turned the door knob and proceeded into the apartment. "It's totally normal. I just need to drink something and lie down for a little bit."

"You look worn out." I headed into the kitchen to get her some juice.

"I went to bed early last night, but when Robbie replied to my email it woke me up. Then I read it and couldn't get back to sleep right away. He wanted me to counter offer. He thinks David is low balling me for my ideas and that I should maintain controlling interest. I didn't put a dime into the place, Joe. But it is all based on my trucks...hell, it's even my image he's using for some of the t-shirts."

"I know." I replied, cocking an eyebrow at her. I held up the pic, which was my new screensaver on my phone. "Sanchez texted me the picture."

"Y'all are a bunch of bastards." She sighed, sipping the orange juice I'd handed her. I crossed to the couch and beckoning her to join me. She followed and handed me her glass so that she could lower herself down to sit beside me. It appeared to be a major production, and I was concerned when I thought about how many weeks she had left to go.

"So, did you counter offer like Robbie recommended?" I asked.

"I was planning to do it this morning, but just as I was about to drift off to sleep Sanchez knocked on my bedroom door."

I squinted. "Should I challenge him to a duel or something?"

She snorted and wrinkled her nose. "No, but that would be

some funny shit. He came to tell me that David and his business partner tried to poach him from me."

"What?" I sat up straight and she did the same.

"I know, right? Trying to steal my chef *and* assuming I'll agree to let him franchise my shit all in the same day? I was tempted to kill the whole deal on the spot."

I turned a bit in my seat to face her. "What did Sanchez say?"

"'Hell no' is what he said. David's partner, Emmanuel, wanted in on our deal. He said so right in front of me. David took him outside and suggested he open his own franchise in New Orleans. I guess the guy owns some commercial space there already. Then David called Dirty S. over and asked him if he'd be willing to go to New Orleans to run Emmanuel's kitchen."

"Wow." Stunned by the audacity of this guy, I frowned. "Wait. Why is this David guy franchising your business?"

"That's exactly what Sanchez said. I think he probably wanted to charge me a finder's fee or something."

I shook my head. "So? Did you rip David a new one?"

"No. I was livid, but mostly because this is a good idea and I didn't feel like I could just spit in their faces and tell them to piss off. You should see the place in Galveston, Joe. It's really cool...it's going to be a goldmine. So there I was, wide awake with my head pounding. Finally, I decided to send an email to Robbie laying out the entire situation. When I woke up this morning, Robbie called me to tell me that *he* would contact David directly. And he did. I guess Emmanuel was also on the conference call. Robbie gave them a counter presentation of how *we* thought things ought to be."

"Damn. I would have paid fat bank to listen in on *that* conversation." I smirked, and Molly grinned and nodded. "How did David respond?"

"He's running the paperwork by his lawyers. One of the

stipulations Robbie is insisting on is that all franchising pro-
posals will be directed to me and approved or denied by me. He
also bumped all of my proposed percentages and is demanding I
get 25% of all liquor profits. David hadn't planned to cut me in
on liquor at all. I guess Emmanuel already emailed Robbie that
he still wants in."

"Shit. Maybe I'll just be a stay at home dad. You can be my
sugar mama." The sound of her laughter tugged at my heart, and
she moved to lie down, resting her head on my leg. Her piercing
blue eyes gazed up into mine and I stroked her dark hair which
fell out over my lap like a long, silky veil.

"Promise to greet me with a martini and my slippers at the
door? When do I get to see this mystery house?" She asked,
reaching out for my hand which rested on her thigh. She moved
it under the hem of her thin sweater to her naval, and I felt small
tremors rumble beneath my palm. A gasp escaped me, and my
vision blurred. My heart felt like it was going to burst with joy as
my children moved beneath my hand. Molly stared at me for a
long moment, and her expression softened as she reached up to
brush my tears away. Her eyes never left mine, and her persistent
eye contact that had once unnerved me so deeply, now gave me
an overwhelming feeling of peace and rightness.

She gasped and her face transformed with shock. I was
about to panic when she shifted my hand around to her side, and
a much more noticeable kick reverberated from under her soft
flesh. She and I simply smiled at one another, as I stroked her
cheek with the knuckles of my free hand. The intense connection
I felt knotting between us felt more intimate…more solid than
anything I'd ever experienced. We waited out the series of tiny
sensations until I could no longer feel anything and our excitement leveled off.

"Anyway, as I was saying before we were so rudely interrupted…" She joked. "When do I get to see the house?"

"Tomorrow morning." I responded, noticing the swelling in

her fingers as I pulled her hand to my lips. It troubled me, as did the dark circles under her tired eyes. "If this house isn't the one, we really need to talk about plan B."

"Let's deal with that tomorrow. Right now, I just want to spend time with you." She slipped up into my arms and I gave her a lingering kiss. She tasted sweet and salty, and as her lips yielded to mine, I deepened the kiss into something more needful. Finally, I pulled away, ready to suggest that we relocate to the bedroom. Molly arched her back and yawned. I chuckled at her.

"You need a nap." I observed.

She gave me a sultry, challenging look that I doubted she'd be able to physically back up. "Are you gonna tuck me in?"

"I *love* this neighborhood." Molly sighed as I turned down the tree lined side street that led to our potential home.

"I know you do." I replied.

"The houses are all so interesting. And we're still close to the shop and to Cas's. This *is* the good school district, right?"

"Right." I rattled off the school ratings for elementary, middle school, and high school automatically. She nodded.

"It's so cold." Molly's teeth chattered as she put her mug of hot chocolate to her lips. She wore a sweat shirt of mine over one of my thermal shirts. She had on gloves, a hat, and a scarf with sweat pants. She pulled this heinous ensemble together with her God-awful furry boots. She looked like the world's cutest, cleanest hobo.

"I know, baby." I flipped the heater to max and shifted my eyes in her direction. Even in her ridiculous get-up, I had a hard time taking my eyes off of her.

The night before, she'd woken up from her nap rejuvenated,

and surprised me with the energy she was still able to harness. We'd spent the rest of our evening proving just how much we'd missed one another. In the heat of the moment, I'd forgotten to set my alarm. Luckily, Molly woke up early when the babies kicked her in the bladder. Naturally, she woke *me* up while prying herself out from under my arm. "Why didn't you wear a heavier coat?"

Her bottom lip jutted forward, and had I not been driving, I would have kissed it. "Neither of my winter coats will zip. I'm too fat."

"We're buying you a new coat today." I remarked, pulling the Mini Coop into the driveway of a charming 1920's Tudor style cottage. Molly's sharp intake of breath was my only clue that she approved of its curb appeal. She flung off her seatbelt and clambered out of the car, with her cocoa clasped firmly in her gloved hand.

Jeff must have been watching for us, because he met Molly at the bottom of the front steps.

"You must be Joe's lady friend." He stuck out his hand, but stared at Molly's crazy boots as if they might sprout fangs and jump him.

"I'm Molly." She smiled, and as his eyes traveled up from her atrocious boots to her face, I witnessed the moment that her sweet beauty won him over. Wearing the dumbfounded expression of a lovesick hound, he led her up to the brick vestibule and she complimented the tan stonework and his choice of lilac for the door.

"How adorable." She gushed. Jeff just nodded at her with that goofy grin of his.

For the rest of our tour, he seemed entranced by Molly. So much so that he nearly walked into a wall at one point. I had to clamp my lips together to stifle laughter.

Like father like son.

Molly asked hundreds of questions and listened intently to

every story he had about the house he'd grown up in. Jeff even had a couple of stories about Nick drawing on the walls with crayons. As he recited an oral history of the home, I watched Molly, trying to decipher her reaction. Her baby blues seemed to take in every nook and cranny. She traced her fingers admiringly over the original built ins, and as we passed lead glass windows in the dining room, she practically drooled. Stepping into the unfinished kitchen, she exclaimed happily when she realized it was set up for a gas stove. The blank canvas had her buzzing with ideas, and she moved to look out the back window.

"Look at that yard, Joe! It's the perfect size. Look at the covered patio. We could grill…and it has a garden! There's just enough grass to play on without having to mow an acre."

I nodded as I watched her step out onto the patio and continue her exhaustive tour. She wandered around the garden for a while, and I could almost see the wheels turning in that beautiful mind of hers.

"You are one lucky man, Joe." Jeff sighed as he hitched up his belt. I nodded without taking my eyes off of Molly, who was circling the shed. Finally, she wandered over to where we stood on the patio.

"Well, I suppose it's time to talk money, Jeff." She sighed regretfully, and he actually blushed, as if he were embarrassed that he'd have to charge her for his childhood home. Jeff admitted that he'd had the place appraised, but it wouldn't be one hundred percent accurate without the completed kitchen. He planned to ask ten thousand above the appraisal price, explaining that he'd designed a gourmet kitchen with a tin ceiling, but hadn't purchased the appliances. He thought it would take his crew a couple of days once he had the cupboards and countertops, and he'd be glad to show her the design. If she'd like to alter it or design her own from scratch, he'd work with that. He added that should we decide the house wasn't for us, he was hoping to list it with a realtor in a couple of weeks.

"That sounds amazing. I'd love to see your kitchen design. And the price seems more than reasonable." Molly glanced over at me. "What do you think, Joe?"

"I think you need a winter coat and I need to get some lunch into you before our babies starve." I replied, trying to send her the silent message that we needed a discussion. She nodded.

"Let me put your number in my phone, Jeff." Molly took her phone out and pulled off her right mitten with her teeth. She typed his number into her cell and waved goodbye to him as I practically dragged her to the car.

"I want this house." She stated the second the car doors were closed. "I want to offer him asking price."

"What the hell kind of negotiation tactic is that, little girl?" I scoffed. "He wants a quick profit. We should offer him the appraised price."

"Joe…" She had the tone of a woman trying to talk a lunatic down off a ledge. Her expression pleaded with me to be reasonable. "How many houses have we been through? We've never even been tempted to make an offer."

"We're saving him a lot of time and hassle. He wants to unload it fast and if we buy it, he won't have to pay a commission to a realtor." I reasoned.

Molly folded her arms across her chest. "The hard work's all done. We don't have time to do a restoration and I can customize the kitchen."

"What about the bedroom layout?" I asked, raising my eyebrows.

"What about it?" She shot back.

I kept my poker face, though I was toying with her. The house was worth every penny of the money. She leaned over the console and captured me with her sky blue gaze.

"Did you see the shower in the master bath? All those shower heads?" Her voice had a husky undertone, and I didn't need her to explain what she was thinking.

I threw open my door just as Jeff was trundling down the stairs. "Hey, Jeff. I think she's ready to see your ideas for the kitchen."

The cold weather had apparently kept the foodies indoors, because when I parked by the food truck to pick Molly up for our appointments, there wasn't a customer in sight. I leaned forward as I slogged into the frigid wind, I was glad that I'd insisted Molly buy the thicker, less fashionable coat in addition to the pretty red peacoat she 'just had to have' the week before. Taking care of my girl was priority number one.

So imagine my surprise when I hopped up the steps of the food truck to escape the biting cold and was greeted by the sight of Molly flat on her back on the floor. Her face was hidden under the sink, so I could only see her from the neck down. It seemed she was doing a little handy work.

"What the hell?" I blurted and I heard a thump and an 'ow'.

"Joe?" She called, and I moved forward, shooting both Stacy and the other employee a disapproving glare. They shrugged, staring at me like deer in headlights. Kneeling down beside her, I tried to get a better look under the sink.

Molly rubbed her forehead with a pained expression, and then went back to twisting her wrench. The spot where she'd rubbed her forehead has a red mark and a small smudge of dirt.

"Baby, what are you doin'?" I asked, and she paused mid motion, eyes wide and childlike.

"What does it look like?" She shot back, and went right back to work.

"It looks like you need to call a plumber." I grumbled and she tossed down her wrench and tried to sit up. I helped her and when her hand went to her side, I tried to act like I didn't notice.

"Joe, if I called a plumber, mechanic, electrician, or any other pro every time some small fix needed done on these trucks, I'd have to lay everyone off. It's part of the job. I have to be a jack of all trades."

"You need to let other people step up and help out." I replied, helping her to her feet.

She busied herself with washing her hands. "Sometimes if you want something done right, you have to do it yourself."

We headed over to Robbie's law office, where Molly signed the papers for the franchises in New Orleans and Galveston. Robbie's hard ass negotiation tactics had paid off, and he got Molly the deal he felt was appropriate for her talent and innovation. Molly held the pen midair and her pensive expression made me wonder if she had a last minute case of cold feet.

"I'm tempted to tell David to take down that damn mural of me or the deal is off." She clucked, her gaze shifting to me for my opinion.

I shook my head feeling a cunning grin twisting my lips. I leaned in close and she turned to look at me with heated curiosity.

"If that picture was of anyone but you, what would you say?" She blushed a little, but I could see the realization dawning in her eyes.

"I'd say it was fucking brilliant." She conceded, and I gently assisted her pen to its proper place on the dotted line. When the contracts were all signed, Molly looked both relieved and elated. She hugged my brother in law enthusiastically. Normally a very low key guy, Robbie took it all in stride.

"You, Robbie. *You* are the man." She said with a fierce, serious tone that would have sounded preposterous coming from anyone else.

"Thanks, Molly. It's a good deal. You did the right thing." He replied, glancing awkwardly at me. I shook his hand without a word. Robbie and I would never be tight, but the fact that he'd stepped up to the plate for Molly like he had seriously elevated his status in my book.

He led us down the hall to a junior partner that he'd recommended to handle our real estate transaction. It took us no time at all to go over the paperwork we needed to sign for the home purchase. We were all set to take possession on December fifteenth, which had our families in an uproar.

Everyone on both sides was stunned that we'd chosen to move in the middle of winter. Why this came as a surprise when we'd been house hunting like we had was beyond me. Tamryn's reaction annoyed the shit out of me, she seemed terribly put out that we were moving so close to the holidays. I wanted to shake the shit out of her.

Tamryn and Betty were conspiring to organize both families to come move us since Molly couldn't paint or lift anything. Molly's friends, Jay and Lisa, offered to pack up the apartment in exchange for pizza and beer. Molly freaked out at the mere mention of this and the first words out of her mouth had been "We need to collect our 'bedroom paraphernalia' and lock it in the fire safe."

"There won't be enough room in the fire safe for all of it. I'll buy a trunk." I had replied, though secretly I was already making plans to hire movers. Mason and Mac would be too busy helping me finish off the painting and remounting some of the wood work that needed a little TLC from me. I wanted to use their help where it would be most beneficial. The way my sister was acting, I wouldn't have asked for help if she was the last person on earth.

As Molly signed the papers, I noticed she was shaking and watched as she reached up and rub her temples.

"Hey." I whispered. "You don't look so good."

"Flattery will get you everywhere, big boy." She joked, but without much verve.

I reached to stroke her arm, not amused by her distraction

tactics. "Do you need some Tylenol?"

"I took some already." She admitted.

"I think it's time for you to slow down, little girl." I brushed a loose lock of her dark hair behind her ear and she frowned at me tiredly.

We headed over to the house to get a look at Jeff's progress on the kitchen. Molly had been totally blown away by his design, which I had to admit was pretty impressive. He used a lot of the original built in cabinets, but painted them white and made the lower bank glass front for a modern flair. He elected to use subway tile white backsplash for a vintage feel, and put up a silver tin ceiling to accentuate the stainless steel appliances. Molly mentioned substituting a double refrigerator, but Jeff said it would be too big for the space and I backed him up.

"You aren't catering out of the kitchen, little girl. You're just going to be cooking for us."

"Fine." She shot back. "But I want my six burner."

"The whole idea of home is for relaxation."

"Says the man who wanders off to carve when he's stressed. Cooking relaxes me, Joe."

Needless to say, her stove was ordered that day before we'd even made our formal offer

When we arrived at our new home, we found Nick there helping his father install the hood for Molly's stove. It caught us off guard, and he looked a little embarrassed to be caught out of his element. Molly hugged him and thanked him profusely for making her dream kitchen a reality. I was surprised and humbled, considering how many hours the kid was putting in at Good Wood.

"It's nothing, Joe. I'm glad to help." Nick replied, as I shook his hand.

"It's not nothin'. I won't forget this." I mumbled as Molly bantered happily with his dad.

As we headed back out to the truck, Molly nearly stumbled

on the stairs.

"Whoa!" I grabbed her and held her tight against me. My heart slammed into the wall of my chest as if it had sprouted wings and decided to take off.

"I'm sorry, baby." She groaned, looking exhausted and a little out of it.

"Molly, you're pushing yourself way too hard." I replied, and I cautiously helped her into the truck.

Forty five minutes later, Dr. Myers backed me up.

"Molly, your measurements look good, but your blood pressure has been elevated at the last two visits. Have you noticed any swelling in your feet, face, or hands?"

"No." Molly shook her head.

"Yes." I said simultaneously, and looked at her in disbelief. Molly whipped her head around in awkward surprise.

The doctor looked from me to her and arched an eyebrow. "Any headaches?"

"Yes." Molly confessed.

"How often?" Dr. Myers pressed on.

"About twice a day." Molly replied softly. It was my turn to whip my head in her direction. I knew she had headaches from time to time, but I had no idea they'd been so frequent.

The doctor pulled up her stool and fixed Molly with a weighty stare.

"I'm concerned." Dr. Myers started. "You're displaying classic symptoms of a condition known as pre-eclampsia."

The doctor explained at length how Molly needed to take it easy, reiterating almost everything I had told her. If she didn't, Dr. Myers promised she'd admit her to the hospital for mandatory bed rest. They reached a compromise that Molly could work for a maximum of four hours a day as long as she took plenty of breaks.

The entire time the doctor lectured her, Molly kept glancing at me, almost as if she suspected the doctor and I were in cahoots. Not that I wouldn't have slipped the doc some cash if I thought it would help slow her down. The doctor said the only cure for pre-eclampsia was delivery, and that it was way too early for that. By the end of the visit, my anxiety level was higher than it had been in a long time.

Our ride home was quiet as we both reflected on our day. We'd been home less than ten minutes when Molly's phone rang. Listening to her side of the conversation, I gathered that she intended to go back out to the truck. Snatching her phone out of her hand, I ignored her look of outrage and informed the caller, who I immediately learned was Carly, that they needed to work around the issue or close the truck for the night. I told her if they were really desperate, they needed to call Sanchez or Stacy for further instructions. Then I simply ended the call. Molly looked steamed. She turned, stormed into the bedroom, and slammed the door.

I immediately followed, and when I swung the door open, she hurled a flip flop at my head. I caught it in midair and dropped it to the ground.

"Okay, I know you're pissed..." I began, but she wasn't in the mood to listen.

"How fucking *dare* you take my phone from me? I'm a grown ass woman, Joe and—" Whatever else she planned to say was lost as I pulled her into a fierce kiss. She struggled for approximately three seconds and then she returned the kiss with equal passion. I finally decided to release her when I felt her tension melting and her body going limp. I guided her down to sit on the side of the bed as her knees buckled. She wore a confused and flustered expression.

"Baby girl," My voice was soft but firm, "I'm a little freaked out right now, so I need you to hush up and hear what I'm sayin'. You're my mate. You say you want me to be real with you, so here goes. Right now, you're ignoring your most important responsibility, which is to taking care of our babies.

I'm counting on you, Molly. I know you're pissed, but I'm not apologizing. You're wrong and I'm right. Now…when you're ready to talk to me like 'a grown ass women', I'll be on the couch."

A look of fear flashed across her face before being replaced by a wary expression of apprehension. I turned and left the room.

I did exactly what I said I would, and when she didn't immediately come out after me, I picked up her baby name book and started flipping through girls names. I got as far as the horrendous moniker Brandissa, when I heard the door creek open. Molly padded quietly into the room. She approached me slowly, like a little kid that knows they're about to get a spanking.

"What do you want to talk about?" I hated the way she was looking at me, like she was waiting for me to strike her, or say something awful.

I sat forward and reached out for her, enfolding her in my arms. I looked up into her eyes. "Molly, I love you."

She looked surprised, as if she expected me to say anything else. I pressed on, stunned that she still didn't get it. "That's something I've said to you a million times, but it still hasn't penetrated that thick skull of yours."

"You sure know how to sweet talk a girl." She said it in a playful way but I saw fear welling in her eyes.

"Darlin', I'm serious. It took a long time for me to understand that you actually think this is some sort of mercy date gone bad…That's crap and it is long past time you accepted that we are meant to be together." I waited, watching her face with unflinching courage. She tried to look away, but I gently cupped her face in my hands. When she finally spoke, her chin quivered and her voice trembled.

"Why do you want to be with me?" Her frank expression as she said it tore through me like drawer full of knives. Her unyielding eyes demanded an answer.

Refusing to back down, I blurted the truth as I saw it.

"You're everything I've ever wanted. I just didn't know it until I saw you again."

She seemed to search me for signs of dishonesty, and I'd be lying if I said it wasn't hard to bear that type of silent interrogation from her after all we'd been through. I steeled myself, remembering what Dr. Greene had reminded me of on more than one occasion. I wasn't the only one with demons that needed to be put to rest.

"But…is being with me making you better, or worse?" I went rigid; dismayed that she would even question this. "You're the first guy I ever loved. I know you think that's just silly bullshit, but it was a very big deal to me. It took me quite a while to even believe any of this was real."

She paused, as if trying to formulate what she'd say next, or maybe how to put it delicately. "I know things have been hard…that I'm difficult. I guess I still have my guard up, but I promise I'm not trying to cause problems between us. The truth is that I feel like you've been backed into a corner. You're stuck with me now, and I hate that. You aren't making me feel that way, but it's how I feel nevertheless. If we keep pushing things and just end up hating each other, I don't think I could—"

"Molly." I interrupted. She looked at the floor again, and I waited for her to meet my eyes. When she didn't, I pulled her onto my lap. A tiny gasp escaped her, and she seemed to be bracing for something, practically sick with apprehension. I smiled reassuringly. "I wish you could see yourself through my eyes. How damn beautiful you are both inside and out. That sad excuse for a life I'd scraped together before us wasn't living. Then one day you were there…and…damn, I just can't explain it. Hell, I can't even understand it myself sometimes. When you're with me, it's like being full of fire and light all at the same time."

I could see tears standing in her eyes, but she managed not to cry. Finally she nodded slowly.

"I just don't know what to do with that." She said, clearing her throat nervously. "I've never had someone treat me like you have."

"Molly." I said, and placed a delicate kiss on her lips. I looked into her tenacious eyes, and watched the courageous girl she'd once been struggling for control.

"I need to tell you some things…so you understand why I'm so messed up." She stated with a slow resigned exhale.

"I don't think you're messed up, Molly—" She shook her head and interrupted me.

"I *am* messed up." The detached way she stated it made my stomach knot. She moved off of my lap and onto the couch next to me, stroking her belly in a calming manner. "It's important for you to understand what the word marriage means to me. What it represents. I need you to get me, because if you do we have a fighting chance."

For the next couple of hours, I listened to her talk about her short and tumultuous marriage. There were times I wanted to tell her to stop…that I couldn't listen to anymore. The thought of this loving, generous girl in the situations she described made my head pound and my blood boil.

She didn't cry, she didn't raise her voice. As she talked, she looked mildly uncomfortable at times, and a little embarrassed. Her lack of response to her own hair-raising stories was almost more disturbing than the stories themselves. She started all the way back at her disastrous wedding night and described Draven's greatest hits, which escalated to him nearly drowning her. She confided that even after she left him, she hadn't felt comfortable taking a bath until she moved in with me. I allowed myself to see this confession as a small victory, but it was clear that we had a lot of damage to repair and huge obstacles to overcome.

When she finally fell silent, I reached for her and pulled her against me. What that monster had done to her made me wish…I put the anger out of my mind and concentrated on Molly. Gently stroking her hair, I breathed her in. "I'd given anything to go back and erase all of that."

"I wish you could, too." She murmured, nuzzling my neck. "Sometimes I feel like I used up all of my energy on him. Like he took the best of what I had to give. I wish I could have given that to you instead. I'm not sure what's left."

"Whatever you have, I want it. You deserved better, baby girl... and you deserve a lot better than a broken down wreck like me. But I promise I'll give you everything I've got."

"I really love you, Joe. With all my heart, I swear it." She replied, but she didn't look in my direction. She was staring at her hands which rested on her stomach. "I'm so sorry for the way things have played out between you and me. I'm sorry we didn't plan this pregnancy a couple of years down the line. I'm sorry that you didn't meet someone simpler, who's more equipped to ease your mind instead of being a pain in your ass. If I were a less selfish person, I'd have stayed away and let you find a girl like that. But I'm not..."

We sat in silence for several minutes and I held her close, waiting for the rapid beats of her pulse under my hand to slow.

"Little girl, you need to listen to me now. Really listen. Since the day you came back into my life, it's been upside down. I've changed everything to make room for you. Not because I felt obligated, but because I love you and can't imagine going back to a life without you."

"I don't want you to." She said without hesitation, and I leaned over, kissing her delicately.

"Good." I replied, and held up the book clasped in my hand. "I think I found a name for our daughter."

Chapter Thirteen

Molly

White Christmas

"CAN YOU NOT scratch up my walls, please?" I snapped at Mac.

My brothers were in the process of removing miscellaneous painting tools from the previous weekend's preparatory extravaganza.

The chaos in our new cottage inspired me to pop two Tylenol and it wasn't even noon. It was going to be a long day. The kids were outside digging up the garden and Joe and Graham had cluttered up my kitchen counters, while discussing which woodwork to mount in what room.

I heard another unfortunate noise from just around the corner where my brothers were barreling to and fro like bulls in a glass menagerie. "Be careful, dammit!"

"Bite me." Mac replied, brushing past me his arms full of

paint brushes and rollers. Mason shrugged as he followed Mac out of the dining room with a small ladder and an oversized can of paint. Now that it had completely dried, the melon color looked even more gorgeous. Joe and I had spent an hour arguing at The Home Depot about my paint choices, but in the end, I think he was pleased with the results. Besides, he got to pick the color for our master bedroom and the living room. I smirked when I thought about how sexy those arms of his looked hoisting those cans of paint into the back of his little old man truck. He seemed to enjoy letting me feel like I was getting my way.

"Molly, where do you want the baby swings?" My mother called, shuffling in the front door. I had to take a deep cleansing breath.

"How about in the nursery, ma?" I called, trying to curb my sarcasm. The sound of my brothers clattering around in the very next room set my teeth on edge.

"Do you think we should go ahead and assemble them? That way Joe doesn't have to later?" She hobbled in my direction, already holding one of the instruction manuals, "Think they'll both fit in that little room?'

"Mom! Let the movers unload everything before you set anything up, alright?" I heard the front door open and spotted Kelly and Francis who'd just wandered inside. Francis held four pizza boxes and Kelly had two cases of Coke.

"Over here, y'all!" I called, forcing a smile as I waved them in my direction. "Go on out onto the back patio. Joe has heaters set up and there are plenty of tables and seating.

I watched as Mac and Kelly practically ran face first into one another. Kelly leapt back as if Mac were a leper and practically bolted from the room. Francis frowned and looked from Mac to Kelly's retreating form before following her out of the room.

"Damn. It's a tad bit nippy in here, isn't it?" Mason commented. "I knew there was a cold front coming thru, but I thought that was supposed to be tonight."

"Shut up." Mac replied.

"Go after her, Mac. Or are you too chicken shit?" I chided. I brought my hand to my lips, as if my pointed pun hadn't been intentional. "Too soon?"

Mason nearly pissed himself laughing, but I felt bad when I saw the truly crestfallen expression on Mac's face.

"Molly." My mother's authoritative voice snapped my head in her direction. Old habits die hard, I suppose.

"What?"

"Should we unpack your bathroom?" I saw Granny appear over her shoulder.

"Fine, do whatever. Christ!" I blurted.

Mom threw up her hands and retreated toward the nursery. Two strong hands touched my shoulders and slid down to encircle me from behind.

"Havin' fun, baby?" Joe's low voice helped pull my irritation needle out of the red and I wiggled around to face him.

"I'm not sure I can take much more of this." I murmured into his ear as he held me close. Graham had led Francis and Kelly out to the back patio where they were plating up pizza. Thankfully, we were alone. Even so, I didn't want to take the chance of starting any drama so I kept my voice down.

"Then let me deal with it and you can go back to our place with Robin. She is about ready to kill Mason anyway. He got paint in her hair somehow. He said it was an accident, but she still wants blood." It was an attractive offer and I almost took him up on it. Then I had a mental image of my mother trying to decorate my house and I groaned.

The front door slammed and Robbie and Tamryn appeared brandishing beer, napkins, and paper plates. The loaded look that Joe and Tamryn exchanged was nothing short of acrid.

"The moving truck is here." Tamryn announced, striding past her brother into the kitchen to put the beer in my fantastic new fridge. "They need you to move your car."

I allowed myself another ten full seconds nuzzled up against Joe's stubble covered cheek. In a hushed tone, I whispered. "Be nice."

"Really, babe. You should go rest." He tilted my chin so that I had to look him in the eye.

"I can go move it for you." Robbie offered, clearly picking up what Joe was throwing down.

"I'll go move it. I need a little air" I replied, seeing the tension in Tamryn's shoulders from across the room. I pulled Joe closer for a moment and whispered in his ear. "I think you should talk to your sister."

His eyes shifted momentarily to Tamryn and he gave me an apprehensive nod. Heading outside, I trundled down the stairs and waved to the hulking moving men. "Sorry, I'm moving it now!"

I parked the Cooper down the street and as I climbed out, I looked up at the overcast sky. So far it hadn't rained, but I suspected we were on borrowed time. Hurrying back toward the house, I figured I'd have a slice of pizza with the nieces and nephews before I started supervising the movers.

"Hey, there!" A high pitched, nasal voice penetrated my thoughts. I stopped at the bottom of the steps, turning to look behind me. A svelte blonde with fairy tale princess hair waved cheerfully from the porch next door. I glanced down at my navy blue sweats and placed a hand on my messy ponytail. I tried very hard not to care that I looked a mess. I saw that she'd turned back to her door and gestured franticly to someone inside her house.

The man who stepped out after her had the weathered look of someone who spent a lot of time outside. His salt and pepper hair spoke of age that wasn't reflected in his muscled frame.

"Welcome to the neighborhood!" She called as they drew near. I realized that she was older than I first thought, probably in her late thirties at least, maybe older. "I'm Penny Madsen. This is my husband, Frank

"Hi, I'm Molly." I replied, smiling uncomfortably as I shook her hand. As I took her husband's hand the babies chose the moment to do some sort of acrobatic maneuver inside me. I gripped my mid-section, practically falling off my feet in surprise. Frank steadied me, his tanned forehead wrinkling with concern.

"Are you alright? Should I get your husband?" Penny cawed, in a voice that could shatter glass.

"I'm fine." I chuckled, trying to lighten the moment. I stood tall to show that I was stable and hopefully move the conversation along.

I heard a door smack shut behind me and saw Joe hurrying in our direction. Internally, I groaned, suspecting they'd talk at us twice as long if we were both here.

"What's wrong?" He demanded, wrapping a concerned arm around me and ignoring the couple from next door.

I gave him a reassuring grin. "The twins were having a fight and it got a little violent."

"Twins! Bless your heart!" Penny shrilly jumped head first into our conversation. She gave me an unsolicited hug, and turned her appraising eyes expectantly on Joe.

"This is Joe." I said as if it was an afterthought. "Joe…these are the Madsen's from next door."

Joe and Frank nodded at each other and shook hands, and I noticed Penny adding a flirty hair toss when she shook Joe's hand. We suffered through a few minutes of polite conversation. We quickly learned the couple had lived in the neighborhood for fifteen years and had two high school age daughters that were very active in extracurricular activities. Penny was a stay at home mom and Frank was some important guy in the oils business who traveled three weeks a month.

Ready for this grating cougar to stop undressing Joe with

her eyes, I explained that we had a house full of family and movers who no doubt needed guidance. Frank smiled empathetically,
and before I knew it, we'd accepted an invitation to dinner after
the insanity of the move had died down. With a silent wave, they
headed back toward their house. As I took the stairs, I watched
Frank give Penny a kiss and cross to the street. He climbed into a
large, newer pickup truck with an oil company logo on the side
and drove away.

"They seem friendly." Joe remarked, waiting for me at the
top of the stairs.

"That's an understatement." I whispered. "She kept staring
at my nose ring."

I noticed a backward glance from Penny. For a fleeting
moment I wondered if she'd heard me, and realized the idea was
ludicrous.

As we came in the front door, I heard Francis' voice coming
from the room we planned to use as an office.

"...now I don't know what happened, All I know is, she
seemed very excited that you were taking her out and she'd been
awfully quiet ever since."

"Francis, listen—"

"No, you listen." I'd heard Francis raise his voice before,
but this was different. Yes, he sounded angry, but with a desperate undertone that stopped me cold. "I let her down, Mac. I set
this precedent, and I can't take it back. If you don't really have
serious intentions, you ought to do the right thing and stay
away."

Joe turned to me, his mossy eyes flashing with concern and
apprehension. I held a finger up in front of my lips. I didn't really know where Francis planned to go with his little talk with my
brother, but it sounded like it was heartfelt. I didn't want to in-
trude on something that was none of my business. Joe seemed to
understand this and we tiptoed through the house and out the
back door to join the pizza party already in progress.

"I can't believe it's our first Christmas and I'm going to spend it without my husband." Stacy sighed glumly, and I felt my cheeks grow hot. Dr. Myers had advised me not to travel and I'd sent Sanchez out of town earlier in the week to train the staff for the Galveston location. He was supposed to leave directly from there and go to New Orleans to help set up the kitchen and interview staff.

Stacy had hinted, in her subtle as a billboard manner, that she wanted to go along. She could have been useful to them, but I needed her with me. We'd had a surprising amount of business considering the time of year. A senator had requested we special cater a committee meeting he was chairing at the state capitol building. He was one of our die hard regulars and he was obsessed with my lemon bars, which I named The Sour Puss. He also wanted me to make enough Cranky Carpenter Wraps for everyone there. I couldn't pass up the opportunity.

Then there was Stacy's bright idea to announce on Facebook and Twitter that we'd do special dessert orders for the holidays. I'd been baking mini Derby and cherry pies and some of my other signature desserts around the clock in the commercial kitchen I rented and the truck itself.

Thankfully, the other employees were all happy for the extra pre-holiday overtime since we'd taken a vote and decided to be closed from Christmas Eve until January second. Even Isaac and Stacy, who didn't cook, helped package the treats in festive wrapping. They also pulled orders off email and took them over the phone. We were in the final push, as it was December 23rd. The cold and damp weather was keeping most people away from the food truck. Almost everyone we'd seen all day had come to pick up their baked goods orders. Though a few got tempted and ordered lunches. After two, the crowd completely died and we'd let Carly go home early. We'd spent the next two hours cleaning the truck from top bottom for the long break and I could finally see the light at the end of the tunnel.

"Stacy I can't tell you how grateful I am for your help these past few days. I know you are bummed about not spending time with Dirty S. But hopefully my present will help cheer you up." I said, pulling out an envelope and handing it to her.

"Molly...you didn't need to..." She began, but gasped when she opened the envelope and saw a plane ticket and cash inside.

"Of course I did." I replied as she jumped up and down and hugged me. "If it weren't for y'all I'd be screwed."

Stacy fanned the envelope in front of her eyes as if it would stop the tears pooling there. "If it weren't for you, I'd still be working in that stupid sports bar in a push up bra having my ass grabbed 24/7."

"No you wouldn't. You're too smart and creative for that. David told me it was your idea about the café and the merchandise." Her eyes flew wide and she went pale. David admitted during a conference call that Stacy had been a resource for all of his market information about Wrapgasmic. Many of the great features about the Galveston location had actually been her idea, including the t-shirts and merchandise. Fortunately, he'd let this information slip before we signed the contracts and I was able to have Robbie make one final change.

I smiled to myself when I thought about the other surprise I had in store for Stacy and Sanchez. They'd learn about it in an email that would be delivered to them Christmas morning. I'd arranged that three percent of everything I made from Galveston and New Orleans to be deposited into their account. Three seemed like the perfect number, with us being the three musketeers and all.

"You're not mad, are you?" She said, twirling a strand of hair tightly around her finger. "Molly, I swear I didn't know he was already building the place, I just told him about the profit margin difference between the truck with and without the bar and mentioned how cool it would be to sell merchandise, since people are always asking if they can buy our shirts. Then he asked to take me to dinner the night of the 5-K so he could pick my brain. It seemed a little weird, but I learned in my online business class it's better to beg forgiveness than ask permission. When he started asking me about who did your website and to talk him through our Twitter and Facebook, I started to get nervous."

I nodded, long over any feelings of betrayal that may have flickered at the time. I knew Stacy always had my interests at heart as well as her own. It wasn't her fault that David had actually put the ideas into place before getting my okay. I suppose he had the same lesson she had in business class.

Stacy glanced at the plane ticket and squealed. "Oh my God! I'm meeting him in New Orleans tomorrow! Christmas Eve in the French Quarter. That's so romantic! Does he know I'm coming?"

"Nope" I took a sip of my sweet tea, and sighed happily. It was such a refreshing change to have a slow day. "That's *his* Christmas present. They're putting him up in a four star hotel, so it should be really nice. I stuck a copy of his itinerary in there so you can surprise him at the hotel."

"I can't wait. I have to go home and pack! What's this money for?" She asked, clearly shocked and delighted.

I shrugged. "Buy something naughty to wear for him."

She tilted her head to the side and the tears she'd been staving off started up. "Molly, I don't know what to say."

"Say you'll lock up the truck so I can get home to Joe. He promised we'd take a break from hanging pictures and organizing the damn house. Tonight, I just want to drink cocoa and watch 'It's a Wonderful Life.'"

As I drove down the surprisingly vacant streets, I allowed

the full weight of work to drop away. What landed in its place was the very real fact that it was our anniversary. One year ago today my ex-husband's crazy ass was hauled off to jail and Joe asked me to move in with him. It seemed impossible to believe that it had been so long ago, but as I did the math and broke it down by milestones it added up. You know that they say. "Life is what's happens while you're busy making plans."

I pulled into the driveway of the house and saw Joe's truck parked out front on the street. As I turned off the ignition, Joe came out the front door and shot me a naughty look.

"Hey there little girl. You're home a little earlier than I thought. Want to go take a nap with me?" The exaggerated wink he gave me made me laugh even as his words sent a rush through my body. Letting him help me out of the car, I pulled him against me, reveling in the feeling of holding him.

"Mmmmm," I groaned in pleasure. "You have no idea how good it feels to be home in your arms." Taking him by the hand, I led him inside where it was warm. Sitting on the couch, I admired how cool it looked settled in its spot in our new yellow living room. He pulled my boots off and spent twenty minutes rubbing my feet and listening to me prattle on about my day. He chimed in that the shop was running like a well-tuned machine, and that Nick and Mac had somehow developed a decent working relationship. When I told him about Stacy's reaction to the present, he got quiet. For a minute I thought he was going to lecture me for throwing money away.

"Baby," he murmured. "You're so good to the people around you. Sometimes I wonder how I ever got so lucky."

I was about to object and counter that I was the lucky one when he twisted his thumb under the arch of my foot. His technique evoked a moan of pure pleasure from me.

"Mostly, I use you for getting things off tall shelves. And for foot rubs. And for other dirty things." He responded with a seductive smile and ran his hands further up my legs. His mouth hungrily found mine, and the foot rub quickly dissolved into a completely different kind of rubbing. Once again, Carpenter Joe demonstrated how talented his hands were, amongst other things. I did my best to show my appreciation, and to reciprocate.

After we'd redressed and regrouped, we cuddled under a blanket and discussed our apprehension about the upcoming holiday festivities. Tamryn had graciously offered her house for Christmas dinner. For *everyone*...both the Hildebrandts *and* the Jensens. She was clear that she wanted a Mulligan for Thanksgiving. Surprisingly, everyone agreed to come. As usual, she was having it catered, so I was only on the hook for a few desserts. I cheated and had the staff make a few more than we needed for our orders, so I could truly relax.

"What sounds good for dinner, Joe?" I ran through my mental inventory, revisiting what we had in the pantry and calculating a couple of different things I could make us. Not that I was looking forward to getting up off the couch. Joe slid from beneath me, ignoring my cry of protest.

"Don't you worry about dinner. I got it covered." I heaved a sigh of relief and snuggled back down into the couch. I heard him in the other room flipping through the binder and then talking on the phone.

Grabbing the remote, I flipped through the channels looking for a good holiday show to watch and settled on 'A Charlie Brown Christmas'. Joe came back in a few minutes later and hunkered down in front of me.

"I have to go outside and take care of a few things in the yard. You stay in here and relax for a bit, okay?" I stuck my lip out and shook my head, trying to pull him back onto the couch with me.

"No, come back and snuggle with me. You promised." Kissing my forehead he easily resisted the force I exerted on him.

"I know, but first I need to clean up a few things outside so that the delivery guy doesn't break his neck on the way up the walk. Plus, I want to make sure everything out there is put away so we can focus on relaxing. Sound like a plan?"

"I suppose. So what did you order for dinner?" He shook his head at me and smiled.

"I'm not telling. You'll just have to wait and see. Now do you need anything before I head outside? I want you to stay on this couch and rest." I had him fetch me some cocoa in my favorite mug and then settled down to watch the rest of the show. My tired eyes swept the room and I smiled. Joe had picked the ideal paint color, and the mix of our furniture looked perfect together in it. We'd picked out a few new mission style pieces, and the house already felt homier than anyplace I'd lived since leaving my parent's house. Soon, I was drifting pleasantly into dreamland beneath the cozy throw.

I woke up to the wonderful scent of smoked meat filling the room. Joe rounded the couch and brought me a plate of mouthwatering food. He'd outdone himself again, reading my mind and ordering exactly what I was in the mood for. Pork ribs from The Salt Lick and Dark Chocolate with Olive Oil and Sea Salt ice cream from his new favorite dessert place, Lick.

"I'm noticing a theme tonight." I remarked, purposely sucking some of the sauce off my fingertips. "Lots of *licking*."

Joe's eyes lit up and he leaned in for a delicate kiss with just the slightest hint of tongue. We chatted more about how to organize the nursery as we enjoyed our delicious dinner. I looked over at my wonderful man with his fantastic lips covered in barbeque and I reveled in how right the moment felt.

After Joe cleared the plates, he put in the movie. Grabbing the remote, he turned it up almost too loud. Snuggling under the covers with me, he resisted my efforts to unzip his jeans, as I innocently suggested it would make him feel more comfortable. He continued to block my passes throughout the impossibly long movie, and I was starting to get a complex by the time it ended. I saw him texting a couple of times on his phone and felt a little defeated. Was I finally too fat for him? Before I could find a way to broach the subject he pulled me to my feet.

"Let's go out back and look at the stars."

Grabbing my new winter coat off the rack, he helped me into it. He was so careful with me, so gentle, I felt foolish for even questioning how much he cared for me. Pulling on his jacket, he took me by the hand and led me toward the back door. Just before we got to the threshold, he paused and his eyes searched my face. Then he opened the door and whisked me outside. As soon as we stepped onto the patio, I froze in absolute shock with my eyes locked on the ground. The white, frosty ground.

All around the yard were piles and piles of white snow. I gaped around in disbelief. The trees and bushes were flocked in white. Our entire back yard was awash in drifts of the pure white powder. Turning to Joe in disbelief, I tried to find the words.

"Snow? How...?" I'll admit it wasn't the most eloquent use of the English language, but I'd dreamed of a white Christmas for as long as I could remember. Even during the decade that I lived in the Pacific Northwest, I'd never had one. Draven hated the snow, and refused to take me to the mountains. Now here I was, living my dream smack dab in the middle of Texas. I was struck speechless.

Joe smiled at my reaction, his eyes twinkling with obvious joy. Taking my hand, he carefully led me over to the bench in the middle of the yard and helped me sit. Taking a seat beside me on the bench, he took both my hands and turned to look into my eyes.

"Molly...do you really like it?"

I looked at him in confusion and then gestured around the back yard. "Wait...you mean...you did this?"

Joe laughed and I felt my heart skip a beat. It was *the* laugh. The one that I remembered from when we were younger.

The laugh of a carefree and happy man.

I felt a stinging sensation in my eyes.

"Yeah, I did. Or I should say I know a guy who knows a guy. I realize it isn't the same as being somewhere with real winter..." He looked so nervous at that moment that I almost couldn't stand it.

"It's amazing! It's even more beautiful than I imagined." The snow glistened in the moonlight like thousands of stars. Joe seemed to exhale a long sigh of relief.

"I'm glad that you like it, baby." He wrapped his arm around me and I rested my head against his shoulder. The absolute wonderment I felt at his romantic gesture left me completely at a loss for words. Pure, raw love overwhelmed me, and I clung to him as we sat in silence enjoying the winter wonderland around us.

Suddenly, Joe turned to me and took my hand again. "Mac told me a while back that you always wanted a white Christmas. I knew right then that I wanted to give it to you, to take you somewhere where we could go and sit by a fire and look out at the mountains. But with the babies coming, I knew it wasn't the right time to drag you to Vale. I know this isn't The Rockies, but it was the best I could do."

I opened my mouth to tell him that this was the most wonderful thing anyone had ever done for me, but he continued before I could get a word out. "I will always give you my best, Molly. We've never been a traditional couple, God knows we've taken a very different path, and it's been a rough one at times. But I think it made me appreciate you even more, and I realize now that wouldn't have it any other way. You bursting back into my life is the best thing that has ever happened to me. You mean so much more to me than I could ever put into words."

Slipping down to the ground, he knelt on one knee and pulled a box from his coat. My heart thudded forcefully as he opened it. Inside was a gorgeous antique style ring that took what little breath I had away.

"Molly, you are the part of me that I have always been missing. Being with you makes every minute of my life better. So I'm asking you now, and I'll keep asking you until you tell me to go the hell away. Will you do me the great honor of becoming my wife?"

As he poured out his heart to me, I felt my blood collect in my cheeks. I searched his emerald eyes, so sincere…so eager…and totally fearless. He was the most beautiful sight I'd ever seen, and him down on one knee in front of me was all of my secret dreams come true. I nodded, trying to swallow the giant frog in my throat that seemed hell bent on preventing speech.

"Is that a yes?" He smiled, his eyes darting back and forth as he seemed to try to see both of mine at the same time.

"Yes." I snuffled, throwing my arms around his neck. Warm tears streamed down my cool cheeks. I pulled back to search his eyes, verifying that this was really happening. He locked his determined gaze with mine, and then my lips were on his. His hands were entangled in my hair, and we kissed until I no longer felt the cold. Finally, Joe pulled me away and picked up the ring he'd dropped in our fit of passion. He pulled it out of the box and taking my hand his slid it onto my finger.

I was crushed when it wouldn't go on past my knuckle.

"Shit." I felt my face fall, but he just smiled at me tenderly.

"You're fingers are just swollen. It'll fit you after." He kissed me on the tip of my nose and slid the ring onto my pinky.

CHAPTER Fourteen

Joe

Full Circle

THE COLD FEBRUARY wind rattled the windows, startling me awake. Spooned up against Molly, I'd instinctively draped a protective arm over her in my sleep, my hand resting on her belly. I'd been dreaming again, but instead of my typical nightmares, I'd dreamed about holding our babies and rocking them to sleep. As if she'd sensed I was awake, she tried to roll over. I edged backward, and made room for her to roll onto her back.

"I'm glad you took out that naval piercing on New Year's." I teased, pushing on her outie bellybutton as if it were a squeaky toy. She batted my fingers away with a tired smile, wrinkling her button nose. "One of those two might have come out with a pierced lip or something."

"It was really starting to pinch." She replied, and I noticed her eyes looked a little puffier than usual.

Pushing my worry aside, I leaned down to her naval as if it was a microphone. I spoke in my sternest 'daddy' voice. "Mornin' Eva, mornin' Logan. You two getting along in there?"

While most couples were out at swanky restaurants or showing off new lingerie on Valentine's Day, we'd spent our evening deciding on names for our children. It didn't take us long. I'd picked three first and middle name combinations for our daughter and she picked three for our son, we traded note-books, and whichever name the other liked best was the one that would be on their birth certificates. We ended up with Eva Rose and Logan Alexander, but we agreed not to tell anyone else until they were born. That way if someone didn't like the names they'd look like an asshole saying anything about it out loud.

At this point in her pregnancy, I didn't even have to lay a hand on her to tell the twins were moving. She was in her thirty-fifth week, and I could see them shift under her skin like some-thing out of a science fiction movie. Though we still had over a month to go, she was much bigger than Jess had ever been.

Molly cried at the last visit when the nurse informed her she'd gained forty-five pounds. I tried to tell her she should be glad, since the doctor had insisted she gain a minimum of thirty-seven, but she shot me a homicidal look. It was very good news, considering she'd had such trouble keeping anything down in the beginning

I marveled every time we had an ultrasound. Based on the size of the twins, it wasn't a surprise Molly was so uncomforta-ble all the time. Jack had been 7 pounds 6 ounces when he was born at eight months, and Dr. Myers was projecting that Logan was already nearly six pounds and Eva was about five. Molly had somehow continued to work part time for the entire month of January and most of February. Just last week I'd finally con-vinced her to quit working all together.

Her headaches were just too frequent and her blood pressure had crept up higher each time we'd been in. At the last visit, they'd found protein in her urine, and Dr. Myers sent her for a non-stress test. Her labs work looked good and the non-stress test looked okay but they sent us home with a jug to collect her urine for twenty-four hours. Molly joked about how glamorous she felt and her remark about the bright jug by the toilet was something snarky about orange being the new black. The babies seemed fine, but the doctor gave Molly a steroid shot to help the babies' lungs to develop. She also put her on a blood pressure pill to manage her elevated pressure, which I religiously reminded her to take every day. Molly called it nagging.

I pressed the doctor on what we needed to do, but Dr. Myers seemed to be under the impression that her preeclampsia was mild. She said if Molly was serious about taking it easy, she wouldn't have to be hospitalized or need bed rest.

Her twenty four hours urine result came back borderline, so the doctor said she could continue to stay at home. She would repeat the tests in a couple of day at her next visit. The doc was recommending modified bed rest just to be safe. Only up to eat, shower and use the restroom. It was driving Molly crazy.

The cherry on top at our latest visit was, when the doctor announced that Molly was already two centimeters dilated. Dr. Myers recommended we stop having intercourse. Not surprising, this added to her mood. Baby girl was especially grumpy.

"Do I have to get out of bed today?" Molly asked with a groan, and I assumed the question was rhetorical.

"You've got about ten women and two gays coming over to shower you with presents today, so rise and shine. At least they're having it here. You just have to get dressed and go look pretty. They'll do everything else."

'How am I supposed to look pretty when I'm the size of the Michelin Man? It's too damn early." She grumbled hissing at the sun like a vampire. She tried to sit up and sort of collapsed on the bed like a slug. "Can you hand me my glasses?"

I'd had a wonderful time harassing her about the thick black glasses. We'd been together for over a year and I'd never seen her in them once. She normally wore contacts, but since her vision had been a little blurry, the eye doctor suggested a slightly stronger prescription. He said the change wasn't uncommon in pregnancy, and should resolve itself after she delivered. She made a lovely nerd, and I called her 'four eyes' as often as I could work it into casual conversation.

I was toasting bagels when I heard her coming down the hall in flip flops.

"Flip flops? It's barely March, little girl. You're toes are gonna freeze right off."

"I can't fit my feet in anythin' else." She said, still sounding unusually drowsy. 'I've got cankles."

I chuckled at her and handed her the bottle of blood pressure pills. She took one and the glass of juice I handed her, I noticed her hands were puffy and white when she gripped the glass, and when I caught a glimpse of her feet, I nearly dropped the pill bottle.

"Baby…I said, looking down at her feet that seemed to have almost doubled in size. 'I think we need to go to the doctor."

"No…I just need to put my feet up." She replied, hoisting her legs onto the chair next to me. I took off her flip flips and snagged her slippers from the closet. They fit on her ballooned feet, but barely.

"Warmer?" I asked.

She nodded, her big blue eyes shining with gratitude. "Yes. Thanks, baby."

A few hours later when Betty turned up on my doorstep, I was still concerned about leaving. But once she arrived, a deluge of estrogen hit my house and I started to feel unwelcome. Or overly welcome, when Molly's slutty cousins arrived.

When Dan turned up with no less than seven gift bags, he started trading snarky barbs with Molly's high school friend Jay. Evidently they were vying for Queen of the Hill, but this development seemed to amuse Molly, so I figured it was a good time to make myself scarce. Besides, Robin was a nurse and most of these women had given birth more than once. Molly would be in good hands with the collection of hens in the house, I assured myself.

Against my better judgment, I'd let Mac and Mason talk me into going out. Considering our last attempt at a field trip, you'd think I'd have pondered this suggestion a bit more carefully. I went into the kitchen to retrieve my keys, and Betty and Granny were putting chocolate bars into diapers and heating them in the microwave. It was the last thing I expected to see, and I almost forgot what I'd gone into the kitchen for in the first place. Returning to Molly, who was propped up on the couch in the living room, I told her what I'd seen.

"Take me with you!" she whispered urgently, clutching her abdomen near her ribs on the right.

"What's wrong?" I frowned.

"One of the babies is kicking me in the ribs." She replied.

"Maybe I should just have them all go home," I whispered back. "We could go back to bed."

Tamryn interrupted us by swatting me on the shoulder. "Get your butt out the door, Joe. We girls need some time without you menfolk around."

"You heard her, Joe." Molly's sassy friend Lisa agreed, handing a beer to each of the slut sisters.

Mason came over to where I stood beside the couch and steered me out the door. We ran face first into the neighbor lady, who held a giant basket that looked like it had been hosed down with pink and blue.

"Hello, Joe." She drawled, sounding like a phone sex operator.

"Hi." I blinked at her over the top greeting, and held the door for her. She ducked under my arm, brushing herself against me unnecessarily.

"What was that?" Mason asked, his eyes the size of saucers.

"Neighbor."

"This is going to be one of those kinky key party neighbor-hoods." Mac snorted, but I saw the amusement vanish from his face when he saw Kelly walking up the street with a giant silver box in her arms. She peered over the green bow at him with a reluctant smile.

"Hi." He said, suddenly looking a lot less cocky.

"Hello, Malcolm." She replied with a slight smile curling the edge of her mouth, but her stride never faltered.

Both Mason and I looked at one another bemused.

"Shut your faces." Mac preemptively interjected before we could even being.

We jumped in a cab and were halfway across town before I realized I'd forgotten to ask Robin to keep an eye on Molly for me. I tried to call her, and a few of the others, but went straight to voicemail. I shrugged, and slipped my phone into my pocket.

The boys had decided that we should hit the Alamo Draft House for a reshowing of Road House. Afterward we planned to head over to Legends Sports Bar to watch a game and grab a beer. It was as good a place as any to hang until the women left my house. We were just at the part where Caretaker, Sam El-liot's character, is found dead when my phone went crazy. I'd put it on vibrate rather than turning it all the way off.

At first, I thought the damn thing was electrocuting me. It was buzzing so damn fast. I jumped up, bumping the table with my knee and spilling beer all over Mac. Pushing my way past several people, I ran out of the theatre, I pulled my phone out and answered it.

"Joe! It's Tamryn! Molly's hurt. She had a seizure. We called an ambulance and they're on their way." My normally unflappable sister sounded like she was on the edge of tears. Cold swept through me like someone had opened a door to the artic inside my heart.

"What happened?" The words barely slipped past the growing lump swelling in my throat.

"I don't know. She was talking and laughing one minute and the next..." It was less what she said and the way her voice caught as she said it. I could hear Jamie sobbing in the background.

"Oh my God, she's bleeding." She wailed, and for a moment I was sure my heart screeched to a dead halt. Then I heard Granny's distinct voice barking orders.

"I'm on my way." Mac and Mason stood next to me with looks of alarm. I ignored them as Tamryn spoke again.

"Joe, the ambulance is here." I heard the noise level drop and assume she had covered the phone with her hand. My stomach was twisting in knots and the popcorn I had eaten was threatening to come back up all at once. A moment later she came back on the line. She told me the hospital they were headed to and hung up.

"Joe, what is it?" Mason looked as pale as a ghost. Mac had a queasy expression that I found far too relatable.

"Molly. She had a seizure. I have to get to the hospital." Mac held up his phone and I saw the app for hailing a cab up.

"One's pulling up outside. Let's go." Mac took the lead with Mason trailing along behind me. The trip to the hospital was a blur. Mason was texting with Robin, who was in the ambulance with Molly.

"She hit her head on the coffee table when she seized, so there was some bleeding." Mason relayed. The boys were jabbering a thousand miles a minute, but I didn't hear much of what they said.

"She's going to be alright." I murmured, and several minutes later I realized I'd been chanting it like a mantra. Mason had fallen into a stoic silence and Mac looked like he might cry. I felt the cold skeletal hands of death wrap around my heart.

Again.

Pulling up to the hospital was like reliving a nightmare. UMC at Breckinridge was the same hospital that Jessica had been brought to after the accident. It wasn't fair to think it, but the place had cost me both her and Jack. Logically, I knew this was a major oversimplification, but emotionally none of that mattered. Frigid chills ran up and down my spine that had nothing to do with the temperature outside. Stepping out of the cab, I focused on putting one foot in front of the other. Inside my head, the demon, composed of pure rage and fear threatened to escape. The bars of his cage were bent and tattered, barely keeping terror from consuming me.

I'm not sure how I got inside to the waiting area. A matronly nurse behind the counter advised us that Molly had just arrived. She took me aside and began asking me questions. Gibbering laughter rang inside my head as the insane monster rattled the last remaining bars but Betty joined us a moment later and somehow we managed to tell the nurse everything she wanted to know. Mason came over as she finished and led me back to the waiting area.

"Robin's with her, Joe." He explained, trying to engage me in conversation. "She said that Molly had another seizure on the way here and that the paramedics gave her anti-seizure medication. Molly's doctor is on her way."

When I entered the waiting room, I saw Tamryn sitting in the exact chair she'd camped in when we went through this with Jess. My mind officially tripped over itself, and I actually froze in place. Dan and Granny sat on each side of Tamryn, and all three hurried to stand when they saw me. I felt a tug on my sleeve and saw Betty had followed me into the waiting area.

"Honey." Betty sniffed, and I allowed her to embrace me, understanding even in my wrecked state of mind that this must be as traumatizing for her as it was for me.

"What…" I started, not sure exactly what I planned to ask.

"We were passing around Dan's cute little sailor suit and Molly had just come back from using the restroom. She kept on rubbing her right side." Tamryn said in a rush.

"She asked me for some Tylenol for a little headache right after y'all left." Dan added, looking shell-shocked. "She was laughing and having a good time, so I thought she must have been feeling better."

"Do you need me to call your doctor?" Tamryn asked, her eyes locking onto mine like laser sights.'

"She's on her way." I replied, sounding as hollow and lost as I felt.

Tamryn reached up and put her hands on my shoulders. "Not Molly's doctor, JoJo. *Yours.*"

I collapsed into a chair, unable to deal with the onslaught. Leaning forward, I put my head in my hands and tried to pull myself together. For several minutes I took slow deep breaths, trying to focus and telling myself we were in the right place and that things could have been so much worse. Thank goodness Molly quit working.

"Can you imagine if she'd been working with those sharp knives?" Granny blurted.

"Or in the shower? Or walking down a flight of stairs?" Dan agreed. My eyes cutover at them, and though I knew they were trying to help, I wanted to pick up a chair and throw it at them. It must have shown on my face, because Tamryn suggested they go get a cup of coffee and call Lisa and Jay who were at the house with all the kids.

I was just starting to get the beast back in the box when there was a ruckus at the nurse's station that drew my attention. Looking up, I saw a young man in a white coat making his way toward me. A moment of pure, unadulterated panic nearly consumed me.

"Mr. Jensen? I'm Dr. Franklin. I need to talk to you. Can you come with me please?" Rising from my seat I looked around and met Tamryn's eyes. She started toward me and I let her take my arm as I trailed leadenly behind the doctor. He led us through a door and motioned us to chairs. "I'm sorry, miss but who are you?"

"I'm his sister. Doctor, can you tell us what's going on?" The man looked at me and I nodded.

"Mr. Jensen, your fiancé has suffered several seizures. We've given her some medication to stop them, and it seems to have worked for the time being." Suddenly a nurse came charging into the room.

"Dr. Myers is here." She interrupted.

"Excuse me for moment." Dr. Franklin said, darting off after the nurse.

"What the hell?' Tamryn grumbled and I simply stood rooted to the spot wondering what the hell myself. Moments later Dr. Myers burst out of the security doors and strutted in my direction. Her younger male colleague trailed behind.

"Joe. Sorry I took so long but I wanted to review the situation in person. Molly's seizures are a game changer. The plan was to induce her, but the position of your daughter has complicated the issue. The baby girl is currently breech and she's the one closest to the birth canal. Molly's still a little confused, which is completely normal following a seizure. I need your permission to proceed with an emergency C-section." Tamryn gasped next to me and squeezed my hand hard enough to crush bones. I felt the room slipping away and concentrated on the pressure of her hand. The universe was tormenting me all over again, but I didn't have time to feel sorry for myself.

"But t…the babies aren't due for another four weeks." I stammered.

Dr. Franklin nodded reassuringly and Dr. Myers shook her head.

"That's true, unfortunately the seizures take us from pre-eclampsia to eclampsia. The only cure is delivery. Both babies are in good shape at the moment and they are nearly full term. All three of them are in more danger at this point if we don't deliver."

My vision narrowed to tunnels of diminishing light and I struggled to breathe. The doctors both reached out for me. Dr. Myers had me sit and place my head down between my knees taking deep breaths. After several moments, I was able to sit upright again.

"What do you need me to do?" The voice that rasped out of my throat was that of an old man. Tamryn struggled to hold back tears, her breath coming in ragged gasps.

"We need your permission to operate. A NICU team is standing by for each of the babies. We have some of the most skilled doctors and nurses in the state." The surreal nature of the conversation was almost laughable.

"And there are no other options?" Molly would want me to be sure. She'd talked at length about how she'd fight to keep the babies from being born premature. It was her main motivation when she quit working. I already knew the answer. They wouldn't have dragged me into a private room to talk to me if there was.

"I'm afraid not, Joe. And the longer we wait the more complicated this will be. I'm afraid I need an answer now."

The sun shone down out of a clear blue sky that made the late morning dew sparkle on the deep green grass. I stepped out of the truck and grabbed the flowers from the seat. Turning I let my feet lead me down the familiar path that wound through the graveyard. Each step reminded me of how unfair life was, how none of us ever had a warning when life ended for us. There was no expiration date stamped on the bottom of our feet. How much simpler everything would be if there was.

The gravel had been replaced on the path and the footing was questionable in areas. I slowed my pace as I got closer to my destination. Frankly, this wasn't where I wanted to be right now. Pain and misery permeated the place for me like rot and termites in wood. With a heavy heart, I came to a stop in front of Jessica and Jack's headstones. The ground to the left was mounded with fresh earth, the sight of it pierced me with sorrow. Sinking down on my haunches in front of the gravestones I placed a hand on each of them.

"Hey Jess, hey Jack. Sorry, it's been a while, I've been dealing with a lot lately."

Taking the flowers I separated them into two bundles and lay one before each headstone.

"The space next to you guys is full now. Jess, I know the plan was to have me planted there beside you when I died, but things have changed…I hope you guys don't mind the new neighbor. I sold the plot to a really nice family. If I'm going to have a chance of rejoining the living I have to let go." I sat for a few minutes, talking to them, explaining about my new family and how much they needed me. After my confession, I rose and retraced my steps to the truck. It felt good…lighter having visited them.

By the time I got back into the truck, I felt like another chunk of weight had dropped away. The last few weeks had been filled with a mind bending number of twists and turns, and I was ready for some peace.

That day at the hospital I'd truly thought I was going to lose my mind. Facing such similar choices with Molly that I had with Jess had driven me to the edge of my sanity. Dr. Greene had arrived shortly after my panic attack began in Dr. Franklin's office. If Tamryn had not had the foresight to call him, I'm not sure what I would have done.

He was able to help me through in his usual heavy handed fashion.

"I don't think I can make the call." I shook my head.

"Joe. This is a no-brainer." Dr. Green's voice was stern and loud. "What would Molly do?"

My eyes shot to his and I nodded in understanding. I immediately gave the okay and the medical staff leapt into action. Tamryn and Dr. Greene took me back to the waiting area. Tamryn fielded questions from both sides of the family while I sat to the side with Dr. Greene.

"I'm proud of you, Joe." He stated quietly, and I looked up at him in utter disbelief.

"Why in God's name would you say that?" I blinked stupidly at him, and he leaned forward, fixing his stern gaze on me.

"You've kept yourself in check. You're letting these people do their job. It shows growth." He sat back and picked up a magazine. The doc and I had already discussed the scenario of a complicated delivery, and I had agreed that I would be in no condition to be in the room if any problems arose. It was one thing to have the conversation in the mellow ambiance of his office, and quite another to be told I wasn't allowed in because she was under general sedation. The thought of them slicing into my girl made my head throb. Though I was irritated to have the doc here analyzing me at a time like this, I could see that, as always, he had a point.

Waiting was pure torture, but at least I wasn't alone. Robin couldn't do it either. She paced the floor, clearly shaken by the experience, and Mason and Mac took her outside to smoke. They came back with a large cup of coffee for me, and she launched into a detailed blow by blow of the ambulance ride that oddly made me feel better. Though her terminology was way over my head with talk of post-ictal states and general anesthesia, it was good to know someone I trusted could speak the language.

An hour later, Dr. Franklin came out and advised that the babies were in incubators in the NICU, but were both doing well. Molly was in recovery and though she was still asleep, she was stable and her blood pressure had already improved. They'd know more when they got her post op labs back.

I was pretty shaky as a nurse took me by the arm led me down the hall to the NICU. She had me wash my hands about three times and gown up and then led me to a chair which I gratefully folded myself into. Two nurses wheeled a pair of rectangular plastic things over to me. Peeking inside, I saw a blue swaddled baby in one and a pink swaddled baby in another.

"Can I hold them?" My voice caught and the words came out in a whisper.

"Of course Mr. Jensen." A matronly dishwater blond with a severe nose, motioned to the two other nurses flanking the babies. With practiced ease, they gently removed them and slowly approached me, placing a baby in each of my arms.

The warmth of the little bundles surprised me. Eagerly peering down at them, I met my daughter's eyes, and a yawn twisted her lips showing bright pink gums. The breathtaking beauty of the little angel nestled against me was unreal. A coo pulled my attention to my son and I looked just as he spit his tongue out at me in a very Molly-like way.

"Hey there you two. I'm your daddy." The nurses had withdrawn a bit and I whispered the words, afraid talking too loud might scare the little darlings. Both of them looked at me with the most amazing expression on their faces, as if they recognized my voice. I sat, feeling the sting of happy tears. I could hardly breathe I was so caught up in the enormity of the moment.

My children. Safe and sound. Molly. Safe and resting.

The nurses let me hold my children for what seemed like far too short a time. I made the most of every second, memorizing their faces as if we were on borrowed time. I whispered many promises to them, mostly about how I'd never let anything happen to them. When the nurse finally insisted they needed to go back under the warmers, I reluctantly obliged and hurried down to Molly's room. I spent the next couple of hours watching my girl sleep. Seeing her beautiful face battered like it was, broke my heart. She had a split lip and two butterfly bandages on her eyebrow. That eye was black and blue and painful to look at, but it was a major relief to hear the encouraging beeps from her monitors. I asked if I could see the babies again, but Molly's nurse told me that I needed to wait for the NICU nurses to get them settled in.

"We're taking care of them, Mr. Jensen, right now you need to be with your wife." She looked so serious for someone so young. I didn't have the heart to blurt out that Molly wasn't my wife.

Dr. Greene stopped in and sat with me for a while after that, but I finally told him to go. He looked pensively in Molly's direction, and then spoke.

"Congrats, Joe. You'll make a great father." He sounded different and I looked in his direction. His eyes gleamed in the light and he cleared his throat before he spoke. "Call me if you need me, okay?" He waited just long enough for me to nod before slipping out the door. It was an uncharacteristic bit of emotion from the doc and I was touched by it. I sat there alone…just listening to Molly breathe. The rhythmic sound lulled me into a doze.

"Joe?" Her shaky voice snapped me to alertness. Her confused expression as she glanced around the room tugged at my heart. Leaning over, I took her hand gently in mine and pressed my lips to her moist forehead.

"Thank God, little girl. You gave me a hell of a scare. How are you feelin'?" Molly blinked vacantly and tried to sit up. I put my hands on her shoulders and shook my head. "Stay still baby, you need to rest.".

"Where are we? What's going on?" Reaching up, I brushed

her hair away from her bruised and swollen face.

"We're at Breckinridge. They brought you in after you had a seizure. Do you remember anything?" Wrinkling her brow, she stared at me in terror, her hand going to her diminished abdomen.

"Oh God! Joe! The babies! What happened to the babies?"

"Dr. Myers delivered them. She took them C-section. They're in the NICU." She gasped and burst into tears, I bent down to embrace her. "It's okay… honey, it's okay. The pediatrician said it's just a precaution, They're small, but they're both doing fine."

I let her cry it out, holding her in my arms with every protective instinct in me firing at once. I figured she needed to process everything I'd been struggling with for the last few hours, and I knew I needed to shut up and just be present. When she started to wind down, I whispered in her ear.

"I was so scared I was going to lose all of you." Her arms tightened around me and I let relief wash over me.

I spent the next 24 hours bouncing back and forth between Molly's room and the babies. I held my children and helped with their first baths, making sure to snap tons of pictures with my phone for Molly. Molly studied every one carefully through her taped together glasses which she'd broken during her first seizure. She forwarded the pictures to Stacy, knowing she could count on her to show them to the world.

On one of my trips over to the NICU, I was surprised to discover my father and mother in the twin's room, rocking them in side by side rockers. They exchanged a nervous glance when they saw me, but their proud smiles won out.

"Joseph, they're absolutely darling." My mother gushed.

"Thank you." I replied, running a hand over Logan's unruly hair.

"We love the names you chose. Very dignified." My father said, and though my first instinct was to sniff at the pretentious comment and question its subtext, I decided to take his compliment at face value.

"We thought so." I remarked.

The following morning, Dr. Myers declared that Molly's rebound after delivery was impressive. She refused to remove Molly's catheter, but her nurse and I were allowed to push her over to the NICU on a stretcher so that she could have her first look at Logan and Eva. Eva was wide awake and in the middle of a diaper change, so the nurse brought her over first.

"Hi, Eva. Molly drew out the "e" in our daughter's name and sucked in a loud breath at the sight of her." Oh, Joe! She's so little."

"Five pounds, one ounce." I informed her, as I took Eva from the nurse and placed her gently in Molly's arms.

"She's hungry." The nurse stated, handing Molly a premade bottle of formula.

The sunny smiled that bloomed on Molly's face was pure heaven. "She looks just like you."

"Poor thing." I snickered, reaching out to stroke Eva's impossibly soft cheek. I thought she looked like a bald, grumpy old man, so I could see the resemblance.

"They're beautiful." The nurse cooed, swaddling Logan and carrying him to Molly. I helped her place a pillow on her lap and Robin assisted her as she took our son in her other arm.

"Oh my!" She giggled, her eyes flying wide. "He *is* bigger!"

"And *he* looks like you." I added, stealing Eva away from her, when she started to fuss.

"Look at all that hair." Molly reached out her newly freed arm to stroke Logan's dark thick faux hawk. "He's enormous! How much did he weigh?" Molly asked, looking longingly into Logan's curious eyes.

"Six pounds." I spouted. "You did good, baby girl."

"Can you imagine how big he would have been if he was full term?" She gasped, kissing Logan on top of his head. He screwed up his face and his tiny fists flailed out of his blanket. Molly's radiant smile as she stared down at his beet red face was the most beautiful I had ever seen.

The following week was a marathon of jumping at every alarm that sounded in the babies' room and changing endless diapers. Molly drove herself mad trying to get the babies to breastfeed. When she didn't have one of them at the breast, she was attached to the double electric pump. On several different occasions, she fell fast asleep while holding one of the twins. Terrified she'd drop them, I stood vigil beside her, nudging her encouragingly.

Seven days after her surgery, Dr. Myers wrote the order to discharge Molly. Unfortunately, the pediatrician wanted to keep the babies for a few more days. I brought Robin back to the NICU with me to translate, and she explained that Logan's oxygen saturation was a little below normal when they took him off his O2. They also wanted Eva to put on a tiny bit more weight before discharging her.

When we broke the news to Molly, she didn't take it well. She marched straight over to the NICU nurses and begged them to find somewhere in the hospital for her to stay. The nurses explained that there were no on sight accommodations for attendant mothers, but assured her that she could come any time, day or night. Molly completely broke down and I was afraid her blood pressure might get too high or that she might pop a stitch. She'd done the same thing a few days before when they'd taken Logan to circumcise him. I'd been so concerned about her reaction that I'd nearly called the whole thing off. In the end, she stayed with Eva and insisted I go with Logan. I did as she asked, though witnessing that procedure wasn't something I was in a hurry to repeat.

The nurses finally paged Dr. Myers, who came in to give Molly a pep talk and write her an additional prescription for anxiety. "You need to go home and get some rest, Molly. They're in good hands. Keep pumping so you can feed those babies, but go sleep in your own bed."

"She's right." Robin agreed, showing professional solidarity. "Between Joe's family and ours, there'll be people here to hold those babies around the clock. The best thing you can do for them right now is to rest up and heal."

The sun was setting when we finally pulled into our driveway. Betty had planned to have balloons in the yard and a welcome home party, but once I got word the babies weren't being discharged, I phoned her and told her to call it off. I knew Molly wasn't in the frame of mind to have company.

The house felt unnaturally quiet after nearly a week in the hospital. Robin gave me a heads up that everyone had stayed behind to clean up from Molly's shower and that they'd had the rug and couch upholstery cleaned. Apparently Molly hadn't only bled on the rug during her seizure, but she'd also wet herself.

"Every one of the kids is going to need therapy." Robin had drawled the day after the C-section. Tamryn, who'd stopped by to take me down for breakfast, had nodded emphatically.

"I'm coaching Jamie not to say anything to Molly about it. You know how she is. No filter whatsoever."

"Gee, I wonder where she gets that?" I'd replied, and her eyes slid sideways. Robin chuckled and Tamryn smirked and tossed a napkin at me.

Everything was spotless when we flipped on the lights. After a quick once over, we discovered leftovers from the shower in the fridge and all of the baby presents were in the nursery.

"You hungry?" I asked her, but she just shook her head woefully." Molly, you've barely eaten since your surgery. Dr. Myers said you need protein to heal. You have to eat something."

"I just want them home, Joe." Her voice wavered, but she crossed her arms and the set of her jaw was reminiscent of the fierce girl I used to know.

"I know, baby girl." I wrapped my arms around her and breathed a sigh of relief when she hugged me back.

CHAPTER Fifteen

Molly

Changes

THERE ARE THINGS that we are prepared for in life. People coach us on taking our driver's test. Older friends prep us for prom night and graduating high school. We prep ourselves for the first time we can go out and legally drink. And then there are the things that we only *think* we are ready for. Like parenthood, for instance. No matter how many books you read, or how much advice you get, you're never ready. Period.

I thought I was getting to know the twins in the hospital, but it wasn't until they came home, ten days after I was discharged, that my real schooling began. Even with all the endless string of volunteers, it was overwhelming...especially trying to breast feed. I pumped and pumped and produced almost no milk. We had no choice but to supplement, but the lactation consultant had a subtle way of making me feel guilty that I was starving my babies.

Mom went to Whole Food and brought back a special tea that was supposed to help and Granny told me to drink a beer. I finally broke down and called Dr. Myers. She didn't seem nearly as surprised as the breast feeding guru had been that I was having trouble. She called in a prescription to help with my milk supply and it did make a small difference. Still, there was no way I was making enough to feed even one of the twin's breast milk and Eva couldn't latch to save her life. Joe told me to quit worrying about it. They'd get what they'd get and they were gaining weight. It was hard not to feel like a failure, but I tried to let it go.

My children were so different, even though they shared a womb. They liked different lullabies. Eva calmed down for me when I sang Let It Be, but Logan only responded to Joe's voice. And they rarely napped at the same time. They had a variety of cries for totally different reasons, and figuring them out was like trying to crack the Davinci code. We just had to learn by doing, and both Joe and I got better at it as the days passed.

Little Eva had Joe's thousand-mile stare, and sometimes it appeared as if she were merely tolerating our presence with righteous indignation. She simply glared at people when they spoke to her in baby-talk. Her regal quality had us calling her HRH, short for "Her Royal Highness".

Logan watched everyone and everything with bright and curious eyes. He ate like crazy, and already had chubby little cheeks and forearms like Popeye. Logan was the mellower of the two, and responded with unabashed wonder when people made silly faces at him. I took pictures of them both daily and was glad I did since they were changing so much so quickly.

Then there was the most astonishing change of all. The transformation of my fiancé. That's something I don't believe anyone could have ever anticipated. Everyone warned me that our relationship would change when we had kids, so I'd spent months preparing for that...mourning our freedom and the erotic heat of our sex life in advance. I figured nothing could spoil the moment more than a squawking baby...except maybe two of them. But the metamorphosis of Joe...was nothing short of re-markable. And like everything else with *us*, it wasn't what one might expect.

About three weeks after our babies had come home from the hospital. I lounged on the swing in the front yard with Robin, taking a sanity break while my mom and Tamryn fed the twins. I should have been napping, but sometimes the need for girl talk supersedes common sense.

"Slow down!" I called after a large SUV that zipped down the road a little too fast.

"Oh Molly-girl, you're such a *mom*. It's like you became a buzzkill overnight." Robin joked.

"I know, right?" I said, watching a dark sedan make a sus-piciously slow journey passed our house. The windows were tinted, so naturally I imagined a psychotic child- snatching clown behind the wheel. "Next thing you know I'll be the president of the neighborhood watch."

Robin chuckled, and then filled me in on the latest gossip. Kelly had finally agreed to a second date with Mac. He'd volun-teered at her school, doing pro bono framing for a construction project that Francis clued him in on. She'd nearly ridden her bike into a tree when she saw him, and when she swerved she crashed on the grassy knoll full of stickers. He rushed down to see if she was okay, and the furious way she leapt to her feet and hobbled away made him realize his presence at her workplace had had the opposite effect he was going for. The following day, he conned one of her coworker into putting a rose in her mailbox in the school office. With it, he left her a note saying he was sorry and asked for a second chance.

A couple of days later she sent him a text saying, "Don't pick me up on your bike. I'm wearing a dress so you'd better make it good." I laughed hysterically, realizing how much I'd misjudged Kelly. She just might have it in her to date my brother after all. The question was whether Mac could handle a woman who could handle him.

Robin and I sat swinging and brainstorming places that Mac could take her that might be an antidote for Chickenshit Bingo when Joe pulled up behind the wheel of a brand new F-250 extended cab. I nearly fell off the swing as I scrambled to my feet.

He'd been on one of his kicks, what I'd begun to refer to as 'alpha nesting'. He'd built the babies a crib that was made to look like a train engine with an attached train car dresser. When I jokingly asked which one of the kids it was for, he looked stricken and a few days later Mac told me he was building a canopy crib for our Her Royal Highness.

Then there was the vehicle situation. Ever since our first car ride hone from the hospital (and wedging two infant seats into the Coop) Joe had talked about getting something a little more family friendly, since his classic Ford could only seat the two of us. He'd even joked that I should trade in my mini coop for a minivan. Even so, seeing him lumber to a stop in this huge gas guzzler took me by surprise.

"What do you think, babe?" He hopped out and leaned back against the oversized air craft carrier that took up our entire driveway.

"What did you do?" I tried to contain my disbelief, but it was impossible. I stared at him, my mouth agape.

"I needed something with a backseat." He turned and eagerly opened the door. "See? I already bought car seats for it!"

"Uh huh." I nodded, blinking rapidly. He was glowing with pride and I hated to burst his bubble. "Joe?"

"Yeah, baby?" He asked almost absently, beaming at his new toy.

"How am I supposed to scale that thing to get the babies into their seats?" I expected him to look devastated, but instead he just shot me a wide grin.

"Easy," he motioned down and I saw a running board deploy as he opened the door. "I got this baby all decked out. I even had them install video screens so the kids can watch movies when we go places."

I stared at him in open disbelief. "But you *loved* your old truck."

"I love our children more. I'd rather they ride inside with us than strapped to the roof with bungee cords." Placing his hand at the nape of my neck, he pulled me in and pecked me on the cheek. Then he bounded up the stairs. "I'm going to play with the kids,"

"It's official. The world's gone completely mad," I said to Robin, following after my fiancé. He'd reverted back to his old self so swiftly that my head was still spinning. Since I'd woken from my surgery, Joe laughed easier and seemed to relax in a manner I hadn't witnessed since coming back to Austin.

"He's downright adorable." Robin called after me, taking a sip of her Coke.

By the time I caught up with Joe, he had a baby in each arm and was wandering around the living room talking to them in an overly enthusiastic tone. They both stared up at him as if he were some fascinating creature that had appeared out of thin air. It was hard not to chuckle at their matching furrowed brows and serious frowns.

"Is Mommy baking bread? It smells yummy, doesn't it? Too bad! Y'all don't get any." Joe murmured to the babies in a high pitched and excited voice. When Eva began to coo at him, he nodded as if he spoke her language. "Hey, don't blame me. Grow some teeth, kid."

"So is it your night to stay, Betty?" Robin asked my mom. Mom, Felicia, James, and Granny were taking turns staying in our guest room. Having a third person to rotate into the night shift was a godsend, and thanks to their help, my incision was healing nicely, and I didn't have to worry about drowsy Joe accidently chopping off his fingers or something. By rotating someone different in every night, we weren't exhausting our help either, and Great Grandma and all the Grandparents got some time to bond with the twins. It was a bit bizarre having no private time at night, but we were nearing the end of this phase. We figured the babies would be sleeping through the night by eight to twelve weeks, and by that time Joe and I *really* would be craving some privacy.

"Nope." Mom replied, smiling approvingly at Joe as he carried on at the twins like some crazed cartoon character. "Mine was last night."

"It's Friday. Friday and Saturday nights are just the two of us." I explained. Joe looked up from his staring contest with Logan and gave me a crooked smile.

"Good." Robin responded. *"My* kids want to take their Grandma out for supper. I think they're a bit jealous of the twins."

"When y'all are ready for a date night, let me know." Tamryn smirked. "I'll bring the girls and we'll stay over. It's never too early to start the subliminal birth control."

"Oooo...I like the way you think. Ditto." Robin chimed in with an evil grin.

Soon they'd all cleared out for the weekend, and Joe and I breathed a synchronized sigh of relief. Somehow with all of his hyperactive carrying on, he'd managed to lull the twins to sleep, or perhaps he'd just tuckered them out with his nonsense. He crept down the hall to tuck them into the same bassinette. We'd learned the hard way that they slept a lot better when they were cuddled up together co-sleeping. Apparently, sharing a confined space for months on end was addictive.

I got busy in the kitchen, throwing together chicken salad sandwiches and fresh fruit salad for dinner. I was watching what I bought at the store a whole lot more carefully these days and swore off ordering in and eating out. I had twenty pounds to lose before I would even *consider* buying a wedding gown. The double stroller Tamryn had given me at the shower was getting a ton of use, and the babies seemed to enjoy long, meandering walks as much as I did. Between delivery, breastfeeding, and not eating ice cream on a daily basis, I'd already dropped twenty six pounds. I still couldn't fit into most of my pre pregnancy clothes, but I was ready to marry Joe, and anxious to start planning for the next big thing.

I sensed Joe's presence before he announced it, feeling his electricity before he even laid a finger on me. My hands stopped mid motion, and then he was there, the length of his body molding against me, his spicy cologne filling my nostrils and immediately raising my temperature a full degree.

"Alone at last." His masculine growl forced my heavily lidded eyes close and I instinctively arched back against him. Physically, my recovering body was nowhere near ready for sex, but every part of me craved him. I missed him with every single fiber of my being and ached to be with him. I could feel him harden against me and sensed how badly he missed being with me. He trailed his wet lips along my neck and a desperate moan escaped me. I turned, my eyes digging into him and he cupped my jaw in his large calloused hand.

Reaching up, I tugged his face down to mine and kissed him possessively. His response was careful...reluctant even, but it wasn't long before he was responding enthusiastically. Soon my hands were wandering south of his belt and with a frustrated groan, he roughly pulled away.

"Your hands are writing checks your body can't cash, little girl." He quipped with a ragged exhale.

"We could do...other things..." My voice was raspy with desire and I let my eyes trail past the waist of his faded jeans.

He took a large step back and raked his hand through his hair. He turned and made a show of pounding his head steadily against the wall.

"This is hard enough without you teasing me." He drawled. It was amazing how he walked the line between cocky and sweet so proficiently.

"You said hard." I taunted with a tiny giggle. I couldn't resist the joke and he turned back to roll his beautiful eyes at me.

Leaning back against the wall he crossed his arms and gave me that damn sexy grin.

"Yes I did. And when you're healed I'll be more than happy to show you exactly how dangerous it is to bait a hungry bear. But until then..." His tone let me know without question that I was cut off. I tried to pout, but he was remarkably familiar with my trickery, and shook his head.

"Three more days." I raised a welcoming brow at him.

"Three more days and I'll fuck you senseless." He fired back, his voice full of virile promise. My heart drummed the way it always did when the animal in Joe surfaced. Then so swiftly it felt like I'd imagined it, his placid expression returned. Placing his hand on the small of my back, he directed me back to the counter. "Now, baby girl: if I'm going to help raise these hungry kids of ours, I think it is long past time you taught me a few things about cooking."

Coming soon!

Say goodbye to Molly and Joe
in the third and final installment of
The Carved Hearts Series,

Heartwood

THANK You!

TO THE BETA readers: Allie Morlan, Andrea Hurteau Barry, Anima-Christi Giraldez, Brett Lewis, Chelle Northcutt, Elaine Mosgofian, Jaimie Rivale, Kara King, Kelly Moorhouse, Laura Wilson, Lee Wright, Linda Cotter, Lisa Andersen Fox, Morgan McNeil Powell, Sally Bouley, Sarah Griffin, Shaina Abbs, Shannon Lewis, Stacey Grice, Stacy Darnell, Tamron Davis, and Vanessa Proehl. Thank you for your precious time and your words of encouragement. Having an audience is a critical part of our process, and we appreciate all of your feedback, whether we took the advice or not.

Robin Harper: our talented cover artist from Wicked by Design. Thank you for the stunning teasers, banners, memes, and the brilliant cover. You have such a great eye and are so gifted at capturing the feel of our story.

Ruby Franco: The most perfect cover model in existence. You, my dear, are drop dead gorgeous. Thank for being so damn easy to work with!

Julie Titus: You make the inside as pretty as the outside. JT Formatting can't be beat.

Mindy Badgett, Schooled Editing: Thanks for being so damn fast and thorough. It helps that you know us well enough to understand our voices so well.

…and a shout out to Jensen Ackles, for effortlessly (and unwittingly) serving as the perfect muse for Joe.

ABOUT THE Authors

L.G. Pace III has spent several decades pouring creative energy into other things besides writing. He began his current journey by telling his two daughters bedtime stories about a magical realm and a hero named Terel. Though that story is still sitting unfinished in the electronic universe he has managed to bring two other stories out of the dark maelstrom of his mind for others to enjoy.

He dwells in the great state of Texas with his wife, novelist Michelle Pace and their children.

OTHER WORKS BY L.G.PACE III

Vigilance
The Lost One

CONNECT WITH L.G. PACE III AT:

Facebook: https://www.facebook.com/LGPaceIII
Twitter: @PACEWRITE

Michelle Pace lives in north Texas with her husband, Les, who is also a novelist. She is the mother of two lovely daughters, Holly and Bridgette, and one uber-charismatic son, Kai. A former singer and actress, Michelle has always enjoyed entertaining people and is excited to continue to do so as a writer.

OTHER WORKS BY MICHELLE PACE

Crazy Love
Something's Come Up (with Andrea Randall)
Fury (with Tammy Coons)
Rage (with Tammy Coons)
The Perpetual Quest for the Perfect Life (with Tammy Coons)
Kiss Kiss

CONNECT WITH MICHELLE PACE AT:

Facebook: https://www.facebook.com/MichelleKisnerPace
Twitter: @MichelleKPace
Webpage: http://www.michellepaceauthor.com

OTHER WORKS BY MICHELLE AND L.G. PACE III

Good Wood (A Carved Hearts Novel, Book One)